A Feast of Narrative

VOLUME 3

Copy Editor: Tiziano Thomas Dossena
Cover Design & Layout By: Dominic A. Campanile
On the cover: The Two Sages; oil painting
by Emilio Giuseppe Dossena (1903-1987)

ISBN: 978-1-948651-18-9
Library of Congress Control Number: 2020931578

Published by: Idea Press (an imprint of Idea Graphics, LLC) — Florida (USA)
www.ideapress-usa.com • email: ideapress33@gmail.com • editoreusa@gmail.com
Printed in the USA - 1st Edition, Autumn, 2020

A Feast of Narrative

VOLUME 3

An Anthology of Short Stories by Italian-American Writers
Edited by Tiziano Thomas Dossena

To my Brothers and Sisters of the
Organization of the Sons and Daughters of Italy in America

ACKNOWLEDGEMENTS

I would like to thank my family for understanding that editing an anthology would force me to sit at the computer at the weirdest hours and my friend Leonardo Campanile for agreeing on the necessity of this project.

The Organization of the Sons of Italy, through their National magazine *Italian America*, which cooperated in the advertisement of this project, allowed us to reach a wider audience, and I thank them for it. Most of all, though, I thank all the contributors to this anthology for showing me how creativity can truly express its existence in so many ways.

INTRODUCTION

Tiziano Thomas Dossena
Editor

When I started with the first Italian American Writers anthology, I was delighted to see that most writers realized this was an effort on my part to focus on our own ethnic group's copious literary production, and participated enthusiastically.

Until recently, no spotlight has been put on them as a group specifically and I believed, and still do, that more of these projects should be initiated and supported by the various Italian American associations. It is, after all, a tenet of most of these organizations to assist their own kind in cultural activities. Somehow, though, I don't see it happen that often, and it's disappointing to realize that there is no awareness of this need to promote our writers, artists, dramatists, and composers so that they may leave a mark of their own.

Anthologies are just one of the tools to allow writers to be known, but they are much more, because they allow writers to 'belong' to a group of 'chosen' people like themselves, people who enthusiastically write because they want to and believe their innermost feelings need to be shared, at least on paper. It makes them realize that, regardless of whether their name is famous or not, they were chosen to be part of something that makes them shine just as much as the other contributors.

A copious number of contributors to Volume Two made it impossible to fit them all in a tome of less than 300 pages, therefore we created this Volume Three, which is being published a very short time after the preceding Volume Two.

Most of the writers of this anthology have an extended resume and their name may be well known even outside of the Italian American community, while some are at their early stages of writing; all of them wrote marvelous stories.

The additional detail in these Volume Two and Three that distinguishes them from Volume One is that the participants are from all corners of United States, and even England and Germany, in which two of our valiant writers are operating at this time. This was the original goal of this project and it was amply achieved.

We hope that with these anthologies we helped, even just a bit, in promoting the writing of Italian Americans to the world.

PREFACE

Tiziano Thomas Dossena
Editor

This anthology contains a very interesting amalgam of different stories and authors. What is common, other than their belonging to the same ethnic group, is the validity of their content and the message they send to the readers. Some stories are funny commentaries on social gatherings of some kind, wakes included, or heartwarming fables, while others address different topics with a more somber tone, such as the constant search for our roots, the worn-out emotions of illegal immigrants, growing up in a large city, the Covid19 crisis, and so on. Regardless of the topic, these writers prove that, besides being Italian American, the passion for writing is the element they have in common with each other. This is their message and it confirms that having them together in this anthology is the proper decision.

I am more than happy, therefore, to present you the authors of Volume Three of "A Feast of Narrative."

"If You Met Him Today" is a moving story by **Cynthia Herbert-Bruschi Adams** about search for one's identity, PTSD, and redemption. In it, there is a very accurate depiction of the mixed reactions our veterans had to face when coming back from Vietnam. It will touch your heart.

In **Bill Aiello**'s "Grandpa's Weeping Willow" a person on the verge of retiring rediscovers his old neighborhood and the tree that was planted by his grandfather. It's a poignant story about remembrance and how important memories are for our mental health.

Lucia Antonucci's "Addio Amore" is a sentimental and bittersweet narrative of a person's lost chance for love. Life makes the protagonist face the brutal reality of a parent's disapproval in 1950s' Italy. It makes you wonder whether things would have been different today or if the main character was just not in love enough to confront his father.

The angst and distress that illegal immigrants suffer in their travel of hope to a new country is gauged through the considerations of an African woman stuck in Malta after a failed attempt to go to Italy. The story "I am Hani" by **Angelo Bummer** is to the point in showing that the process of deciding to emigrate to another country under terrible, almost inhuman conditions is dictated by desperation.

Maria Teresa De Donato's "My Name is Freedom" presents killer whales through a soliloquy by a young one of that species. It's a very efficient mechanism and it entails an explanation of how these animals see themselves, an author interpretation obviously, and how we err in judging them as aggressive. It is a very charming story that could possibly turn into a book for young people.

I would define "David" by **Debbie DiGiacobbe** "a fresh breath of air." The story aims, very successfully indeed, at humanizing the figure of the homeless, which unfortunately has been often depicted as people with mental or drug problems or as slothful individuals. It is a valiant effort and it will make you all warm inside.

Dave Di Lillo's "The Steamer Trunk" is a visitation of times gone by but never forgotten, a rediscovery of the family's roots, the grandparents' sacrifices and the enormous obstacles they had to overcome so that they could offer a decent life to their children. It's a nostalgic story in which many readers may seem traces of their own ancestors' sagas.

New Yorkers may find "Garbage Park" narrative reminiscent of their years growing up in Queens or Brooklyn or even The Bronx. The locales maybe would be a little different, but basically the premises would be very similar. The exchanges and interchanges among young people, the 'unwritten rules" of their way of communicating are very well described in this story by **Mike Fiorito**, a veteran at reconstructing teenagers' tales and their emotional state.

How can an encounter with your distanced father in a bar when you are not eighteen yet turn out to be unique? It will be when a star of the music world who you adore is sitting at the next table, surely. Those premises bring a lot more to the table than it may seem in "At The Saloon," an intriguing story by **Cecilia Gigliotti**.

Starting as a semi-nostalgic tale of people attempting to reconnect with their roots, "The Immigrant's Grandson" turns out to be a man's desperate struggle to uncover the reasons for his grandfather's crime that forced him to flee Italy and emigrate to USA. **Joe Giordano** narrates the exchanges between this man and a newfound Italian relative at the airport of Naples with gusto and surprises the reader with an unexpected, amusing ending.

Thomas Locicero's "The Little Man Who Was Almost There" is a witty tale of aging and learning how to use the down sides of that process to your advantage. The conversation is so well-built and realistic that one may recognize part of it as something that he or she has heard in the past when dealing with some older relatives of their own.

LindaAnn LoSchiavo's "A Worthie Woman All Hir Live" touches an unusual subject, a break-in. What's unusual, though, is not the break-in in itself but the reason that initiated it. By reading this well-developed story one will discover there are hidden motives and maybe even undiscovered crimes. The conclusion of the story holds a very refined humorous connotation.

Anthony Michael Malara's "Motta" could have been just another narrative about searching for one's roots, but the developments of the story bring so many more emotions when the protagonist discovers his family's origins are from Italy. Visiting that country, his life changes completely for many reasons. The author does justice to the complexity of the feelings connected with the discovery of one's own heritage and all the possible ramifications connected to this finding.

"This is a simple tale, told by a wise and wizened wanderer, alone on the road he is destined to follow." This overture to a fairytale or folktale type of narrative, which is how this story could be categorized, opens "A Christmas Story Allegory: The Fire and The Trust," a fascinating story of a mother's fight for mental sanity and the power of faith, by **Maria Massimi**. It's a powerful tale of belief, trust and hope.

A father's observations about his two daughters' piano recital, starting from the beginning of their learning experience, are thoroughly entertaining and genuine in "Four Hands" by **Steve Piacente**. The father being an orchestra conductor makes the story even more intriguing and believable in its details.

Within a story about finding the real joys of life by discovering what makes other people happy and dropping prejudice about foreigners, **Paul Salsini** introduces humorous but true annotations by Italians about the COVID-19 situation in the USA in "The Tour Guide." The author also points out in his narration that sometimes bad situations bring good things and one should not give up hope no matter what the circumstances may be.

Marylouise Serrato's "Evil Spirits" is a captivating tale of superstition, small town's gossip and forbidden sex. The premises that the deformity of the daughter can be only explained by the visit of evil spirits are used to introduce the mother-daughter duo, who is soon joined by the son, a recently anointed priest. The death of the local magistrate brings unexpected changes in the family's balance of life and to their relationship with the town's other inhabitants.

Football being a religion of sorts for some people is the premise of the story. The main protagonists of "Hillbilly Bikini Bottom" are high school football players on the final game of the season and they are definitely being worshiped by the locals. **Stephen Siciliano** inserts the dealings, or absence of them, by black teenagers with the local white girls in the development of the story to show how subtle and devious racism may be. It has a very accurate description of Southern States' mentality, hopefully superseded by now, in relation to the race-relations issue.

Mark Spano's "Peckerwoods and Altar Boys" scrutinizes with a pointed style the interactions between Italians and other ethnicities in the Kansas City of years ago and the moral duality of the catholic kids of the time, who saw no conflict at all in committing a sin right after attending church. The descriptions are very convincing and the situations, even when serious, are tinged with a fine sense of comicality.

John Suriano wrote a story that is reminiscent of the Outer Limits TV episodes. His "No Fix, No Pay" is a delightful tale in which a mysterious lady fixes problems for a more than reasonable fee. The protagonist's doubts about the origins of her strange capabilities may not be cleared, though, as his life's predicaments and requirements become more complex.

Within an Italian American family in which the mother hates to cook and is at the same time very defensive of her own kitchen, many surprises may occur. **Tim Tomlinson**'s "Excuse Me" is a story of unrequited expectations and denial of reality presented in a fresh and pleasant fashion.

Bob Trotta's "Brothers in Arms" brings us back to a time of turmoil, when the US government decided to leave Vietnam, and the effect a day of reckoning for the last remaining American citizens has on two families entwined together by the friendship of their sons and he tragedy that had plunged upon them.

In a continuous line of thoughts and topics, **Leo Vadalà** addresses yet another wake and viewing in "Dies Irae." Just as he did in "The Viewing" in Volume Two of "A Feast of Narrative," he analyzes the possible thoughts of a person at what should be a revered function and the absurdities that enter his mind, filling this story with hilarious brashness.

Based on a true story, "Nanu" is a classic tale of the reality of life's economical situations forcing people to accept jobs that they never thought about. At the same time, the story introduces the inevitability of growing up all of a sudden when misfortunes come across one's family.

Elizabeth Vallone demonstrates once more her capability of conveying strong emotions to the reader.

These authors prove that within the Italian American community, writing is thriving. We hope that by discovering their validity and enjoying their stories, the readers will keep that in mind, look out for additional literary production by these authors, both past and future, and promote them by purchasing their books.

INDEX

If You Met Him Today

by Cynthia Herbert-Bruschi Adams

*This is the story of a conflicted young man who leaves friends
and family behind to find himself while fighting in the Vietnam War;
but the war only inflicts more damage. He struggles through life with little
joy until the day he finds redemption in an unanticipated encounter.*

If you met him today you would see a man who does not appear well. His body is too thin with flesh hanging loosely and little sign of muscle mass; calves resembling more of a turkey's neck than the rounded globes of athleticism that once he had possessed; severe damage to one leg, one arm and the side of his face. His color is too pale and his hair too sparse; but if you spoke with him you would hear resonate tones shaping the exquisite words of a well-educated or highly intelligent man. You would notice politeness, kindness and a startling sense of humor.

How did this person come to be in such a condition? To answer "it was Vietnam" might be too simple for the trouble started before then and was even responsible for getting him sent to Southeast Asia. Ben is literally now a fallen star who refused to be caught or properly helped. He had always seen his father as gifted and envied his dad's luck with business, with being a skilled pilot and early on attaining scholarships and many accolades.

1

It seemed natural that Ben would follow in those lofty tracks but the aura he had created around his dad's supremacy frightened him; utterly and completely filled him with a crippling dread. And the closer he came to attaining the prize of an Ivy League scholarship, the more self-recriminations echoed in his head. Doubt consumed him; would the world see him as worthy? He had studied, was a letterman in three sports but could he handle this? Would his dad acknowledge him with pride, hold him in esteem, demonstrate his love? Yet the school had made its offer and he was expected to go off to Prestige U in the fall. The local papers regaled him along with his teachers and classmates. Home town boy headed for success! There was only one thing he had to do and that was to complete high school.

During the last months of his senior year he began skipping classes, smoking a little weed and in general just not showing up. The teachers and the principal were horrified. This got his dad's attention. The school tried to work things out so that a couple of Summer School courses could prevent his academic collapse and allow him to graduate appearing to be "on time". But he did not get with this program; he steered around the steps destined to lead him to a beautiful life. When his friends went off to trade schools, state schools and a few private colleges, he did not collect on his scholarship, he did not pass go. He suddenly went off to the Army acting cheerful and proud and as though this was a wonderful option, a noble duty.

Why not a war hero he asked himself. Thus he set up an entire new pyramid to climb. He loved athletic challenges so boot camp went well. He could endure and exceed the physical demands. He could show respect and be polite to the officers and exceed expectations in classes. He was a born leader and soon took on increasing levels of responsibility. Ben then found himself in a war zone; his letters home were vague and infrequent. He found peace in the anonymity and the company of uniformed men. It all felt like a deer hunt complete with sleeping on the ground. Then the deer shot back.

He was wounded but not seriously. By the time people at home knew he had been injured Ben was already back to the war. Months of jungle life went by. His feet grew strange things and his boots were glued to his feet. Somewhere within their depths the boots emitted an odor like the sludge of a garbage can on a warm summer day, decidedly fermenting; perhaps even giving rise to fire. Still he fought on with determination. The war had a certain pattern and a flow. He hated the Army, he loved the Army. And then his platoon hit a land mine. Parts of Ben left him forever. Visions of his dying friends would never leave him.

His friends at home heard that he had been killed in Vietnam and the high school crowd took it hard. He had been much loved and thought to be indestructible. Someone sought to confirm the rumor and discovered that a person with his name had been killed but was listed as a resident of Virginia. He was from Rhode Island. There was hope. Then a letter arrived that he had written quoting Mark Twain "Rumors of my death have been greatly exaggerated." They rejoiced thinking he still even has his sense of humor. He must be fine. They went on with their lives finishing degrees and getting engaged and protesting the war.

When he was discharged he hunted up a group of his old buddies. They were glad to see him and tried to include him in their continued lives. He now had the GI Bill so he became one of them taking a few courses. But it was too soon. He still felt glued to the jungle, afraid of loud noises, afraid to be out in open spaces, anxious when walking down a path. Ben was not sure of what to do so he quit school and went home for a while.

He came back to the campus to party on weekends and would get fixed up with girls for a night or two. His friends were planning their weddings and he was asked to participate. But inside he felt like a leader, why just be a groomsman, so he asked one of these dates to marry him. She said yes and they rushed to the altar with a plan for him to then continue school. She got pregnant and he flunked his first term examinations. She complained that he drank too much and that he wandered the house in the dark. The marriage lasted six months.

Alone again and ashamed of failure he was having trouble picking up the pieces. He drifted to friends' homes eating and drinking everything they had and didn't offer to help. He seemed disinclined to bathe and soon became an unwelcome guest. He made his way back to Rhode Island's coast being careful to avoid his parents' home where the pain of his shame seemed painted on their flag and run up the pole. He felt the flapping in his heart.

He worked on a fishing boat. The employment was seasonal as the tourists and restaurants ate most of what was caught. He didn't care. They let him sleep on board so he acted as a deterrent to vandalism and had no expenses, no one cared how he dressed or noticed his hygiene over the smell of fish. When he was laid off, he slept in the back of a coin operated laundromat and was paid a few dollars for repairing the machines and making certain only the owners collected the coins. The fishermen knew how to find him when they needed any help. If he wasn't in "Soap and Suds" he was at the "All you can eat for $1.50" restaurant.

This went on for several years. The former high school hero thought of himself as the village idiot without a clue as to how he might change things. Then one day his dad came looking for him. His mother wasn't well and wanted to see him. Recognizing the situation his father gave him two hundred dollars and advised him to get cleaned up and buy some decent clothing before he came home. Ben stared at the money. He had no transportation but it was a short walk to a tavern. That's how far he got the first time.

The next time his dad came with a friend and they brought clothing and took him to a hotel room where they waited in a car while he went inside to shower and shave. To his credit he did not sneak out the bathroom window and hide in the woods; he got dressed and went to see his mother. He had trouble looking at how her body had deteriorated but being with her was sweet. She had never demanded too much from him and seemed to still love him. Her love made him feel warm for the first time in a long time. He wanted to cry and tell her he loved her and that he had killed some people in Vietnam and that he had seen his friends blown to bloody pieces but nothing came out except a tear and a hug. That was enough for her, she said. That was all she wanted. He promised to come back soon but never quite made it. He tried not to think about her too much.

But he stopped drinking. Somehow he realized that being sober would be the only way to break out of his life. He had committed some petty thefts and never wanted to be caught. Sober was the way to be plus he would need less money. He still slept in the back of the laundromat but now rigged up a one-burner hot plate and eventually scavenged a boat-sized refrigerator out of the town dump. In this way he began to eat a little better and think more clearly. He checked with the VA and found someone to take him to meetings where he could talk about the memories and God if he wanted to.

A letter with several stamps and addresses was waiting for him under the Soap and Suds door when he got back from Maude's Fish and Chips one evening. It was written by his long ago wife and told the story of their son whom he had only met briefly. It said the boy had been no trouble to her growing up but now he had asked to meet his dad. As he was about to turn 18, she thought maybe it should happen at least once.

Ben didn't know whether he was thrilled or frightened. There was a number to call and he knew where there was still a pay phone so after a few days of worry he called. Arrangements were made for a meeting two weeks hence in which she and the son would drive to Maude's to meet him. He wanted to pay for the meal and to be spiffy looking. He put the clothing he had worn to see his mother into one of the dryers so that the dust would shake out, cleaned his shoes and teeth and planned on a haircut and shower the day before the meeting. He collected every can he could find in a three mile radius to help fund the meal additionally getting his fishermen friends to let him scrape off barnacles and do some painting for another few dollars. Thus he had his nest egg.

. . . .

The boy was really a man. He looked the way Ben must have looked when he was a senior in high school. Ben was proud and thanked them both: his ex-wife for her hard work to rear a child and the son for visiting. The son was gracious and kind and seemed moved to actually touch his father's arm as that hand was missing three fingers so they didn't actually shake. He told his dad where he would be going to college and asked if he could see him again. He ended by saying how proud he was to have a dad who fought for his country and was a real hero.

When they left Ben could not stop smiling.

Grandpa's Weeping Willow

by Bill Aiello

Sometimes a little bit of bad luck can turn into good fortune.
A traffic jam and a return to an old neighborhood bring back memories
for a man about to end one chapter in his life and begin another.

It was late Friday afternoon, and Pietro was on his way home from work; a hot, steamy, lazy July afternoon. He had left his job at the advertising agency. Midsummer, not a busy time, except for a small number of companies that profit from the summer trade. Companies like airlines, travel destinations, beach equipment... Pietro had been in the business almost all his adult career. He knew it well.

The work wouldn't pick up for another month. That's when the children went back to school, fall fashion kicked in, people bought furniture and holidays were coming. But here, in mid-July, with the temperature at the boiling point, Pietro had experienced it for so many years. It was high in temperature, but not in workload. So when the work and contracts and ad designs would begin coming in, in another month, he wouldn't be there. Pietro was retiring. He had just one more week to go after this. And then he'd close another chapter in his life.

The office wasn't busy. Almost half the staff was on vacation, or hiatus. And then, like the end to school vacation, right around Labor Day, the office crowd would return.

Except this year, he wouldn't be there to hear the stories of what people did for summer vacation. The trips to the beach, the lake, Europe or mountains in Alaska. Who went camping to which national park, or toured the city on a new ten speed bicycle, or who saw three Broadway shows. For the first time in decades, this year it would be different. A new life for him was right around the corner.

And on this steamy, humid afternoon, as he was driving home, he was also caught in traffic. For a few brief moments he laughed to himself. The office crew isn't at the job. They are all here on the highway.

Pietro turned on the radio for the traffic report. It wasn't good. The hot summer sun had caused the road ahead to buckle, and just beyond that, an accident. Traffic was backed up for miles and miles. Pietro had to exit the highway and take another route home.

It seemed like an eternity to the next exit, but he got there, left the highway, and called his wife to notify of his delay. He'd find a place to buy a small snack, just enough to keep his stomach satisfied until he got home. But it wasn't a total disappointment. This road off the highway was not entirely strange to him. It was the town where he grew up. Many, many years ago. Decades ago. Pietro knew the town, he knew the streets; he didn't need a map, GPS or to ask anyone for directions. It would take him longer to get home, but he was by no means lost.

He found himself driving down a busy boulevard, one he had been on so many times before. This was where he grew up, where he lived with his family. It was where he attended school, went to church. He saw the park where his father taught him how to ride a bicycle, and after he learned, he rode down these streets hundreds of times.

Just a few more blocks, and came the street where he lived in his youth. It had changed a bit, some new homes, and stores, and businesses. Places that sold cell phones, computers and a bank with ATMs. There weren't any of those when he was growing up.

A feeling of nostalgia came over Pietro. He just had to pass the home he lived in as a boy. He did. A tear came to his eye.

This was a big Italian neighborhood when he was a young boy. He could tell from the shops and businesses that Italians were no longer the predominant ethnic group. But they weren't entirely a group of the past, either. When he came to the first intersection, there was an Italian grocer, and a meat market.

And to Pietro's utter amazement, two familiar sights. The *pasticceria*, which served as his family's source of cakes and cookies that nearly every Sunday they enjoyed with coffee and tea, was still in business. Across the street, the pizzeria, the same one, with nearly the same façade, looking almost exactly as it did when he came here all those Saturday nights after he played pool at the bar.

The temptation was just too much. He had to go into both. After he parked his car, he looked at each, almost as if he was reunited with two old friends.

Did the same families own the businesses? Should he identify himself? Would anyone remember him? Did he, perhaps, know more about the glory days of these two establishments than the present workers do?

He entered the bakery first. It all came back to him. He smelled the cannoli cream, the powdered sugar. He remembered waiting on line, with his grandmother and mother. His grandmother would place her order in Italian. His Mom did so in English. He remembered the woman behind the counter who'd give him a free cookie every now and then. When Pietro got older, he'd go in and pick up orders on his own.

But no one behind the counter looked familiar. Pietro asked if the Capitola family still owned the shop. Yes, they did. But no one from the family was there at the time. So he ordered a few pastries. And on his way out, he saw what he didn't see on his way in. The photos of the town in Italy where the Capitola family came from. And photos of some of the old crowd who bought their cakes and pies here, every week. Old friends, neighbors, customers.

He recognized many. There they were, the photos still lucid, lively, brilliant. Just like they were so, so long ago.

The employees behind the counter, and a few customers noticed him and his devotion to the memories on the wall. For a brief second he was going to speak, but felt that no one would understand. He looked one more time, and he was out.

Now he was on his way to the pizzeria right across the street. The bar and pool hall where he spent many a Saturday night, where he met his wife, were gone. But the pizzeria was there. Like a hero who has returned home, he went in.

And once again, the aromas overcame him. The sauces, the cheese. The conviviality of the crowd, the customers chatting, the activity behind the counter.

Once again, he asked if the owners were the same as when he spent his youth here. He remembered the first names. They were Dominic, Angelo and Ciro. The family name escaped him, but he asked. Yes, it was still a family business. Dominic had retired and moved out of state. Angelo had died, and Ciro lived a short distance away. Their grandchildren now owned the restaurant. But none were there at the moment.

Pietro ordered a slice and took a seat. The memories rushed to shore. The old jukebox was still there. The telephone booth was now a charging station for cell phones. The old red table tops looked new, but of the same color.

It dawned on him. Italians still own businesses, but they don't seem to be present much. Someone else runs the store and serves the customers. Times change.

Then he finished his pizza and it wasn't quite as late as he thought. There were still two places he wanted to revisit.

One was the schoolyard. The schoolyard where he played soccer, handball and smoked his first cigarette. The schoolyard where he fell off his bike and scraped his knee. Then he was off to the church. It was here that he would have his biggest revelation. At the bake shop, pizzeria and schoolyard, there had not been that many changes. But here at the church, particularly the vast lawn moving away from the convent, rectory and garden, it seemed ethereal, almost surreal. He remembered all the church carnivals, concerts and graduations that took place there. He remembered the lawn sloping down towards the railroad tracks. He remembered the bright orange sunsets and pink skies whose beauty he didn't appreciate then.

And then, there, off to one side, he felt a rush of wind and heard a voice calling. It was not clear at first; it seemed to be broken by the wind, the train passing, and the flutter of birds overhead. Then it got quiet, awfully quiet, frighteningly quiet. And still. Not a leaf blowing, nor a bird chirping, nor a car passing. Pietro saw a familiar sight, heard a familiar voice. That tree at the edge of the property. That weeping willow, he remembered it.

His grandfather, Carmelo, had planted that tree when it was a sapling. Carmelo was the church gardener, and Pietro came here one Saturday when he was seven and helped his grandfather plant that tree. He recalled Grandpa telling him in Italian how to dig, fertilize and water the young plant, which someday would grow into a big, handsome, strong tree.

The sun beginning to set in the west, the same bright orange balloon of a sun gave a pink reflection to the adjacent sky. Then, under the weeping willow he saw the image of his grandfather, who at the time the tree was set into the ground was the exact same age he is now. There was the smiling image of his grandfather, beaming from ear to ear, pipe in his mouth, eyes brilliant as the sun. In Italian, he heard his grandpa say how proud he was. And to Pietro's absolute incredulity, the Italian he seldom used returned to him, as he spoke with his grandfather the same way he did over half a century before.

It was only the sound of the passing train and some noisy blue jays that signaled to Pietro that it was over. It was time to head back to the car.

The interior of the car was hot and heavy from the summer heat. Pietro stepped in and waited a few minutes before turning on the ignition. And when he did, he realized that one chapter in his life was about to come to an end while another had reemerged, if only for a few brief minutes.

Addio Amore
(Farewell Love)

by Lucia Antonucci

This story describes a profound relationship
that transcends continents and time.
If you have ever been in love, this poignant tale
about its joys and tribulations will touch your soul.

I had just graduated from medical school from the University of Bologna. It was the year 1949. The Second World War had ended a few years earlier, and Europe was trying to get back to normal. After graduation, I returned to my home in a village outside of Naples, Italy. I had planned to take the summer off before resuming residency at a hospital in Naples. It was my dream to become an engineer, but it was my father's dream that I should follow my older brother and become a doctor. My father wanted to open a clinic for the two of us in our village. During the Italy of my youth, you did not debate with your parents, they always knew best. I went along with my father's decision and attended medical school. I graduated number one in my class and was happy with my accomplishments.

I had many friends in my village and among them some nice young ladies. However, my heart never skipped a beat for any of them; they were just friends. In those days, parents kept an eye on families that had a daughter whom they felt would be suited for their eligible son. My brother had an arranged marriage, which seemed to have turned out OK for him. My younger sister is a school teacher and my other brother is at the university with his eye on law. My mother is a retired schoolteacher. My father was fortunate to have acquired a great deal of real estate in our village. He owns many buildings and businesses. Recently, he opened the first open aired movie house like they have in America. It is very successful featuring many of the American movies, which everyone here loves to see. On weekends the lines to enter the movies are endless. All in all, we are a fortunate Italian family living in a beautiful villa, with a maid and gardener.

One particular day, I went to visit a doctor friend of mine, to return some books I had borrowed. I rang his office bell and he answered "Avanti," meaning come in. Upon entering, I noticed he had patients. I excused myself, saying, "I'm sorry, I didn't realize you had patients," to which he replied, "Come in, it is our friend Peppino and his wife."

I greeted Peppino and his wife, whom I hadn't seen in a few weeks, and noticed a lovely young lady seated on the examining table. Peppino quickly introduced me to her. "Franco" he said, "this is my cousin Theresa from America. Do you remember the last time we met, I told you my cousin would be visiting?" "Yes," I said, but I had assumed she was an older woman, not a young lady. I shook Theresa's hand and welcomed her to Italy. She turned bright red, and my heart started to skip a beat.

My doctor friend, nicknamed Mimi, explained the reason for Theresa's visit. In America she had knee surgery at age 13 and still experienced much discomfort. Her father suggested she be seen by a doctor in Italy to determine if there are other issues. Dr. Mimi did not see anything wrong, but suggested she see an orthopedic specialist. Dr. Mimi told Theresa to explain her knee problem to me. Since I am a doctor, he thought I might find it interesting. Theresa blushed even more, while explaining her condition in the dialect of Naples, which I found to be delightful.

Dr. Mimi again suggested that the next best course of action was for Theresa to be seen by an orthopedic doctor, to which I replied, "I am acquainted with an orthopedic specialist. I will be happy to make the appointment. In fact, this case is quite interesting. I will accompany Peppino and Theresa to the doctor." Peppino thanked me, as did his wife and Theresa. As they said their goodbyes and left, my friend and I went on his balcony and watched and waved as they departed.

My friend said, "Franco, what do you think of the American?" I said "she seems nice," but in my mind, I thought she was delightful. Once again my heart was beating faster.

A few days later, I went to Peppino's house, since I was able to make an appointment for Theresa with the specialist. Upon entering, I was disappointed not to see Theresa, when suddenly Peppino called, "Theresa, come, Dr. Franco is here." Theresa entered. She looked beautiful, dressed in a long yellow caftan, her slippers matched her dress and she wore a yellow ribbon in her hair. She was dressed like the actresses we see in the American movies. I was taken aback by the sight of her. This time, she extended her hand and seemed more relaxed.

We talked and talked for a long time and since I like to joke and she liked to laugh, we got along well. It was after midnight, and I knew I had to leave but it was not easy for me to go. I could have stayed all night listening to this American with a Naples dialect. We said our good night and planned to meet at the doctor's office in two days.

On the day of Theresa's appointment we met in the specialist's office. After a thorough examination, the doctor prescribed some vitamin injections and felt Theresa would benefit from keeping her leg in hot sand for fifteen days to remove some liquid on her knee. Of course, I went to Peppino's home each day and gave Theresa the injections. My father owns the cabanas at the beach in our village and to my delight Peppino rented one for a month. I joined Theresa and her family at the beach periodically and I took care of her knee in the hot sand. She seemed to be feeling better.

The days we spent at the beach were delightful. We rented a row boat from time to time and, together with her cousins, we had an enjoyable time. Italy, at the time, still held on to old world traditions, and she and I were never left alone. We were always with family. We attended mass every Sunday, and it seemed the whole village knew I was smitten with the American. Yet, it was difficult for me to express myself to her, but she knew. Much to my delight, Theresa remained in Italy for five months.

When the time came for Theresa to depart, her cousin Peppino was sick with fever and asked me to accompany her aboard the ship, together with family, to make sure her papers were in order, her cabin was acceptable, etc. With a heavy heart I did so. When we arrived aboard ship, everything was fine. Theresa's cousins decided to tour the ship and Theresa and I walked and talked. I told her I would write often and one day I would come to America.

The sound of the alarm for guests to leave the ship was truly the alarm that broke my heart. All of the cousins had said their goodbyes, and tears were unending. I was the last to say goodbye. Seeing Theresa so sad was devastating to me. I tried to joke, but it didn't work. She told me she would write as soon as she arrived home. I left the ship and Theresa stood on the top deck so we could all see her and wave. As the ship sailed, the band played "non ti scordar di me" meaning don't forget me; who could forget?

When Theresa arrived home, her dad sent Peppino a telegram informing us that she had arrived safely and all was well. We were all delighted. Theresa and I wrote each other often and I also wrote to her dad. He and I had become great friends. I tried to get a visa to go to America, but at that time, there was a quota and my request for a visa was denied. Theresa asked some of her doctor friends if they would sponsor me, but of course not knowing me, it was not possible. Theresa's letters to me were sent to Peppino's house, because I didn't want my parents to know of my plans so early. When I found it was not possible for me to go to America, I wrote Theresa and asked what I could not ask in person. I asked for her hand in marriage. To that

I also asked a second question, "Theresa, would you consider living with me in Italy?"

I waited anxiously for the next letter to arrive from Theresa. The time which passed seemed like an eternity. When the letter arrived, I was filled with so many emotions as I began to open it. Reading the letter, I found that my questions were answered. To my delight, Theresa said yes. I was the happiest man in the world, but such happiness was short lived. Upon speaking with my parents, World War III broke out in my home. My father said "If you do not distance yourself from this American, you will be disinherited, there will be no clinic, and you must leave this house." This was the Italy of my youth. As I was unwilling to disobey my father and risk my future, my next letter to Theresa was what Americans refer to as a "Dear John" letter. While I cannot divulge the full contents of my letter in summary it read, "Dear Theresa, forget the proposal, forget all that we have meant to each other. I am reaching for the impossible dream. Perhaps one day we will meet at the fountain of God."

Theresa was heartbroken. Her father wrote me a letter, which to this day, tears at my heart. His words were quite succinct, "How could you break my daughter's heart?" He wrote many other things, which only an Italian would understand. I wrote back to tell him I loved his daughter but Italy had a different mentality. He was angry, as any father would be, and demanded I send back all of her letters, pictures, discs, etc. I complied and gave everything back to Peppino. He seemed to understand the situation I was in.

Time went by, a clinic was opened, I met a young lady my parents approved of and we married. I am a well respected doctor and have operated on many of Theresa's relatives. My wife and I have two sons, one a doctor and one an attorney, of their own choosing. Although my wife is Italian, she lacks the sense of humor I found in Theresa. Her Italian dialect is not delightful in the same way Theresa's was. The years have gone by and there isn't a day that passes that something of Theresa doesn't enter my mind. Most especially I recall her eyes, which truly understood love is a many splendored thing. "Addio amore!"

I am Hani

by Angelo Bummer

*"I am Hani" recounts a young woman's journey through
the perilous migration route from East Africa to Southern Europe,
and her separation from her husband when she goes into labor
during a rescue mission in the Mediterranean Sea.*

The nurse showed me the information card that the officer placed at the foot of my hospital bed and explained to me that she would return to record my information, take my fingerprints, and ask me questions. She said I did not have any identification on me when they rescued me, even though I distinctly recall having papers when I left Tripoli.

My husband told me about them asking questions and taking fingerprints. He said this is a trick. That the fingerprints will prevent me from being able to move, and that these questions would try to trick us into saying we came here looking for work, which would give them reason to put us in a holding cell and deport us.

How he knew this, I did not know at the time, nor did I know the significance of it.

But now I have this child, that I do not want, that was given to me by this man who is now in a different country. Italy, I am told.

My husband is weakened. How will he ever make it on his own without me? He will crack at some point. This is what the journey does.

I do not even like him. I had to marry him because he had sex with me and gave me a child. But I can't tell anyone of this. I can't risk it, just like I couldn't risk not going along with the marriage to save him from prison and myself from being beaten or worse. Who knows if I would have survived? Some do not. And others are permanently deformed, sentenced to live out the rest of their lives in shadows, with secret friends, rotten food, trying to avoid society one day at a time, like my poor brother. I've seen it happen several times, and I knew what I had to do in order to get out.

As soon as we were married, he put me on a 4X4 with forty other people, mostly men and boys. We carried as much water and gasoline as we could and drove as far as we could until there was no more gas. And then we walked. I was lucky that I was pregnant. The men gave water to the children first, and since they knew I was pregnant I also drank first. I also happened to look like a child, even though I have been a woman for almost six months.

But we had to ration the water because we did not know how long the journey would take. Some said it takes three days; others said it takes two or even three weeks. For us, we drove three days, and then walked three days. We drank hot water for five days, ate rice for four days. I thought I would die at some point, like the young man we called Cannon because he was able to sprint faster than any one we have ever seen. Even in the desert sand.

But the thirst and the exhaustion and the sand eventually got to him. We tried to spit what we could in his mouth, because we were out of water by this time, but with the wind much of this turned to wet sand that clung around his mouth and vacuumed into his throat when his spirit coughed and gasped for life.

And then again. With Goat Man. We called him this because he was only a teen but had the face of an old man, and his face did not change expression. He was determined and unfazed, the last man we thought would fold. We would play this game to try to make him laugh or at least smile, and we did manage to do this once, when Cannon tripped over his own feet and fell into another traveler who was trying to pee. They made everyone think they were going to fight. Even I believed it. And when they finally let us in on it, we all burst out in laughter. That was the day Goat Man smiled.

Goat Man simply did not wake after the fifth night. Luckily, one of the young boys noticed his shoes sticking up in the sand early that morning. Otherwise, we would have never known how he disappeared. That the desert had overtaken him.

When we encountered the men at the Libyan border, I was so relieved. I did not know how much longer I would last. They brought us to their house and gave us cold water and hot rice. I was so thankful!

And then they became cruel. They had guns and required money. At first, they wanted one thousand dinars, and when everyone said there was no way they could come up with the money, they eventually went down to five hundred dinars. And when everyone remained silent and thwarted their eyes, the men began hitting them with the butts of their rifles and taking whatever belongings they had in their pockets and bags.

Some had cell phones in their pockets, others small amounts of cash. Bags were mostly filled with clothes, which the men emptied. Some photos and papers flew out of their pockets and the bags with the clothes, along with other items like toothbrushes and tubes of toothpaste and small bags of dried lentils and fava beans that broke and scattered on the littered concrete floor. When two of the men decided to run, they were shot rather easily. I can see it so vividly now. Everything was silent and still moving. But I did not move. I could not move. Nor could I speak. I heard nothing.

I was thankful that I wore a head scarf. I knew I would need to in order not to attract particular attention to myself, and honestly I was used to doing so. And I was thankful that my husband spoke several dialects of Arabic. The officers began taking each of us, one by one into a room while one of the officers remained on guard threatening us with his assault rifle. My husband was able to convince them that we came together, so we were able to stay together as the officers tried to extract money from us.

We were brought into a hot, empty room that had trash and bottles strewn across the floor. I did not understand everything at the time since they spoke in such as foreign dialect, but another man who was not an officer eventually came into the room. My husband told me later that he had to make a deal with that man.

The officers said we needed to pay one thousand dinars, that they were cutting us a deal because we were married and had a child on the way. They said that if they did not get the money, then we would be separated and put in prison where they could not be responsible for what happened to us next.

The man that walked in was a business man. He said he would loan us the money to pay the officers, and that my husband would have to pay him back with interest. We had no choice but to accept the offer. Of course.

Then, the man gave us a cellphone to call our relatives and ask them to wire us money. He called his parents and his brother, but no one would answer. He had me call my father, but my father said that I am married and it is the duty of my husband's family to wire the money. In the end, the businessman had a backup plan to keep us moving. He had a truck arranged to bring us to a work location just outside of Tripoli. We could continue to try and reach our relatives but in the meantime he would have us work to raise money to pay off the debt. He also put us in contact with smugglers who would get us and others across the sea to Europe, for two thousand dinars each.

All of us crammed into the back of a pickup truck. All except the two who were shot. I do not know what happened to them. They were probably buried in the desert or just left there. Maybe they just threw them in a pit. I don't know. But I'm sure that their parents and families are still wondering where they are, wondering if they are okay, if they are happy, if they are eating well.

We had to stand up in the back of the pickup truck in order for all of us to fit. This was the most excruciating part of the trip. More so than traveling through the desert on the 4X4 or being on the boat nine months pregnant. We still needed to travel through the desert to get to the main roads, but on this day the wind whipped the sand around and all I could do was cover my mouth and eyes and remain standing. I closed my eyes and prayed the entire time.

The trip took a day and a half, and we did not sleep. When the driver slept, he had his friend drive, the one who also had shown us his gun to make sure none of us ran off. But no one would run off. Where would we go? This businessman was our safety net. He would get us to Tripoli. He saved us from the officers. He said he would find us a boat and get us safe to Italy. We just had to be willing to work and to wait and to give him money.

We stopped whenever the driver stopped. When he did, we peed and drank water and washed our eyes and mouths. And then we had to jump back in the truck before the driver left. He would just go. He would not say anything, not even look at us. We had to watch him constantly.

I did not know when the truck would stop, so at times I just peed standing up, praying with my eyes closed. I imagined others doing the same. I remember opening my eyes a few times when I felt the truck slow. We were passing through villages and small towns, and I remember everyone in the town following us with their eyes, looking at us. I was so ashamed. At that point I wondered how I ever got here. I felt like the lowest of the earth.

It was here that I really began to hate my husband. Here I realized that I would have been better off without him. I hated him for having sex with me, for forcing himself on me, for marrying me, for taking me. And I hated my parents for letting it happen. For going along with it. For saying it was the best for me. It was there that I realized that I could only place my loyalty in God, and that I could not put my trust in anyone. I resolved to look after myself at that point, to leave him whenever I got the chance, whenever it was safe.

I imagined meeting a kind man in Europe, one of those pink ones that smiled at everyone when they walked through my village. One that would let me do whatever I wanted to do and would not yell at me and tell me how I should act. One who had money and would help me finish my degree and become a lawyer or make lots of money with computers. I could create an app, one that tells others where they are if they are in danger, or an app that shares with others their prayers, a Prayer App, to those in distress. And I could do all sorts of good and it would make me famous, and everyone would know who I am and that I have a duty to God and people.

I could return home and bring my family and friends to a nice place, an island, or a big city like London or Tokyo. On the airplane. I could get them documents because I would have money. And money is what allows you to cross any border and go anywhere in the world, even Hollywood.

We stayed on the outskirts of Tripoli for several months. My husband's family was able to wire one thousand dinars within a week; they had to sell some livestock to do so. It turns out that this was a normal routine for the businessman. He must have been very wealthy, having truckloads of travelers pay him money, or at least those who were able and not sent to prison or sold. He was also able to connect us with the boat people, very quickly and easily, and he must have also been paid some money for doing this. A very wealthy man he must be.

Luckily, my husband was able to get work as a butcher and raise enough money to pay the smugglers four thousand dinars to get us on the boat. During that time, we stayed with other travelers, all from different countries, Mali, Sudan, Syria, Eritrea. Many young boys and teenagers. I made a friend who was from Palestine. She had two small children with her, so I helped her take care of them while the men and boys were out working or trying to find work or out drinking on the streets.

There were about fifteen of us all together living in that small apartment. The water in the place was inconsistent, turning off for long periods of time and then turning back on, so I always made sure to fill up jugs of water for when this happened. Food was a problem too. Since we lived with so many people, and not everyone pitched in with their fair share, we decided that we all needed to take care of our own food. This only became a problem when some of the boys had been drinking and would come in and search for food to eat. They did this occasionally, and would get hit in the head when they did. One time the Palestinian husband got very mad and beat one boy with a pan real bad.

During that time, I mostly survived on broth made with lamb bones that my husband would occasionally bring home from his work at the butcher. I also cooked lentils, fava beans, and pasta, sometimes making a soup with the broth. But that was what we ate for the four or five months that we were there.

And then one night, the boat man came and told us that we had to go. It was dark out, dusty, sticky, and still. Those of us who had already paid, followed him. There were about eight of us, and when we went outside, he told us to get in the back of his truck where there must have been a hundred other people standing up. It was a large flatbed truck with boards streaming up the sides and with roofing tin hammered to it. I got splinters in my palm holding on as the truck bounced up and down driving through the neighborhoods and picking up more and more people.

When we got to the port, we were shocked at the boat we were being put on. "Don't worry, this one will take you to a larger boat out at sea, one that will take you all the way to Italy," the captain said. When we asked for a life vest, he said we would have to pay extra. 250 dinars. My husband paid for one, that was what he had money for. And he gave that one to me. He could have bought one for himself as well but he did not want to arrive in Europe with no money at all. He was willing to take the risk.

Then the man rushed us onto the boat, cramming more than can fit, as if he were loading cargo. There seemed to be hundreds of people on that boat, but I could not see everyone because it was dark, and we were packed on and I was shorter than everyone except the small children. We were all confused and panicked at that time, but we all had to remain still because it felt like that boat would turn over if we started to move and protest.

The captain shouted something that I could not understand. And then we were off. He did not come on the boat with us. He simply walked off. I had a water bottle with me, and I hid it between my legs. At one point, I almost fainted from exhaustion. That's when some of the people were able to guide me to sit down at a nook on the side of the boat.

I can't remember much from that point. I think that was when I started to go into labor because it was hard to comprehend everything around me, and I just closed my eyes. It had probably been six hours when I began to feel extreme pain, and I did not know if or when we would reach Italy. We did not even reach that larger boat the captain spoke of, and I did not know who was steering this boat.

I remember drinking my water at some point, and I remember looking up for a brief amount of time. I was wet and shaking, and the boat smelled like piss and vomit and salt. I think it was my own vomit and piss, but I'm not sure. And then I saw some of us getting on a large boat, a blurry white mass in the dark night. I later realized that that white mass was a rescue boat from Malta.

I remember there was a lot of screaming, from both the travelers and the Maltese. The boat was swaying back and forth and I saw them use a lift to aid the children to board. And I remember being moved and carried over the others to reach the rescue boat.

That was the last time I touched my husband, I believe. I had imagined he, along with everyone, eventually made it onto the rescue boat. But I was told otherwise. There was a second rescue boat that continued to collect travelers when mine was full, this one from Italy. We assume our separation happened in this manner as there is no record of him departing with us in Malta.

For me, there was nothing but silence on my boat. They had separated me from the others and brought me to a small room. Two other people were with me, and I recall the constant grinding of the boat's engine, the sickening sway of the boat, and the brief, muddled exchanges between the two looking down on me.

I must have been on some sort of makeshift mattress, and I remember curling up when the stabbing pains shocked me to consciousness at moments, but I did not quite know where I was all the time, and I did not understand what was being said as other voices came into range. But at one point, I think I saw the face of my child.

To this day, I am not sure if my child was born on that boat, or if she was born in the hospital, here in Malta. She is healthy. That's what I am told by the strange nurse that checks in on me. When I ask her about my husband, she says he must be in Italy, but that Malta will not let me go to him. I cannot leave this island because migration laws forbid it.

But now I have a child, a child that I do not want, and a husband that I would prefer to have right now, but cannot. A child, that is all I have.

My Name is Freedom

by Maria Teresa De Donato, Ph.D.

*As humans we take too many things for granted. We assume that we are the smartest species on Earth and, as consequence, that we know what is best for everyone else. But what if Nature and Animal Kingdom could talk?
For instance, what would an Orca raised in captivity tell us while speaking about being deprived of its freedom and jailed in some sort of open cage?*

This story will provide you with the answer.

Hi there! My name is Freedom and I was born a decade ago in the cold waters off the coasts of beautiful Norway.

My mom and dad are amazing swimmers. Since I was born and for the following couple of years I spent most of my time swimming next to my mom. She taught me all I need to know to enjoy life in every possible way. So far, I have learned how to have fun alternating diving into cold and deep waters and emerging from them while happily chasing at an incredible speed motor boats or quietly swimming below and among people kayaking.

People can be quite funny: they usually look at me with admiration, awe, and fear. They seem to see power, beauty, greatness, and charm in me and at the same time it appears as if I can scare them to death. I will never understand them!

You might recognize me and all other members of my family for our striking color pattern consisting in a black dorsal/top that contrasts with the remaining white areas of our pretty massive body and an oval eyepatch behind and above our eyes.

I know, we are simply gorgeous, aren't we?

And let me make one thing clear: although some of you might call us "Killer Whales" we are not whales at all! In fact, we are the world's largest species of dolphins, with our closest relatives being the Irrawaddy family.

Swimming along the coasts of Norway is extremely exciting. With its breathtaking views, the magic of its fjords and amazing mountains and the beauty of its overall landscape, this country must be one of the most fascinating on earth.

I am sure I am not the only one thinking this way. In fact, besides its populations and annual visitors who might agree with me, I myself have plenty of friends that share my view. We, however, prefer to enjoy its sea and swim off its coast all year round. For a few months during the winter, some of us even venture inside the fjords, in the Northern part of Norway to have a big party together. Of course, our favorite meal is made of herrings. There are plenty of them for all of us each year.

Due to our ability to adapt to all kinds of water temperatures, you can find us almost anywhere: from the ice-capped waters of the Arctic and Antarctic to the much warmer waters along the Equator and besides oceans and seas, every now and then you might find some of us enjoying the fresh waters of rivers.

We are very social, like to stick together and live, swim and go hunting in groups of up to 40 individuals. We pretty much depend on each other... just like you, our human friends.

Despite our bad reputation of being dangerous and killers, we usually do not attack humans. When we are hungry, we hunt to eat enough food to survive. We do need tons of it each and every single day. That is not an easy goal to achieve. This, however, has nothing to do with being evil but everything to do with Nature and how things are supposed to work so that a state of balance within species and the environment is preserved.

Some of us, on the contrary, have experienced evil from humans.

We are born to be free, to fully enjoy a great life in the waters where our massive body can move without constrictions or limitations, swim for thousands of miles, plunge into the depths of the oceans and seas, jump out of the waters while proving all the splendor and agility of our majestic body even when nobody is watching.

Sad to say, some of my friends have been captured by your people, raised in captivity and deprived of the love of their mothers and relatives and of the chance of enjoying life to the fullest as it is intended to.

As consequence of this unfortunate circumstance, from time to time frustration and sorrow might have built up in them. Furthermore, some misunderstandings caused by living in an environment that is far from being natural, let alone ideal for us, and where we might erroneously interpret some of the signs and behaviors of our human friends, especially of our trainers, have sometimes ended up in tragedy.

For instance, when we see our beautiful lady trainer jumping up and down while calling us by name and her ponytail swinging back and forth or from side to side, we are going to interpret that as an invitation to play. As a result, we might emerge from the water of the pool, grab that very ponytail with our strong teeth, pull our trainer-friend and dive with her into the water. It is like sharing a toy and playing a game we have been invited to.

Life in a pool, far from the greatness and vastness of oceans and seas can be very unhealthy, disorienting, boring and frustrating for us.

How can you people think, even for a minute, that we wish to kill the person who cares for us the most after we have been separated from our mothers, fathers, and relatives? That is heartbreaking!

The problem is that none of us was born to spend its life in a pool as well as none of you would survive living your entire existence in your closet and never getting the chance to explore and enjoy the amazing Nature and open spaces surrounding you.

Hi there! My name is Freedom. I am an Orca and I hope you will all read and meditate on the validity and fairness of some choices of your fellow humans…

David

by Debbie DiGiacobbe

This story takes you inside the heart of a homeless man, his trials, tribulations, and his ability to keep resolute in spirit. David spends his days sitting by the grave of the great Benjamin Franklin listening to his stories, and studying those who come to visit as they do the same with him. Many people cross David's path each day; however, it is the kindness and compassion of a young teacher that leads to a surprising and unusual friendship that benefits them both.

He did not expect to be here sitting on the sidewalk alone, knees pulled close to his chest, his head heavy like a bowling ball falling forward from its weight, his body hunched over like a tree beaten by the wind. Attached like a vine, his back hugged the red brick wall. From the corner where he sat, the wall traveled three feet before it was interrupted by a wrought iron fence. The fence extended for ten more feet to meet an adjacent wall, which continued down the block around three corners, returning to where it began. Likewise, a sidewalk circled around the encampment like a moat. Inside the fortress, the grounds were pristine. Lush green grass swam between stones that marked the lives of those gone before, each etched with an epitaph trying, but unfailing, to sum up each life. —Pastor. Faithfully Led his Flock. —Firefighter.

Dedicated to Saving Lives. —Loving husband and father. In between, perennials sprouted the colors of the rainbow marking the return of spring and new life. Sunlight sliced through leafy green trees grabbing hold of the flowers and the dead, pulling them up to the sky. Outside the gate, weeds pushed through cracks in the old cobblestone where the man sat. He did not expect to be sitting here.

For over 200 years, the cemetery attracted visitors, mostly strangers. Among the final resting place of the most ordinary, lay one man who did not need an epitaph. The most superfluous and generous words could not sum up all he had accomplished. Through the iron bars, strangers gazed upon his raised tomb, which sat on top of the earth distinguishing his importance.

Approximately the same size as the man in the tomb, the man on the sidewalk appeared smaller. Like a shadow slowly being erased by the clouds, he was barely visible. Next to the him, a bronze plaque displayed a long list of accomplishments: statesman, author, diplomat, inventor, postmaster, and philanthropist. Hundreds, if not thousands of visitors, were drawn each day to the grave of Benjamin Franklin.

This is a good spot, thought the man. *People's pockets laden with change.* As he counted on their goodwill, he watched as one after the other tossed their pennies, nickels, dimes and quarters through the gate, a superstition which they believed would bring them prosperity and good luck. Just inches away, the man sat alone and hungry.

—A penny saved, is a penny earned.—Benjamin Franklin. The man would save his pennies to buy a meal.

It was barely noon when the temperature had already reached a scorching ninety degrees—a typical summer day in Philadelphia. Underneath layers of clothing, the man baked in the sun. Pain shot up his back from sitting on the ground. He did not complain. He tried to feel hopeful, but it was difficult. In between naps, he occasionally looked up to observe those who passed. He liked seeing them—their presence comforting. He recognized many familiar faces, people who worked in the tall office buildings that towered over the low historic structures of the past. There was the tall man with his dark hair slicked to the side in a pinstripe suit carrying his laptop in a man-bag slung over his shoulder, his head bowing quietly as he passed; the short lady in a mismatched outfit, designer flats with red curly ringlets that bounced as she strutted joyfully, always smiling and saying hello; the young musician with a loose tee shirt tucked in his tight black jeans, sporting a beard and tattoos who sometimes stopped to chat; the young girl in her tight yoga pants struggling to walk five disobedient dogs who was too distracted to turn her head. He knew they saw him, maybe even prayed for him—he hoped.

Living on the street took its toll. Constant exposure to the elements was rough not only on the body, but on the mind and spirit as well. With the passing of time, the man's body grew tired and weak, his mind struggled to focus, his soul fell into a deep pit, his spirits suffered. Moving kept his body from growing stiff. His calves were sturdy, his arms strong, but his heart was frail. He was finding it hard to remember. Reminiscing, what he could recall, no longer brought joy, just constant questions of decisions made and those not. Days passed meshing together, becoming one. It was easy to lose track of time. The man roamed the streets like a lost puppy, begging for food, searching for a place to rest.

The corner, which he discovered recently, turned out to be a good spot. Most who stopped were generous, providing enough change to buy a meal. Their kind words fed his spirit. The stories engaging his mind as he wistfully listened to them as told by the tour guides.

"...A young Franklin worked for his older brother. As his apprentice, he learned and mastered the publishing business from James. However, James had limited Ben to the task of printing, not allowing him to write. Cleverly, under the alias of Mrs. Silence Dogood, Ben was able to get his work published in the New England Courant. With only two years of formal education, Ben drew inspiration from books and from others. Excited for new opportunities, Ben ran away to Philadelphia when he was just 17. After three long days aboard ship, he arrived at the dock on High Street with just a few pennies in his pocket, barely enough for breakfast—a loaf of bread," the tour guide explained.

As the man heard these stories, he challenged himself to remember them. He replayed them in his head like a movie, keeping his mind keen and giving himself something to think about. The stories fascinated him, and he never tired of listening as each storyteller highlighted a different aspect of Franklin's life—Ben the inventor, Ben the statesman, Ben the philanthropist, Ben the father. He liked those stories the best; he too was a father.

There were some things the mind never forgets. Yesterday was often like a fog, yet the past could be beckoned in an instant. He thought about his son, Michael, who would be 35 this year. As a child, Michael was smart and curious. He questioned everything. Why are the stars so secretive? How come they only come out at night? Why do bats sleep during the day? Why do Nonno and Nonna only speak Italian when I am around? Together, they would read to find all the answers, except for the last. The man had taught his son everything. Eventually, Michael grew up, went to college, found work, got married and moved away. Like time, the man lost track of his son.

As he reminisced, his heart filled with sadness. He had all the time in the world. But what good is time that is idled? Each uneventful day brought long, unbearable, tedious hours—hours that turned to days, days that turned to months, months to years, years to decades— five to be exact.

The present was unkind, the future seemed bleak, but sometimes the past could be sweet. The man reached back further in his memory trying to recall his own youth, searching for happier times. He closed his eyes tight until he saw it in his mind. Red bricks connecting a row of two-story homes that stretched from one end of the block to the other. A small porch with brick pillars on either side supporting a front bedroom that hung over the porch. People gathering on their stoops out front with family and friends. In the rear yard, too small for people, was as an outdoor greenhouse. Pots lined the perimeter interspersed with flowers and spices: parsley, basil, oregano. In a large planter, a small fig tree boasted sweet figs, which he loved. The community made up of immigrants, although different in ethnicity, shared similar values. They were Irish and Italian, on opposite ends of the neighborhood of course. He was on the Italian side.

He could picture himself sitting on a swing dreaming of all the possibilities of the future. In first grade, he had wanted to be a fireman; by third, he had dreams of playing in the NFL; by fifth, he was going to join the army; in high school, after writing a paper about his ancestors, he envisioned being a writer. There were many stories to tell while growing up. He had notebooks full of them. He wished he had them now. They would help him remember. Instead, he sat on the street letting time pass by.

Lost time is never found again. — Ben Franklin. *The man on the street had lost so much time; time he would never get back.*

The park was an oasis in the city. Tall trees dense with leaves hid the hot summer sun providing some relief to those who slept on its benches. Pink tulips lined the curved paths which cut through the sharp rectangular architecture of the block. Like an alarm clock, birds began their interlude signaling the conclusion of night and the start of day. It was sweet to the man's ears, a sharp contrast to the sour stiffness he felt in his body as he rose slowly, sitting first then standing, all the while trying to feel grateful even as his body complained. Like he did each morning, he packed his bags just before dawn trying to avoid the park ranger who would politely ask him to leave. "Sir, you have to move along." It was bad enough being homeless; however, being asked to leave, made him feel even more worthless—if that was possible. Like many cities, Philadelphia relied on its revenue from its tourism. Its financial success determined by its image. Seeing the homeless man and others like him was bad for both. Wearily, the man wiped his eyes, gathered his two heavy duffle bags, and with his body drooping from the weight of his belongings and the world, he shuffled slowly down six long blocks to sit by his friend, Ben.

The human spirit was unpredictable. After all this time, he was still surprised by the dissimilar reactions of those who passed, from the ones who uncomfortably looked down to those who stopped to offer a kind word. He was always grateful for the latter. But it was the children who were the most predictable, for whom he was the most thankful. He could always count on their kindness. They were innocent, not yet tainted by the world. Their caring words and gestures lit up his days. With their sympathetic eyes, they would look up to their parents, tug on their sleeves, ask for something to give. Many acquiesced, while others drew them close, pulling them away. He was not upset; he understood. He too was a father. The man hoped he would see the children today.

• • • • • • • • • • • • • • • •

Like a colony of ants, the children worked feverishly, separating themselves into groups for daily dismissal: those who rode the buses, those who walked home in small groups for safety, and those being picked up by parents who didn't trust the world or at least some of the people in it. It had been a long day. The teacher felt the exhaustion of Snow White when she bit into that juicy red apple. Unlike the unexpected nap that befell the princess, she would welcome sleep. Sara had survived her first St. Mary's School Field Day, their version of the Summer Olympics, not quite as organized, but a lot more fun. Normally, Sara would stay late to do work that she could not get to during the day: planning, marking papers, catching up on emails and parent communication, but the day had sucked all the energy out of her. She would go home, eat an apple, and go to sleep.

Sara normally rode the bus, but today she decided to take the train. Although it was more costly, it was more reliable and would let her off closer to home, a small reward. She could not wait to walk in the door and kick off her shoes. She reached under her desk for her flats, gathered her work, and made her way down the long, quiet, and finally deserted hallway. After a quick reprieve in the air-conditioned building, which tuition helped pay for, she opened the door only to be hit by a wave of heat. She hardly walked a block before sweat began to bead down her face. She wrapped her long straight blond hair into a ponytail giving her neck some relief, and hid her head under a baseball cap to protect her blue eyes and her fair skin from the sun.

To get to the train, she would walk through the historic district passing some of her favorite places: Independence Hall, the Liberty Bell,

Betsy Ross's House and Ben Franklin's Grave. In the near distance, she spotted the cemetery. Like so many, she marveled at the greatest of men who had done so much for the people of Philadelphia and the country. She too wished to accomplish great things. Her head housed a storage closet filled with ideas: feed the hungry, stop global warming, fight for criminal justice. Like air fueling a fire, passion fueled through her veins. Unfortunately, work was so consuming, she had neither the time nor energy to complete even the smallest of tasks let alone fight for a cause. She wondered if others were weighed down by the daily demands of life.

—Energy and persistence conquer all things. —Ben Franklin. Sara had energy and WAS persistent. She was conquering all things...at work.

. . . .

The man sat on the ground. His body limp like a delicate flower starved of water, his clothes shabby and loose. A cup tilted in his hand, his fingers wrapped around it lightly, his nails long and embedded with dirt. He was thin and frail, olive in complexion either from ethnicity or the sun. She reached in her handbag and pulled out all she had. Sara placed a few dollars in the cup and said a shy hello. The man opened his eyes slightly and muttered, "Thank you."

Sara had moved to Philadelphia from Midway, a small rural town in Kentucky, about a year ago. It was a culture shock at first, but in a short time, she came to love everything about the city: its theaters, art, restaurants, bars, but mostly its people. She had never experienced a group so outwardly passionate. Their loud enthusiasm rang for their sports teams, new restaurants, and small businesses. It celebrated a neighbor's new job, birthdays, graduations. It fueled protests for climate control and criminal justice. There was nothing not to like about this small city which had earned its title, City of Brotherly Love (and Sisterly Affection).

. . . .

The morning train seemed faster as it zipped through the many neighborhoods that sewed the city together, each boasting their unique style of architecture and people. Her neighborhood, in South Philly, was made up of old timers, mostly Italians, who for the most part welcomed the newcomers who had revitalized the community by opening up new shops and restaurants, replacing the quiet with noise and their energy. They had brought new life to a fading community, increasing the value of people's homes and their lives.

Sara walked two blocks before passing Betsy Ross's House. She stopped to participate in the short flag raising ceremony which was performed each morning promptly at 8:00 AM. A short block ahead was Ben's grave. As she approached the corner, she noticed the man from the day before. She chastised herself for not having anything to give him. Her generation relied on credit and debit cards, Venmo and PayPal. She rummaged in her leather bag gathering the few coins she had and dropped them in his cup. She felt embarrassed. She had so much while he had so little. As the man looked up with a grateful smile, she observed the lines that traveled his face. She wondered what paths had brought him here. "I'm sorry I don't have more," she said. "Thank you. Every little bit helps," he replied.

And as she walked away, her heart was heavy and sad. He was not a young man, not that that mattered, but the streets had to be difficult for someone older, although it was hard to guess his age. Life on the streets had a way of aging a person.

•   •   •   •   •   •   •   •   •   •   •   •   •

Months had passed since Sara met David, five to be exact. Sara had fallen into a new routine. She decided the train was the best way to commute. It was faster, more direct, and the time she saved, she would use to visit with her friend. Each day, Sara prepared two lunches, one for herself and one for David: a sandwich, fruit, bottle of water and a Tastykake (a pair of prewrapped desserts unique to Philly). Sometimes she would bring him something she made the night before. He loved her fried chicken. On her way to work, she would stop and leave him lunch. After work, she would visit with her friend sitting down next to him so they would meet eye to eye, a small gesture that allowed him some dignity. David always looked forward to seeing Sara. Sara felt the same.

—*A man wrapped in himself makes a very small bundle. —Ben Franklin. Sara may have been small in size, about five-foot two, but she was NO small bundle.*

"Morning, David! How are you doing today? I brought you a small pillow to sit on. I hope it helps your back."

"Thank you so much, Sara. I could use that," he said gratefully.

She handed him lunch and some other things: clothes, toiletries, books. David loved to read.

"How's work going?" he continued.

"Work is good. We had our Author's Lunch today. The children shared their stories. They did a wonderful job. I felt bad for Shari though. She had worked so hard on her book, but her mom couldn't make it. Luckily, I thought to record her presentation on my phone," she said spiritedly. "I will email it to her tonight. Some of these kids have so many problems. It's so sad. I wish I could fix them all."

"You just fixed one," he said.

David always had a way of making her feel better. She often felt that she benefited more from their relationship than him. That's the thing about giving, the giver always seems to benefit the most.

As time passed, their friendship grew. Day after day, they shared stories and dreams. David told Sara how he broke his leg horsing around on the monkey bars, and how his mother had overreacted by not letting him go back to the park without her for months. It was humiliating for an eight-year-old. Sara told David how she drove her bicycle into her dad's car while learning how to ride. Boy was he mad, she thought she saw smoke come out of his ears, but he got over it fast. David talked about his family, specifically his son who was an editor for a publishing company. He was so proud. He wondered what he was doing now. Sara told David about her parents and her older brother, John, who joined the army and was stationed in Syria. She was worried about him. David described how he worked as a carpenter and electrician, how he lost his job, how he had come to live on the streets, and how he hoped to work again. Day in and day out, they talked until they knew almost every detail of each other's lives. To those who passed by, it might have appeared to be a most unlikely friendship, but for David and Sara it was the most natural thing.

• • • • • • • • • • • • • • • • •

It was July 4, 1776, Congress had just signed the Declaration of Independence. A new nation was born. The document was written by Thomas Jefferson, with the help of Ben Franklin, of course. *We hold these Truths to be self-evident, that all Men are created equal, that they are endowed by their Creator with certain unalienable Rights, that among these are Life, Liberty, and the pursuit of Happiness...*

Sara thought about her friend who had lost those rights, not by action or choice, but by circumstance. The land of great opportunities... for some, she thought. This certainly was not what our forefathers envisioned, especially not Ben. Sara pondered. It is not always about the choices you make, sometimes circumstances choose you. David tried everything to change his circumstances.

The city was filled with people who tried to advocate for those like David—church groups, organizations, individuals like Sara. Still, it was not enough. Sara did what she could. She encouraged David to go to a shelter, to stop by the local church for a meal, to meet with a social worker at a nonprofit just a block away. She even tried to take him, but he refused. Being on the streets left him skeptical and untrusting. Sara was his closest ally, but still, she was unconvincing.

• • • • • • • • • • • • • • • • •

Fall turned to winter, and as the temperature decreased, Sara's worry increased. A coat, blanket, hat and gloves provided minimal protection from the cold. Tonight, it was expected to drop to sixteen degrees. David hated going to a shelter. "They are loud, dirty and unsafe. People steal your stuff," he would say. It was only on the coldest nights that he sought refuge. Sara prayed he would seek shelter on this frigid night.

"Where are you going tonight?" she asked.

"Don't worry, Sara, I am going to My Brother's House," he confessed.

"You have a brother?" Sara replied.

"No, it's the name of a shelter," said David.

Sara felt silly. She knew he had no one. Hope had filled her heart for a short minute.

Sara jotted her cell number down on a piece of paper again. She had done this numerous times. She knew how easy it was to lose things when you were constantly on the move. David put the paper in his bag. At the corner, David turned south toward the shelter while Sara turned west toward the train. "Be safe, David," said Sara. "Don't worry, Sara. I'll be fine," he replied, like always. Sara went home to her quiet, clean and safe apartment.

• • • • • • • • • • • • • •

It was 7:00 AM when Sara got off the train. The corner was empty. Where was her friend? Rushing as usual, she would have to stop after work. She was sorry David wouldn't have a meal today, but there was nothing she could do. Her day would be filled with long boring meetings. She would rather spend it with her students. It was less exhausting and more fun. Instead, she'd have to listen to her colleagues as they rambled on about policy and curriculum. She was resolved that they loved hearing themselves talk. Like a mouse pleading its case to a lion, compromise and agreement were never achieved. The constant back and forth gave her a headache that not even a Tylenol could fix. She was happy to see 3:00 p.m. Everyone one rushed to get home, their enthusiasm ending with the clock. Sara liked to stay late in her classroom where she was surrounded by the work of her students and quotes from Nelson Mandela, Helen Keller, Dr. Martin Luther King—all of which inspired her. Although she had much to do, she decided against working late. She would leave on time so she could catch David. She grabbed her handbag, laptop, some important papers, and headed home.

As she exited the building, cold air smacked her in the face. The wind tried to knock her down, and she leaned forward to fight it. Four blocks seemed like a mile as she pushed against its current. Approaching the corner, she saw no signs of her friend. Where could he be? It was odd, but it wouldn't have been the first time he was missing. Sometimes he grew tired of sitting. Occasionally, he would walk away leaving his empty lunch bag and his small sign politely asking for change—indicating he would be back soon. Sara walked around the block, but there was no sign of him.

On the train, her mind raced. What if he's lost? He was becoming more confused. What if he's hurt? Crime is everywhere. He would be an easy target. Maybe he's sick? He does have health problems. Sara poured herself a glass of wine to help her relax. She prepared herself dinner, a small plate of cheese and crackers; she wasn't very hungry. She sat by her living room window, which overlooked the street, gazing out at her neighbors, who like herself had everything, and thought about how one circumstance could change your life—like it did for her friend. She tried to quiet her mind, but it was impossible. Finally, she distracted herself with her work, and with papers on her lap and a red pen in her hand, Sara gave in to sleep.

• • • • • • • • • • • • • •

The same song repeated in her head at least a dozen times before she realized it was her phone. It was still dark. Who could be calling at this hour? She glanced at the clock. It was 1:23 AM. She began to worry as her head started to clear.

"Hello. Is this Sara Stevens?"

"Who's calling?" she asked.

"I'm Doctor Lee, from Jefferson."

Sleep still in her head, Sara tried to focus, her mind slowly catching up with her body. Sara listened as the doctor, who in her most compassionate voice, told Sara the news. Not quite sure she had heard correctly, she pleaded with her to repeat what she had said hoping she misunderstood. Finally, fully awake, she realized she was not dreaming. Her eyes filled, as the doctor explained that David had passed.

Sara struggled to comprehend as the doctor retold the events. By foot, he barely made it to the hospital. Collapsing with severe chest pains, he went into cardiac arrest. They tried desperately to save him, but it was too late. They did everything they could. Sara took a deep breath. When she was finally able to think, she asked, "How did you know to call me?"

"We found a card in his pocket with your number and your name."

Sara sat quietly and wept.

· · · · · · · · · · · · · · · ·

It had been a couple weeks since David died. Every time Sara passed Ben's grave, she looked for him. There was a hole in her heart. He was a good man. She felt sad that no one would remember him.

Sara shared the news with her students who knew him through her stories. They each made a heart with words of sweet condolences. She glued them around the perimeter of a poster to create a plaque. She put on her flats, grabbed her laptop, picked up the poster and exited the building. And just like the day she had met David, she was greeted by a wave of heat. She hardly walked a block before sweat began to bead down her face. She placed the poster down long enough to wrap her long straight blond hair into a ponytail giving her neck some relief, and hid her head under a baseball cap to protect her blue eyes and her fair skin from the sun. When she reached Ben's grave, she placed the small memorial next to Ben's, right where David once sat.

David Williams
He was a kind man.

He worked hard.
He was a master carpenter and electrician.
He drew inspiration from Ben Franklin.
He loved the children.
He loved fried chicken.
He loved to read.
He had a family, a wife and son.
He had a best friend, Sara.
He will be greatly missed.

• • • • • • • • • • • • • •

The weekend flew by. Monday morning came quickly as it always did. Sara woke to the sound of her alarm. She showered, dressed, grabbed her coffee and headed to work. The train was packed as usual. Sara stood for the short 15-minute commute. She was tired already from grief. She walked her usual route, passing first Betsy Ross's House, then The First Firehouse, followed by Arch Street Meeting House, and finally Ben's grave. When she neared the corner, she observed what appeared to be debris. However, as she got closer, she was shocked at what she saw. Surrounding David's Memorial were flowers, pictures, and cards. —He was a nice man. He said I should work hard in school. —He told us things the tour guide didn't know about Ben. —He was smart.

Sara's felt herself smile. They did see him, they did care. And just at that moment, the sun peaked its head out from behind the clouds, stretching out its hands, reaching down, and like it did with the flowers and the others, pulled David up to Heaven. She could see him smiling down on her and hear him saying, "I'm okay, Sara."

This story is dedicated to all those who are homeless, and to those who advocate for them.

The Steamer Trunk

by David M. DiLillo

*"The Steamer Trunk" is a story of a young couple's decision and journey
to emigrate from Italy to America in the early part of the twentieth century.
Their steamer trunk becomes a symbol and backdrop to their story
as their future generations grow and prosper as Americans.*

It was always just there. This flat-black nondescript cube to be dealt with, walked around, or maybe slid out of the way a bit, omnipresent in our Weymouth house's attic. It was built with strong wood. It had to be. It had to make it across. There was two rough hand-cut leather handles bolted to each side. The heavy, recessed lid was mounted to the body of the trunk with two sea-worthy hinges and a solid brass locking latch. Was it stashed away and disguised as something functional in our Lilliputian sized apartment in Roxbury or relegated and forgotten to our small storage section in the basement? It was invisible to me. But to my sisters, it was alluring, beckoning. Foreign and old looking, something from another time or world it was mysterious, spilling over with possibilities of secrets or unimaginable treasures. Where did it come from? Whose was it? Even after all of their speculation, they never opened it. They never dared to.

We had sold my parents' house. They were both gone now and after almost forty years living and gathering things in this house the time had come. It was on that last morning in my parent's house when for the first time I really saw it and registered that it could be no more than some old black homemade wooden chest. All us siblings, and our sons, were cleaning out the family home and removing all traces of us ever having been there before. The closing was the next day. My parents, God Bless them, were both first generation Italians and children of the Depression.

They couldn't bear to throw anything out, "You never know... Maybe we could fix it... Or we could use it for something..." So, the attic and the cellar became the depository for the tonnage of misfit toys, sewing machines, clothes, old shoes, bolts of cloth material, zippers and buttons, and items I've never seen anywhere else except my parents' attic or cellar.

One of my parents' obsessions was to save all and every Christmas gift box that came into that teeny tiny ranch house since the actual birth of Christ. "Hey, what are you crazy? Oh no, I'm not paying for boxes. I got plenty up in the attic!"

We children didn't think the new owners would appreciate the gold mine of *"perfectly good"* gift boxes that we'd *"throw in"* with the place. So, out they went, decades of careful and deliberate saving, gone. Plastic bags were another coveted shiny object for my parents to hoard. There were plastic bags full of plastic bags and then they had plastic bags inside more bags! Enough plastic bags saved in that attic to kill a couple of more Earths. The plastic bag trove, quickly and without tears, joined their gift box attic mates in the dumpster.

My parents also loved those racy hot pulpy paper back novels of the fifties and sixties. This literature needed to be retained and stored, too. "They're good stories!" Cartons of these mildewy scorchers with their heaving loins and forbidden steamy taboo affairs laid out on each page were all just there for the taking. These, too, certainly could not be left in any Welcome to the Neighborhood Basket for the next owners. These rare finds and so, so much more all had to be sorted with some care and diligence because who knows what "diamonds" and "nuggets" may have been wisely squirreled away up there in the safe attic, disguised in empty gift boxes or my father's overcoats and zoot suits from the 40's.

Their master plan was to foil thieves in a break-in. "Hey, it could happen! Who the hell is gonna think to look up there?" So, this took time and we didn't have time. Thoroughness and selectivity had to be couched for speed and mass disposal. We established a fire brigade up in the attic. One squad up and one down below and as we sorters and schleppers marched like Sherman to the sea through all that the attic concealed.

We all had seen the trunk as we climbed up into the attic. It was impossible to miss it, sitting there like a sentry right near the attic pull down hatch. We tried to deny it was there and that it would have to be addressed and dispatched. It was the last big thing and it had to go down and then out. We all stood there for a few seconds looking at it. First, it had to be emptied. At least we were going to see what the hell was in this stupid trunk. We got kind of excited that after all these years we'd discover what my parents had ferreted away in here.

I forgot who opened the trunk. The latch was unclasped and pulled back. We lifted the heavy lid and looked in to see old sheer curtains and bed spreads and other "linens" used long ago from our time in Roxbury. These linen heirlooms sat in that trunk forty years because, "Hey, we paid good money for those. You never know, we might need them...We could still use them! They're still good!" It was a letdown.

I started, "Okay, does anybody want any of this stuff?"

"No?"

"No."

"What are we gonna do with it?"

"Throw it away."

"What? You can't just throw it away. It's all still good!"

"Oh my God. Do you hear yourself? Okay, do you want it?"

"Well, no."

"Okay, do you want it? Do you? How about you? No. Okay. Toss it."

"What about the chest?'

"Christ."

"Okay, does anyone want it? No? No? Okay, bring it down to the street with the other stuff."

The other stuff was forming a small mountain in the dumpster. We all took turns jumping onto it, futilely, to try and compress it. The tide of it threatened to spill over the sides. The remainder of what we couldn't shoehorn and jam into the container we piled up out on the curb. The jumbled pyramid spanned along the sidewalk the length of my parent's lot.

The next day was trash day, luckily. My sisters decided to be there in the morning with tips for the trash men to handle those of my parents' treasures not reclaimed by strangers. We were grateful that there was no rain in the forecast for that evening. We hoped people driving by would stop, because mixed in with the bags of plastic bags and gift boxes were bar stools, end tables from their living room, old favorite dolls, and games and toys long forgotten, a rocking horse, that favorite coat or sweater that our parents always wore. We wanted people to take a good hard look and reclaim and maybe cherish the good stuff and there was good stuff in there, too. It was just stuff none of us could use or wanted anymore.

My son and my nephews being younger and stronger than us wrestled this black bear of a trunk through the small attic opening in the hall ceiling. Two of them down below and two in the attic above lowering this Goliath down the flimsy pull down ladder, and then out to the sidewalk to the top of the pile.

We started walking back to complete our mop up and one of my nephews yelled, "Hey Uncle Dave, look at this!" He spotted it on the side of the trunk, "Look!" We all missed seeing this pasted on label. The size of the label was about 8 x 10" and had a background of white and in the middle of this field was a huge red star with blue printing across it, "White Star Line" and in the lower right corner, "Napoli to Boston."

It made me gasp. This was my grandparents' trunk! My mother told me their story but I never put the puzzle piece of the steamer trunk together with them. She told me that my grandparents got married in Italy and then came to the States on their "honeymoon." This was the trunk they had built to take all they owned to America! I looked at my siblings and all our children standing in the middle of all these discarded possessions outside on the curb. I thought of my mother, my aunts and uncles and all my cousins. I thought of my grandparents who died so young that none of my generation ever got to meet them. I thought about all our families, all of us, everything we have and ever achieved. All of it got started out of this chest.

· · · · · · · · · · · · · ·

He marched into the middle of the six man tent, stomped on the ground and sprang to attention. Settled into their bivouac the other five men gawked agape as he sounded off, "Mi Chiamo Rocco Visabelli," the handsome ramrod straight stranger said with a military snap of his boot heels. On his left heel he slowly pivoted to access his new quarters and squad mates. His querying, intelligent eyes observed that he had commanded the room's attention. He thrived on the attention. With a smile, a bow and with a wave of his pith helmet, he stated, "Comrades, I am here to win this war single-handedly, if I must. Visabelli will rule the day. I am Romano. It is my destiny!" The other five men answered this Roman rooster's crowing with hoots, catcalls, and mock applause. He was not to be deterred. Visabelli looked at each man, slowly, individually, locking eyes with each; Marseglia the baker, Nicolini the carpenter, Carlozzi the shoe maker, Guerrini the tailor and Morganelli the laborer. They were all poor southerners from Calabria, Puglia, Campania and Abruzzo. Visabelli in birth, education, and privilege was profoundly different from his squad mates. As he shook hands with the others, Visabelli smiled hearing the men's southern accents. Their accents certified his and their class divides.

"So, my brave, strong comrades, I see and I hear you are all from the campagna, yes? Well, well, well! If I may ask, who is guarding your goats and chickens and your cows while you dress up and play soldier, eh? Your women? Well my Southern Comrades, we'll all see , yes we will see very soon of what you are all made of, yes soon enough."

The squad suggested what sex act he should do to himself or where on his body he could shove his head. They'd have to take this Roman's condensing bullshit throughout the war. The southerners collectively groaned. *What luck*, they thought! Romans were all the same; too good to be even considered even just Italian.

Visabelli spied the last open bed and took in the man lying in the bunk next to it. He turned the force of his personality onto Michelangelo Morganelli, looked him up and down and appraised him as just another poor paesano, "So, Morganelli, you made sure to save me a place next to you huh? I know, Morganelli, I know! You are already jealous of Visabelli. As soon as I entered the tent I could see it in your eyes, your gratitude and feverish hope, maybe...even an answer to your prayers that simply by being near me, my Roman courage and intelligence will rub off you, yes? Maybe by some blessed miracle it could also happen with my looks, too paesano, but no, no paesano for you, only God can help you there, no? Don't worry, Campo. Visabelli is here. I will take you under my wing. Protect you and teach you. Don't worry!"

Michelangelo responded confidently. "You know, I was just telling my brother campos here, before you graced us with your regal entrance, that if God doesn't bless us and send our unworthy little squad a Siciliano, then please Dear God send a Romano! And here you are! A gift from God himself! Men, it is destiny. We are saved. God sent us our very own Romano!" Gazing adoringly up Michelangelo, imitating classic Italian art, he extended both hands to the Heavens, "Grazie, Dio! Thank you for this gift of Visabelli. You have anointed us with the sacred privilege of existing in the same army as Visabelli and for all his joyous gifts that he brings to us, your and now his, humble servants! So, dear Lord, we say thank you for sending us this little Caesar of a yapping dog. Long Live Caesar!"

The rest of the squad stood and joined in a chorus, "Long Live Caesar!" Visabelli from then on become Caesar to all and he loved it. Caesar and Morganelli smiled and embraced after their verbal fencing match. Fate had driven them together and they both needed to know 'who is that man beside me,' because together they would meet the Turks and their fates.

. . . .

Michelangelo laid on his bunk and wrote to Maria. He wanted to make sure she knew he made it and he loved her and he was going to survive. Maria could read. None of their parents could. She'd tell them everything. He and she made a vow that they would be married as soon as he got back to Benevento. He tried not to think that maybe it'd be his first and last letter home and about never seeing her and his family ever again.

"Hey Michel, already writing your sweetheart, eh? Tell her how beautiful Africa is with the palm trees and stench of camels and Turks. Yes, this would be a fine place to take your bride on the honeymoon, eh Campo? Did you tell her all about me? Did you dare? So, Campo, she may now start to ask for me in her letters. It is unavoidable. She will be amazed at your good fortune of you serving with a Romano, a handsome warrior-god and with the knowledge that I will let you tell people that you are my friend!," Caesar smirked.

Morganelli smiled sadly, shook his head, "Caesar, please, this will be a long war. It's the first day. Save some energy for the Turks. Why don't you clean the sand out of your ears or practice your saluting, or ass kissing officers' culos? That would be a more productive use of your time than breaking my gulgliones, eh. Right now, you're making me tired."

"Ah, Campo, you know, I'm making myself tired, too. Madonna! I did not enjoy the crossing. Two days crossing the Mediterranean from Italy to Libya and not in a luxury suite that I am entitled to expect. This was all much too much to ask me to lower my standards.

I survived but, confidentially, I got seasick on that dirty tub of a ship. Disgusting! You know, too, how The Mediterranean is a rough sea. They will hear of it in Rome, believe me! What about you, Campo? How did you fare on the high seas?"

"Hey, Caesar, for a poor campo like me who's never been out of his village before, never mind going off to Africa to fight in a war, ah not too bad. And, I did not get seasick either this being my maiden steamer trip; eh, you spoiled brat! I never got the chance to know luxury from shit, so it was okay for me. But hey, now we gotta survive this two week indoctrination at the hands of the Italian Army and then it's on to face those son-of-a-bitch Turks!"

The Italian army kept the new arrivals in the Tripoli garrison for two weeks upon disembarking from the troop steamer. This fortnight was spent gathering rations, weapons, ammo, and medical kits and perfecting the final battle plans. In the safety of the garrison, tales of false bravado of the punishments shouted in oaths detailing what was to be meted out to those dirty Turk from their gun sights or at the end of their bayonets. But at night, alone in their bunks, in the long, hot, starry African night, they suffered moments of abject total fear. Most were from small villages, boys coming off the fields and out of apprenticeships in shops, gone for the first time in their lives so far from home. Now, they were infantry soldiers in the 57th Infantry Regiment, a re-enforcement force, sent to Libya to capture territory for Italy from the Turks. For what? Maybe for an excellent chance to be killed or maimed in action for a cause they really didn't understand or did not have any impact on their day to day lives. Caesar and the southerners all continued to torment and tease each other. It built camaraderie. The squad jelled and became a unit. Their survival hinged on it.

The six man squad got their marching orders and they and the rest of the 57th moved out. The first objective, fight their way into the Benghazi garrison and re-enforce troops there. Carlozzi and Marseglia did not survive this first engagement. The regiment stayed in Benghazi in a defensive posture for most of their time in Libya. As their hitch was coming to a close, they were re-organized and fought through Derna's trenches to get back to Tripoli to disembark back home. Guerrini and Nicolini perished in close order fighting in these trenches. Morganelli and Visabelli were the only two of their squad to survive their almost year-long deployment in Libya.

Now, safely back on the troop carrier steaming back to Napoli, Michelangelo stood at the ship railing looking out at the horizon. He took out his pipe, a gift from his father and carefully packed it with the army issue tobacco, struck a match and waited for the nicotine to calm him. His mind wandered back to Libya. He'd seen things in Libya. He did things in Libya. He wasn't the same young man who left his village an eternity ago and he wasn't afraid of anything anymore. His heart raced and he started to relive the squad's march to Benghazi to reinforce the garrison, which was on the verge of collapse, brutalized by the Turks and their Somali allies. They had to fight their way into the garrison and then repel attack after attack by these madmen. He could feel his chest heave and breath coming shorter and shorter to him.

Caesar sauntered up beside him and mercifully snapped him out of the brutal flashback of Benghazi, "Hey, Campo, daydreaming again of your fame and fortune as a conquering Centurion? Paesan, I see that look on your face. It's okay. It's over. You and I made it! Hey, we even got promotions to corporal! Think of the bonus we'll get once go through processing in Napoli! Hey, look what I pinched!" Caesar pulled out a bottle of wine. "That Siciliano chooch, Grasso, left it unguarded. I got tired of him shooting his pig mouth off about how smart he was to smuggle it on board, so your emperor took his tax, eh. C'mon let's eat those sandwiches and drink his piss Siciliano vino."

A faint smile was Michelangelo's response to his fighting comrade. He and Caesar had been through too much, together. "Mio Dio, Caesar. What we did there in Benghazi. I can't get it out of my mind. It haunts me. I can't sleep!"

"Hey Michel, snap out of it! You can't think that way! Jesus Christ, what we all did! What we all had to do to stay alive. We had to fight for our lives, goddam it! We did what we had to do. We did what we were trained for, what our instincts led us to do. It was gonna be either us or them and by God we picked it to be them. We did your duty!"

"Duty! I shot a man point blank in the face and you bayoneted another as he was coming at you. Christ, I can never forget their faces. The look in their eyes at that the moment..."

"Campo, Thank the Good Lord you saw them coming over. If you hadn't seen them and we didn't stop them dead in their tracks, they would have breached and you and I would have joined the others, morti! Those Turk pigs! They're animals! You saw them shitting in the streets like dogs. Mother of God, the smell of them. Pigs! That smell. I tell you, I'll never been able to be free of that stench. Mannaggia! Hey, that scum and this shitty war is not worth another thought in that pea-sized head of yours, eh! You and I saved ourselves, goddam it, and we got stripes for it, too. That's bravery under fire!"

"Bravery, I shit and pissed myself and so did you! Okay...Caesar... you're right, it's behind us now. Let's drink and let's never talk about this ever again, ever."

Michelangelo reached for the sandwiches and unwrapped them both and gave Caesar one as he poured the wine. Looking at each other, they clinked glasses, "Salute. To Grasso, that chooch!" The two men sat silent looking out at the now calm Mediterranean Sea eating and drinking their stolen wine.

"When we get into Napoli", Caesar started, "we go to headquarters, get processed, turn in our weapons and get our pay vouchers. Then, that'll be it for you and me, Paesan. I catch the train to Roma and back to civilization, Thank God! And you, back to your family and beloved, eh? What about your padrone in the campagna? I'll bet he misses you, too!"

"That pig Don Alphons and that elephant he married, Livia, they'll be waiting for me. Those gavones we pay with our blood, the bastards. I'm not a famous Roman doctor's spoiled brat of a son like you who never had to work a day in his life. Back to field like an ox for me. Hey, Caesar, tell me, why the hell did you join the army? I'm sure Papa could have pulled on all those little strings and kept his bambino home and safe sucking on the tit of life in Roma, eh?"

"Ah, Campo, you are correct, I could have ducked it but I wanted to join and fight."

"You ass! For what? The greater glory of Italy? Please. It was all a colossal pile of shit, sand, and blood slammed together like one big huge putrid jumboth. At best, we fought to a draw with those animals. Even when we dropped bombs on them out of our aeroplanes they didn't stop coming at us. Ah, I shkeeve the very thought of every one of those bastards and that piss hole country. It's not even fit for Don Alphons' pigs"

"Well, Paesan, I did it for a couple of reasons. First, there were two women in Roma...so an exit strategy was needed to dodge a trip to the altar with either. And I was bored. I craved adventure, to feel something. Getting shot at, people trying to kill me and me trying to kill them, well, that fit the bill for me Campo. Besides, I think I might get into politics and with war time service on my record, well, it would give me a great advantage, proof of the brave Romano Centurion that I truly am, eh?!"

Michelangelo shook his head in disgust, "Jesus Christ, I endured all that shit and almost got myself killed so that a giamoke like you can end up running things? Oh, Sant'Antonio, save us from Caesar and the rest of his crazies in this crazy world! Okay, Paesan...Very well...I'll play along. What's your plan? Would you join a party and which one?

"Socialists of course!", replied Caesar with pride, "There's a young left wing socialist in Roma, a big time anti-war politico, Mussolini is his name. Now, he is supposed to do great things for Italy's future. My papa knows him. Treated his mother. I'll attach myself to him and his clique and see what happens. A genius like myself, I'll get noticed by him soon enough and I will quickly rise to be his right hand man, eh?! Have you ever heard of him?"

"Yes, Caesar, even in the campagna we get newspapers and I can read too, chooch! Jesus Christ...to think you could have anything to do with being in charge of things someday. Now, I'm really depressed!"

"It is just one plan, Campo, just one of many...", Caesar casually suggested, "For a man of my charms and abilities there are many doors that will burst open for me to lead me along countless other roads to choose from and to seize my fortunes. Alas, yes, I am lucky. I do not have Alphons and Livia waiting on my return. So, is that your plan, Campo, return to the yoke?"

Michelangelo smiled proudly, "No. I have another plan."

Amused, Caesar smiled and egged his friend on, "And tell us, Aristotle, what of this plan you speak?"

"As soon as I get back to Benevento, Maria Grazia and I will be married and immediately we leave. We're going to immigrate to America! We decided all this before I left. We've been working out the fine details in our letters ever since I shipped out. It's given us both hope through all this shit. We're to tell our families right away. That will be the hardest part. Especially mine, since I've been away so long fighting in this goddam war. They all know it's for the best. There's nothing there for us. After Libya, I can't stomach Don Alphons' shit or anyone else's any more. I fought for more for myself and Maria and someday, God willing, for our children! No! We're gonna make a break. America is where our future and our lives will be."

Caesar stared hard at his friend. Looking into his eyes, he reached for both Michelangelo's hands and grasping them, "Michel, I know you. I know the man that you are. It's the only plan for you. I know you'll succeed. I know you'll prosper. You'll conquer America! She will be lucky to have you as her new son! Buona Fortuna, mio fratre, Buona Fortuna!"

The troop-ship arrived with great fanfare in Napoli. Cannons sounded as they entered the port. Bands played, government officials and their beautiful wives and daughters warmly greeted the returning heroes as they exited down the gangplank. The two friends moved agonizingly slow through the laborious Italian circus of organized mayhem to be processed and dispatched out of the army. They had time for one last meal before Caesar's train left to Roma and Michelangelo's bus to Benevento. One of their regiment comrades, DelTufo, a local boy, suggested a nice restaurant. Said it was his favorite and the best in Napoli. Caesar complained bitterly all through the meal and what a stupid tasteless ass DelTufo was to recommend such a trough of inferiority, "I can barely choke down this Neapolitan swill and piss for wine", but not a crumb of bread remained or a dish left umopped. The two friends embraced and each went their separate ways.

• • • • • • • • • • • • • • • •

Michelangelo and his bride Maria Gazia Mercuri-Morganelli arrived in the port of Boston sometime in the Spring of 1914. They left from Napoli and landed twelve days later at Long Wharf in Boston. The journey in steerage across the Atlantic was not one of luxury. Beds were bunked in a large common area. Ventilation and privacy were non-existent. The newlyweds staked out a corner that offered a modicum of space and the illusion of privacy. The food was atrocious and foreign to their Neapolitan palettes. They survived. Neither of them got seasick or worse caught anything from their steerage mates, and mercifully no one in their compartment died on the voyage. Upon docking in Boston, Michelangelo and Maria held each other and trembled. They made it!

The cost of their voyage over for both of them and their steamer trunk was $40.00 and they had $20.00 in cash, all of it a fortune. The cash was sewn into Maria's petticoats for safe keeping. The bulk of this fortune came on the back of Michelangelo and his service in Libya. He knew he was going to be drafted. There was no escaping this obligation. The Royal Italian Army was offering bonuses to all those who signed up early and volunteered to fight in Libya. He calculated since he was going to be drafted anyway, why not sign up and get every cent he could. His field promotion to corporal along with his combat bonus gave them the head start. Maria's small dowry got them closer. Michelangelo's family commissioned the village carpenter, Anastasio, to build a steamer trunk for the crossing. They decided on the size. Anastasio selected beech wood. To cut costs and to not attract the attention of greedy eyes and prying fingers, there was no decorative or fine detailed hardware on the outside. Just two rough leather handles securely bolted in place and heavy duty hinges and latches. Anastasio decided that it should be painted flat-black to help camouflage it out in the open. He wanted nothing about the trunk to catch the eyes of the curious. Everything they owned and needed would be in that trunk.

Steerage class disembarked last, which meant almost another entire agonizing day waiting to get off the ship. Michelangelo had written to the Italian Protection League of Boston. The League was established by wealthy Boston natives who had a social conscience to help new Italian immigrants navigate their first critical days and weeks being in America . The League would meet them at the dock. But first, they needed to get off the ship, claim and store the trunk and lastly, pass the health exam by the medical staff on Long Wharf. These were monumental and excruciating challenges for the young couple; as they didn't speak or read a word of English, now they were left to the mercy of harried Italian countrymen-translators. Finding and processing the trunk was a nightmare filled with heart wrenching chaos for the honeymooners with misdirection and frantic chases from one end of the wharf to the other. At one point, they were told that there was no record of it ever having been loaded onboard in Naples! Finally, with the trunk safely in their possession, they found the agency and it was off to their office to register them and take the free room assigned to the couple for the week. The League suggested they settle in the North End of Boston. Most of the Italians, without family in Boston, settled there to start out. The League loaned the couple the down payment for their first month's rent. The League also acted like an employment placement service for new arrivals. They had contacts in the warehouses, the docks, in kitchens, with the utilities, local farmers, and the many shoe factories. These employers were always on the lookout for people who were desperate and were willing to supply cheap labor for work no one else would do. Michelangelo was a farm laborer all his life but he was intelligent, a military veteran, and well-read for living in a small village. So, with this advantage and his persona and confidence, the League set him up with one of the city's utilities as a laborer. It was a huge break. It was the biggest utility in the city, had benefits and most importantly steady employment.

By the end of the week, with the League's help, they found a little one bedroom apartment on Salem Street. Michelangelo had a job and they were on their way in America!

Michelangelo became known as "Mike" to the crew of his utility truck and he was learning to speak and read English. It was little tougher for Maria to sharpen her skills because everybody spoke only Italian all day but she and Mike practiced at night trying to speak English only to each other. They were focused on becoming American citizens.

As much as the North End was a refuge to the young couple, the Black Hand was always close by, ready to prey on ignorant and scared Italian immigrants. They had tentacles everywhere, always watching, waiting, tempting, and ready to "help," for a cost. Maria hated them and was frightened by their greed and indenturing allures. Mike and Maria worked hard and saved and within a few years bought their own home in Roxbury. These two Italian immigrants from the fields of Benevento had earned their own American dream.

. . . .

Thirty years after their arrival, Michelangelo and Maria Grazia both passed. Both never made it past their early fifties. Maria Grazia suffered complications after a surgery. Michelangelo less than one year after she died. My mother said he died from a broken heart. During that time, they both became citizens and raised seven children.

Mike, with his quiet dignity, worked hard, said little, and eventually became the boss of his truck crew. He parlayed his laborer's salary and with economy raised those seven children and then bought a three decker house at the top of their street as an investment. He and Maria wanted to give their children a strong start, a foothold. This house is a touchstone for all our family. We simply refer to it by its street number, "28."

Now, my mother and all her siblings are also all gone. They all took their turns living, starting out on life's paths, chasing their own dreams at "28." My mother was the last of the siblings to marry. When the time came to sell the family home, my mother ended up with the trunk to carry all her treasures and eventually took the trunk into her new life with my father when they married. That's how the trunk ended up in our attic.

The steamer trunk is one hundred and eight years old and is still here with us. What and with whom will this chest see over its next one hundred and eight years?

Garbage Park

by Michael Fiorito

*"Garbage Park" provides an unflinching exploration
of the racially charged world of the NYC projects in the 1970s.
Garbage Park should make the reader uncomfortable,
especially in the context of the current time.*

At 3:00 a.m. the garbage trucks pulled into the depot.

While the Ravenswood Project slept, great caravans of junk loudly rolled into the station. I woke up and—wondering how anyone could sleep—got out of bed and walked to the window. Pushing it open, I watched the trucks creeping back to the depot, like defeated wolves returning from the hunt, hunched over, ragged. Great white heaps, they looked tired and dirty. Backing up into the garage spaces, they beeped loudly, huffing, making honking sounds.

"What's the matter?" my brother Virgil asked from his bed. He slept next to me, his bed perpendicular to mine, our heads nearly touching as we slept, as if the coils of our dreams were intertwined.

"Nothing," I said. "The noise is bothering me."

"Go to sleep," he said. "It'll stop."

As if he commanded it, the clatter suddenly ceased. From our third-floor window, I looked across from the Department of Sanitation to the adjoining park. We called it Garbage Park. There were basketball courts, handball courts and a full-sized cement baseball field behind the basketball court. In the darkness, the ground in the park looked clean and perfect. Far above the hallowed ground in Garbage Park loomed the Manhattan skyline.

I felt as if I was being lowered into the ground, plumbing the historical depths of Garbage Park.

There were stories that long ago, when Queens was farmland, black people were tortured and buried alive in Garbage Park. Matty Jordan said that Moses Murphy, a slave who had escaped to the North, had been captured, beheaded and buried in the ground that is now Garbage Park, along with his wife and children. It was said that many slaves lay hidden in the earth beneath Garbage Park.

Evil lurked beneath the cement surface. As kids, we had no idea that our basketball dribbled atop a burial ground. That the echoes of our feet rumbled the ground below.

That night, as I looked above the empty park and gazed at the Manhattan skyline, the buildings were standing erect and blinking like spaceships. The Empire State Building proudly pointed to heaven, decorated in red, white, and blue. From our view, the Chrysler Building stood sentry next to it.

There were no birds chirping, no signs of life. You might hear night birds in some other places on the earth, but not in Garbage Park. All the saints in heaven couldn't make them sing. The garbage trucks had chased them away. Papers twirled in the air, lifted by the trucks whooshing by. The street was dark blue, like a river of tar. Other than the movement created by the legion of trucks, the summer air was dead.

At any one time two dozen garbage trucks were lined up on the sidewalk in front of the depot. Inside the garage another few dozen trucks slumbered. The entire neighborhood had become inured to the foul stench; the rotting odor of the garbage was no longer detectable.

It was in the handball court of Garbage Park, a few years later, that my brother Virgil said he could take Jethro Malone in a fight. Jethro and Virgil were both twelve, two years older than me.

Coming from one of many brothers, Jethro was stout and tough. Even though he lived only a few blocks away, in the Queensbridge Projects, he'd only recently started coming to our project block in Ravenswood. One day he was a new kid playing basketball with us in Garbage Park, and the next day he was the leader amongst us.

The day after Virgil had said he could take Jethro, Virgil and I had come home from Saint Patrick's grammar school, books in hand. Jethro had stewed for twenty-four hours over Virgil's comment; he had the taste of blood in his mouth. We had no idea this idea had taken form; there was no warning. Jethro's dreams had mingled with the rotting garbage; the ghosts from his mind crawling out of his skull and slinking down Twenty-first Street. In a heap of refuse, his pain began to shape into an anger, a fury that, by consuming everything in its path, only grew larger. The trash contained the decapitated skulls of slaves, the bodies of blacks hung from trees, the ghosts of sins that lingered still in these Ravenswood Projects. The trail of death seeped into Jethro's brain at night and fed his fury, until it was too large to contain itself, and came tearing at us.

His rage was fueled by breathing in the dirty air. The stink worked its way up through our nostrils to our brains, invading our minds.

As we approached, Jethro stood in front of the lobby waiting for us. All our friends were there: the Vasquez brothers—Phil, Eric and Lou-ie—Teddy Guzy, Simon the Zealot. But to my surprise, they were not there to stand with us, but to cheer Jethro on.

Across the street, a garbage truck blared and huffed, its lights blinking wildly, parking in front of a garage door, trying to warn us of the coming doom.

"So, you think you can take me?" Jethro shouted at Virgil. Before Virgil could say anything, Jethro punched Virgil in the face. Virgil staggered backwards and fell to the concrete floor, his palms flat on the rocky stone.

"And you!" he said, now coming towards me, "What do you think, you're a tough guy?" and slapped me with the back of his hand. I put my hand up to my face and felt the heat from the smack. I wasn't scared.

Hearing all the ruckus from the street my mother opened the window of our third-floor apartment.

"What the hell is going on down there?" she demanded to know. She'd frequently open the window to tell us to come up for dinner. Once she opened the window and yelled at us not to cross in the middle of the street. Her voice boomed out of the window so loudly that a row of kids stopped in their tracks, walked to the corner, and crossed at the green light with us, like a colony of obedient ants.

"I said, what's going on," my mother repeated, no longer asking a question, her voice thunderous now, like the voice of a prophet coming from heaven.

Pointing at Jethro I said, "This fucking nigger just hit us." We didn't use that word at home and never outside to each other. It was a word black people called each other. But I was so angry that Jethro had picked a fight with me and Virgil, I hoped saying this would slice through his heart and kill him on the spot. Perhaps right here, on this very spot, was a slave burial ground. As we stood atop the concrete, below its surface lay the remains of buried slaves, of abandoned children, some killed at birth, some dead from starvation. The bodies of women, raped, beaten, and the discarded bodies of men who crossed a white devil, lay twisted and tangled in the dirt below the surface, strangled by the earth, silenced. I didn't know what any of this really meant. All I knew was that I could marshal a legion of hateful angels by dropping that word. That word lay at the bottom of a great rubbish mound, accumulating power over the centuries. Just one word could tear the world apart.

It only made Jethro angrier.

"What did you say, you little motherfucker?" he said, as he stepped towards me with his backhand across his chest, ready to hit me again.

Suddenly, walking towards the lobby entrance, we saw Charlie, my friend Vernon's older brother.

Looking at the worried eyes of the kids standing in a circle around us and the slap mark on my face, Charlie knew something had happened. As he looked up at my mother hanging out of the third-floor window, she pulled in the window and shut it.

"Why don't you boys go upstairs," said Charlie, pointing at me and my brother.

My brother and I walked into the project lobby, defeated. We took the elevator in silence.

That night, as we climbed into our beds to sleep, we talked around what had happened, not wanting to discuss it directly.

"You shouldn't curse," Virgil said. "And it was wrong of you to use that word. You could go to hell for that kind of language."

I became silent like I was listening to his sermon and taking it all in. Although I loved the crosses and red-eyed Jesus relics from Catholic school, the teachings about God and sin seemed unreal to me.

The sounds of the garbage trucks honking and beeping filled the room. Their red and green blinking lights flashed on the ceiling of our bedroom.

"Did you hear me?" he asked, noticing that I was staring into space as he spoke. "You shouldn't say curse words."

"I don't say no curse words," I said.

"Yes, you do; you say them to me." He paused for a moment. "You said them today."

"No, I don't," I said. "I don't say them."

He looked at me, knowing I was lying.

"Fuck you," I said. "I said it for you. I said it for us."

"Stop," he said. "It's wrong, you'll go to hell."

"I said it for us to make that asshole stop."

Virgil sighed and looked at me, disappointed.

Knowing I wasn't going to make my point, I gave up trying to be serious.

"Fuck you, fuck hell, fuck, fuck, pussy, pussy, fuck, fuck you, fuck, cunt, cunt, cunt, fuck."

Virgil turned over and put the pillow over his head so he couldn't hear me.

I smiled and turned over to go to sleep. It was the only victory I'd had that day. I fell asleep to the shadows cast by the trucks marching into the depot all night long.

· · · · · · · · · · · · · · · ·

Weeks after Jethro beat us up, Eric Vasquez found me in the project lobby. I had to fight my battles early to get them out of the way.

"Jethro says you're not allowed around here."

"What are you going to do about it?" I shot back. Eric's eyebrows arched in surprise. Eric pushed me and I pushed him back. Then I grabbed his shirt and pulled it up over his head and pummeled him with punches saying, "Fuck you, you fucking scumbag." I wanted to punch his eyes out of his face. I had a few more skirmishes, being cornered in the project lobby, or threatened in Garbage Park. I addressed them directly.

We played a game Virgil made up coming home from school. The game was "who can walk the fastest." We played this game because the kids in the neighborhood were still taunting Virgil. If we walked quickly, he figured, people would have less of a chance to see us. As we took short quick steps, Virgil and I would look over our shoulders, left to right. We never talked about the game and why we played it; we just did it. Virgil's nervous energy washed over me and made me nervous too. If they were coming after him, they were coming after us.

"Where's your brother?" asked Ronnie Green, as we played basketball in Garbage Park one day. "He don't come out no more?"

Though Ronnie stood a foot taller than me, I shot him an angry look and didn't say anything. I wanted to kill him right then and there; my eyes were red on fire. If you talked about my brother, I hated you. I might have tortured my brother; but he was mine to torture, no one else's.

"But you ain't afraid of no one," he said, reaching his hand out for me to shake. "Yeah, you alright."

I shook his hand just to get rid of him, mumbling "asshole" under my breath.

A year later Virgil went to high school in Manhattan, on the Upper West Side. You couldn't see his school from our apartment window; it was nestled in the canyons and valleys of Manhattan buildings. The smell of the garbage couldn't reach that far across the East River. Virgil joined the wrestling team. He wasn't the scared skinny kid anymore. Lifting weights and training had made him muscular and confident. Going to high school in Manhattan, he was seen around even less. People would say, "I saw your brother walking from the train station; man, he looks different."

As Virgil got stronger from lifting weights, and with puberty raging through his body, he even put his foot down with me.

One time, playing basketball in Garbage Park, Virgil intentionally stuffed my shots, towering over me, making it impossible for me to score or even shoot.

After struggling for a few minutes, I threw the ball at him saying "fucking asshole." He took the ball and scored.

"You going to complain or play?" he asked. After a few more smackdowns, I waited for one more, then I took a swing at him, punching him square in the jaw as I had many times before. This time, he reached back and landed a punch right on my temple. My right hand automatically let go a counterpunch but went adrift as soon as the impact from his knuckles made my knees buckle.

• • • • • • • • • • • • • •

Many years later I saw Jethro Malone playing handball in Garbage Park.

"How's your brother doing?" he asked. Having long ago made amends with Jethro I said, "He's good. You know, he's in school, playing sports." My brother hadn't been around the park in years. You see, Virgil had escaped Garbage Park. But many of us were still there, breathing in the dust from ancient bones. We had taken in the stink of death from our nostrils for so many years, our skulls were like cages littered with poisoned bats. The soot clogged our brains so badly that it even oozed out of our eye sockets. When we choked, we coughed up the bile of a thousand years of hatred.

"Do you think he could take me now?" asked Jethro.

"Yeah, Jethro, he could take you and me and the rest of us."

All I could think about was the silent bones buried in the dirt below the surface of Garbage Park.

At the Saloon

by Cecilia Gigliotti

In the summer of 1958, a college-bound teenager spends an evening with her estranged father and unexpectedly witnesses something extraordinary.

I'm not looking forward to dinner with my father. Today marks seven hundred and forty-eight days since he moved out. He called once, at the ninety mark. My mother answered, listened a few seconds, and hung up. She didn't say a word to me, but her mouth wouldn't harden over like that for any salesman on the line.

Then again yesterday. I knew because she used her fighting voice for five minutes before calling me into the living room. She said that I didn't have to see him if I didn't want to. That I was almost eighteen and could answer for myself. She kept saying it even after I said yes.

I've never trusted the phone, how it allows voices to invade private spaces, how it distorts sounds you think you know. Even when I'm the caller, I end up flummoxed and overexplaining myself to the stranger who can get me the person I want. I must not want anyone badly enough.

Three months back I had an acceptance letter from City College. They started taking girls in fifty-one, less than a decade ago. I stood in the cramped yellow kitchen, barefoot in a pool of sticky sunlight, re-reading, wondering when and how he would find out.

Heat oozes in between the buildings. June heat. Hostile heat. It's worst, as everything is worst, on the subway. A sweaty current carries me out onto the platform, office duds desperate for a drink, tourists desperate for shelter. Even so, I'm in no hurry to reach Grand Central. I tune in to the rise and fall of concrete beneath my feet. Times Square roars from blocks away. Coca-Cola ads and street vendors pushing scalped Broadway tickets. They still won't shut up about *West Side Story* and it's been here a year. I can avoid this particular circle of hell if I stay east of Seventh.

I cross the street with the crowd and duck into the Waldorf Astoria. Circling in the door and then straight up the soft green and gold incline, into the tall cool hall. People who don't look like they could ever belong stand around craning their necks or hefting cameras, and the bellhops are ready to tear off their white gloves. The green and gold underfoot slicks into marble. I slip out down the stairs and follow Park until it collides with Vanderbilt. Ten minutes later I'm heading for the station entrance when my sleeve catches.

"Hey, where you going?"

I turn, and there he is. His brown eyes grin with his mouth, his face has more lines here and there, his shoulders don't fill out that beige suede jacket quite how they used to.

"Dad," I croak.

The corners of his eyes crinkle and I don't react quickly enough to escape a hug. Then he stands back, holds me at arm's length. "Would you look at you."

I giggle, nervously, idiotically.

"God, am I happy to see you." He grabs my hand. "I know just the place."

I want to ask *Where?* but we're off, me tripping over my own two feet to keep up. I'm dizzy from heat by the time we arrive at a brick cube balanced on the intersection of Fifty-fifth and Third. A faded white scrawl on the side wall. P. J. Clarke's. God knows how many bodies are packed inside, but I hold my tongue.

My father sidles expertly up to the bar to order a pair of beers. I have to remind him I don't turn eighteen for another month. "That's right," he murmurs. "You look so mature."

I order a Coke.

A waiter ushers us through to the dining area. From a table tucked into a little alcove, we can observe the whole room. Lined with sconces, peppered with red-and-white gingham tablecloths. I slide into the seat below the large roman numeral clock.

"Just so you know"—my father lifts his pint—"this is it for me tonight."

I nod and drop my eyes to my menu.

"I mean it, Leela. I'm getting better, I swear I am."

Yeah, right, I want to think, but I'm too blindsided by the nickname. I'd invented it as a baby, trying to say "Lydia." He's not allowed to do that.

We lapse into a silence that would be painful if we were alone. I wonder how much violent entertainment this place hosted when it was founded, how many issues of honor boiled over as cups were drained, how many Hamiltons and Burrs were egged on by their rowdy fellow patrons. Nothing that happened here could stay secret for long. According to my mother the three of us came once or twice when I was very young. Then they went a few more times and left me with a sitter. All I remember is the thin line of my mother's mouth when she would arrive home. I've lost track of how long it's been.

"Leela?" my father's voice cuts in. A waiter is standing there. Realizing I'd been buried in this menu without reading a word, I scan it and pick out a burger.

My father is pleased. "That's the one I ordered."

The waiter nods and vanishes.

We sip our drinks until he speaks. "How's Helen?"

Oh God. I'd even sooner talk about my mother than about Helen, how my school plans and my unraveling family somehow meant my childhood best friend had to become my ex-best friend. She would cancel on me and blame her straitlaced Christian mother. Helen's mother thought I was studious to the point of being unladylike. She thought my mother's bake-sale cookies were never up to par. It was only too clear what she thought of my father. And yet the prospect of my parents divorcing is enough for her to keep her daughter away. "She's all right. Working full-time at her mother's bakery."

"That's always been her strong suit, hasn't it?"

"Yup."

The bustle has swelled a bit. Over my father's shoulder, a woman with a bronze face and thick dark hair takes a chair facing me. A guy who looks not much older than I am, and unsettlingly familiar, takes a chair across from her.

"And you, Miss College. I can't tell you how proud I am. I knew you were destined for greatness. Think about how times are changing. You're on the front lines of that."

"You know me...downright revolutionary."

My peripheral vision is excellent. The guy turns his head and the lamplight catches his glasses. Instantaneously I place his voice, the voice I've heard on records at parties and in all the shops for the past ten months. Well, besides *West Side Story*. I'm not prepared to see someone like him in the flesh, nor is anyone peering over their menus. But there's no need to panic over whether he notices us, given how he leans in. His date is young, but something in her face says she's seen more than maybe she should have. She must be telling him a heck of a story. He slides an elbow onto the table—my mother always scolds me for doing that—and rests his chin in his hand, half listening, jiggling his knee. I trace the gingham squares with my index finger and hope the heat isn't visible on me.

"These past two years have been a real doozy," says my father, like he's been talking the whole time.

"Mm-hm." I lean over the glass that has refilled in front of me and suck through the straw. The cold hits the roof of my mouth and dissipates into shivers.

"Any plans yet for the course of study?"

"Uh..." I put my elbow on the very edge of the table and touch the back of my neck. I don't exactly want to get into it with him. "I'm weighing my options."

"Lydia. If I know you, you've been scheming for ages now."

He does know me, too well. "All right. Art, with a concentration in photography."

His eyebrows rise, like he's won a bet with himself. "Really?"

"I like taking pictures. I'm sure you know *that*." I can't help a little bitterness. Most photographs I've taken have been of the family. Lots of candids.

"Well, I remember some good shots." His voice is gentle, kind. "On the Sound that summer, fifty-four? Every time I see those sunsets it's like I'm back there." He glances down for a second. "With the two of you."

My heels drum quietly. The next sip is so long it gives me the hiccups. Our plates arrive, and I'm suddenly ravenous. I try to pace myself and draw out the silence. It's several degrees too warm for comfort.

"How are things with your mother?"

"Same as ever." I wouldn't have mentioned her first. The Coke is near dregs by now. I should ration it out, but a couple moments later it doesn't matter what I should do.

Across the room, he's glancing back and forth between the girl and the kitchen door. Finally he gestures for her to stay and darts off, past the bar. It isn't just that he's tall; I've never seen someone so *gangly*. Her eyes close and she tugs her cardigan tighter around her shoulders without putting her arms through the sleeves. He straightens his jacket, adjusts his tie, bites his lip, touches the back of his neck, and I have to lower my eyes. By the time I raise them the door is swinging.

"You still like rock and roll?"

I nod, straining to bring my eyes back.

"Who're you listening to these days?"

I swallow. My voice is whispery. "Buddy Holly."

"Oh, good. I like him. Are you sure you're okay?"

"Dad, you're going to think I'm insane."

"Why? What are you looking at?"

"He...he was over there."

"Who?"

"Buddy Holly."

He shifts in his seat. "Honey, all I see is a girl."

"*Stop* it." I hit him on the arm. "That's his date."

"Who's she?"

"I don't know! I don't know everything!"

"Does he live in the city?"

"I didn't—think so—"

"Lydia." I can feel his eyes on me. "You seem upset."

My words can't come fast enough to beat the emotion rising in my throat. "He just left the room, he'll be back any—"

Speak of the devil, here he comes, bounding back in. I never thought I'd see a grown person bound. It's as if he's got electrodes for nerve endings. I spot red petals and a metallic glint before he reaches her and drops to one knee.

Someone gasps. I'm sure I would too if my throat hadn't caught itself. My dad turns to me. There's a good deal of clinking and clattering and scraping backward against the floor.

She smirks in a poor attempt to hide her astonishment. "Do you want to get married now or after dinner?"

The way people are starting to lose their cool, you'd think he proposed to *them*. My glass is empty; it quivers in my hand.

"I'm serious." He's talking louder now, but so is the rest of the room. Again we all hardly register with him. "Tomorrow morning—"

More snatches of words. The girl touches her cheek. He slides the ring off the stem of the rose and takes her left hand and puts it on her finger. Then he whirls her up and kisses her and the place erupts in applause. I'm on my feet, a roiling sensation in a spot I don't customarily acknowledge. My father shakes his head and laughs, his eyes crinkling, a too-vivid snapshot of those vacations I captured. The heat feels like delirium. I can't force myself back down into my chair, so I snatch his half-full pint glass and drain it down, down, barely pausing to gulp, goldish droplets spilling over the lip and plinking onto the tabletop. It's like drowning. I hear my name, but I don't stop until I see foam at the bottom.

When I lower the glass my father is staring at me and I'm staring at them. They seem like one person. His mouth is against her ear. That's all I can take. I leave my father and Buddy Holly and fiancée there, shove out into the sweltering night, feeling as if the stem of that rose is stuck down my throat.

The Immigrant's Grandson

by Joe Giordano

A man searches for his roots and gets a surprise.

Wearing jeans and sneakers, rumpled traveler Nicholas Robustelli, stirred in his coach seat and ran his hand through salt and pepper hair. The Boeing 747 descended below the clouds that cast blue-green shadows across the double-humped caldera of Vesuvius, dulling the turquoise sparkle of the Bay of Naples.

In Arrivals, a slim man with a deep chin cleft wearing a tailored olive sports jacket and an open-collar white shirt, not a hair or thread out of place, held up a sign with his name.

Nicholas extended his hand. "Doctor Abandonato?"

"Cousin, call me Salvatore." Abandonato shook hands, then grasped Nicholas by the shoulders. "Welcome to Napoli."

"*Grazie* for meeting me at the airport."

"It's nothing. You look tired. Why don't we get a coffee?" Abandonato offered to roll his suitcase, but Nicholas refused. As they walked, Abandonato said, "This is your first time in Italy?"

"I've been to Milan on business, but this is my first trip to Naples."

The brightly lit coffee shop had a few wooden tables. Most patrons stood at the black-marble bar. Payment was in advance. Abandonato asked what Nicholas wanted.

"Cappuccino."

Abandonato smiled. "That proves you're American. In Italy, only women have milk in their coffee after *colazione*. In the afternoon, we drink espresso."

Abandonato paid and the barista turned to the espresso machine.

Nicholas spoke over hissing geysers of super-hot steam that dribbled amber liquid into white cups. "I've been flying since yesterday. I need more than a finger of coffee to wake up."

"For you it's breakfast time. *Saluté.*"

Abandonato downed his coffee in a gulp and clicked his cup onto the saucer. Nicholas sipped his cappuccino and daubed away a foam mustache.

"I'm so glad you found me through Facebook," Nicholas said. "My aunts had some contact with family in Italy, but they've all passed away. I never took an interest when I was young."

"Your grandfather Niccolò was the only member of our family to emigrate to the United States. My grandfather was his stepbrother. Our entire family now lives in Pozzuoli."

"That's an exclusive suburb. Things have improved for the family. My grandfather was a tenant farmer in Caserta. I have a grainy picture of him in a doughboy's uniform from World War I. That's how he became a U.S. citizen. After the war, he brought his wife and my six-year-old father to New York."

"How was life in America for them?"

"Niccolò was a ragman recovering trash and what was thrown away when people died. Rags crusted with filth were hung on lines, washed by the rain, and bleached by the sun before being sold for paper making. During the Great Depression, my father had been out of work two years when he landed a job in a warehouse. Working rapidly to impress his boss, he grabbed a box, knocking over a glass ashtray that shattered on the concrete floor. He was fired on the spot."

"What a shame."

"We first generation Americans stand on the immigrants shoulders. My father had no education, so he insisted I did. Your e-mail invitation rekindled thoughts about my roots, and I thumbed through some old photographs. My wife Carol said, 'Go to Italy,' so here I am."

"The family is excited to meet you."

"Great. While we're alone, I'd like to ask about a specific piece of family history."

"What would you like to know?"

"After my grandfather died, my father hardly spoke of him. An aunt told me that Niccolò came to the United States aboard a merchant steamer. He skipped off without papers and tried to disappear into the Lower Eastside of New York."

"Ah."

"The cops in Manhattan grabbed him and he was given the choice to enlist in the army or be deported back to Italy."

Abandonato's eyes diverted.

Nicholas continued. "Whispers were that he left Italy in a hurry. Strange that a man would leave his wife and son in Naples to try and disappear in New York."

"Yes." Abandonato shifted nervously on his feet.

"You hear things as a kid when the adults don't think you're around. My father told his sister that Niccolò was a wanted man."

"Oh?"

"Niccolò had a dispute with an aristocrat in Caserta. My grandfather was accused of stealing, and he shot the landowner in the face with a shotgun."

Abandonato stiffened. "What do you want from me?"

"There must be newspaper accounts. My Italian isn't good enough to search the archives. Would you help?"

"If the story is true, and I don't say that it is, why in God's name would you want to unearth the past?"

"If my grandfather committed murder, I want to understand why. Was he falsely accused of stealing? Was it a matter of honor? There had to be a police file."

"It happened a hundred years ago."

"Yes, but his life, my father's, and mine turned on this single incident. Did I become a successful American because of a crime? I want to know."

Abandonato retreated a step. "I'm so sorry. I've made a terrible error."

"What do you mean?"

"Facebook is unreliable. There are so many people named Robustelli in America. I made contact with the wrong person."

"Are you joking?"

"This is so embarrassing. We're not related. I should've been more careful before allowing you to come to Napoli. I'll pay for your airline ticket and drive you to your hotel, but I'm afraid you're on your own."

The Little Man Who Was Almost There

by Thomas Locicero

The wife of an old ex-boxer battling dementia must decide between nudging him back into reality or allowing him to live in a false world that brings him joy, all the while manipulating him to help her to recapture her lost youth.

Clete had been angry before. He learned that anger offered a sense of irrational power even while locked in weakness, that it provided an overdramatic largeness from the incendiary fragments igniting in the smallness of veins; the result, according to him, was the shattering of jawbones, cheekbones, and orbital bones, which settled like marbles in a mask, and fingers, too, his own, like splinters in gloves. His wife, Greta, knew that it had been decades since he'd actually fought anyone. He was in his early eighties now. His days of chasing gas station robbers with tire irons or dislodging the teeth of elevator muggers were supposed to be behind him by now. When he shared his adventures, he always mentioned, as casually as an insignificant afterthought, that he'd learned something.

In the Navy, he had been the boxing champion of every ship on which he had been stationed. Before then, on the streets of Pittsburgh, he had been the enforcer with the fierce left hook, the protector with the pressed collar and boxing glove cufflinks.

"You should've known me then," he said to his wife, forgetting that she had known him then. "I was something to behold. A Dapper Dan, a ladies' man. I had a body on me."

"Whose was it?" was the standard joke from the corner boys to whom he boasted, each time telling the story as though it were the first time.

"Was it dead or alive?" was Greta's favorite response, though she'd yet to share it with him. In sixty-one years of marriage, she had never shown him what she referred to as her light side. She never actually thought that she might become a victim of his anger. She just didn't want to be responsible for causing him to reminisce.

"I used to spar with Billy Conn's trainer's son" had been modified to lose a character at a time until the comment underwent a metamorphosis: "I fought Billy Conn."

"If you keep telling people that you fought him, Cletus," Greta once warned, "one of them is liable to look it up."

"Are you saying that I didn't fight him?" he had responded.

"Just tell people you sparred with him and leave it at that."

Clete went for a walk and perceived a young man to be shadow-boxing. "You're doing it all wrong."

The young man clutched him. "They're trying to break my arms."

"Who?" asked Clete, tightening his slight frame and sniffing through his one working nostril. "Where are they?"

Two policemen turned a corner, their batons drawn, and dashed toward the young man, who pushed Clete to the ground. One of the policemen continued his pursuit while the other helped Clete to his feet.

"Are you all right?" the officer asked. "Do you need an ambulance?"

"I'm fine, I'm fine. I fought Sweet William. Do you think a young punk is gonna do me harm?"

"Sweet William?"

"Billy Conn. Don't you know your history?"

"I thought they called him The Pittsburgh Kid," the officer said.

"'They' did, but I called him Sweet William. Hell, I gave him the nickname myself.'"

They reacted to a grunt and turned to see the pursuing officer tackle and restrain the young man.

"What'd he do?" asked Clete.

"Tried to rob a convenience store," the officer replied. He patted Clete on the shoulder. "We couldn't have done it without you, old timer."

"Damn straight. He's lucky I didn't break his jaw."

When Clete returned home, he said, "Turn on the TV! Turn on the TV!"

"Why are you so excited?" asked Greta, obliging. "You shouldn't let yourself get so excited."

"I'll tell you why I'm so excited," he said, grabbing the remote from her hand and pressing numbers until he found the local news. "You're never too old to learn something, and today I learned something. Timing is everything."

"Cletus, honey, you're eighty-two, and you're just learning this now."

"I knocked down a robber."

"Are you telling stories again?"

"What do you mean 'telling stories'?" He held up a hand, which was conveniently scabbing at the knuckles. "A punk robbed a convenience store. I just happened to be there at the right time, and I knocked him down."

"You did not," said Greta, placing a hand to her mouth.

"It'll be on the TV," Clete said. "You'll see."

"Were there cameras? Were you interviewed? Oh, this is so exciting! Should we call your mother?"

"She's a hundred and three. I don't want to excite her."

"So, what kind of questions did they ask you?" asked Greta. "You didn't mention Billy Conn, did you?"

"They asked me where I learned to fight. Of course I mentioned Billy Conn."

"What did you say exactly?"

"That I sparred with him."

"You said 'sparred,'" Greta said, "not 'fought'?"

"Of course I said 'sparred.' I never fought Billy Conn, you know that."

"That's right," Greta said, averting her eyes, "I forgot."

They watched three hours of news. There was no mention of his heroics.

"Maybe it's too soon," offered Greta. "Maybe they'll have it on the late news."

On the late news, a reporter mentioned an attempted robbery of a convenience store after which the suspect fled on foot, knocking an old man to the ground before being apprehended by police. Clete clicked off the television.

"He made it sound like you were knocked to the ground," Greta said.

"That wasn't my story," said Clete, truculently. "Weren't you listening? He said it was an 'attempted' robbery. I knocked down a *robber*, not a 'suspect.'"

"Well, maybe it's on the late late news."

"The late late news?" said Clete. "What do I look like to you? An owl?"

Clete went to bed. Greta turned the television back on and watched the late late news. Toward the end of the program, after the weekly weather forecast, a reporter told of an attempted convenience store robbery and of the mysterious old man who innocently happened into the robber's path, slowing him down enough to expedite his capture. And then Greta saw Billy Conn. She looked at the bedroom door, then back at the television. She decided not to call her husband for fear that she might startle him. Another reporter said, "A similar incident occurred thirteen years ago to the day, when our own William David (Sweet William) Conn, better known as Billy Conn, the Pittsburgh Kid, at age 72, decked a young man who robbed the Uni-Mart on Beechwood Boulevard in the Squirrel

Hill section of Pittsburgh. Conn, the former light heavyweight champion of the world, was voted one of the top ten boxers of the twentieth century. During his career, he compiled a record of 63 wins, 11 losses and one draw. Conn is best known for having lasted to the end of the thirteenth round against a much heavier Joe Louis in what many boxing experts consider to be the greatest heavyweight match of all time. Billy Conn, the Flower of the Monongahela, died in 1993 at the age of 75."

Greta lay in her bed that night and watched her husband sleep in his. Then, when she thought sleep might come, a separate, uninvited thought came to her. It made her smile, though she wasn't sure whether it had come from her light side or her dark side. She tried to justify her acting upon it: *It wasn't my idea to have separate beds*, she thought. Seven years is a long time. She needed to remember before she forgot.

In the morning, just before dawn, Greta rose to prepare breakfast. Clete was in the kitchen hurriedly searching the newspaper for the article hailing him a hero.

"I watched the late late news last night," said Greta, "and you won't believe what I saw."

Clete closed the paper. "Was it about me? Why didn't you wake me?"

"No, it wasn't about you, and before you ask me again, I didn't wake you because you know how fast those news stories go. If I went to wake you, we both would've missed it."

"What was it?" Clete said, his anger rising. "What did you see?"

"A feature on Billy Conn."

"Billy Conn?"

"Billy Conn."

"What did they say about him?"

"They talked about how sweet he was to his wife," said Greta.

"Sweet William," Clete said. "How was he sweet to Mary Louise?"

"He never got angry with her," answered Greta, "and he pleased her in every way. *Every* way. He didn't let age slow him down in that department."

"They said that on the news?" said Clete. "Why would they say something like that on the news?"

"You know the news these days," said Greta. "Who can tell what reporters might say?"

"I remember when they kept Roosevelt's polio a secret," Clete said. "You remember that?"

"And now they're talking about Billy Conn's tender time with Mary Louise?" His voice was now rising. "Which station was it? Which reporter? I'm going to pay that no good pervert a visit he won't soon forget."

"I don't know which station it was," Greta said. "It was late, I was tired. Some cable station. Nowhere near Pittsburgh."

Clete rolled his neck and his shoulders. He inhaled through his nose and exhaled from his mouth; a mist of saliva dissipated in the air. "It's just wrong!"

Greta measured her words carefully before speaking. "Another way to look at it is...well, it's a compliment. I'm sure there are a lot of people who still look up to Billy Conn, people who want to be like him. Some of them, after they reach a certain age, are afraid to...you know... but if they hear about Billy...you never know."

That night, Greta went into the bedroom to find that the beds had been pushed together. Clete emerged from the bathroom shirtless, flexing his chest and abdomen. He took Greta in his arms.

"Let me freshen up," she said.

"No need," said Clete, undressing her.

He caught a glimpse of himself in the mirror, then faced it and stared.

"People used to say I looked like him, you know," he said.

"Who?" asked Greta.

"Billy Conn."

"I know you meant Billy Conn," Greta said. "I mean who? Which people said you looked like him?"

Clete's eyes darted from side to side. "You know, people. From the neighborhood."

Greta was embarrassed to see her reflection in the same mirror in which her husband admired himself. She wanted to say something, but she didn't want to anger him. Especially now. Throughout the hour, Clete's body refused to cooperate. Greta tried every trick she knew. She even tried some things she had read about, ignoring her husband's inquiries: ("Geez, woman, where did you learn that? I may be losing my memory, but I definitely would have remembered *that*.")

Finally, Greta said, "Get angry."

"What do you mean?"

"There's the anger that makes you think too much and the anger that causes you to not think at all. Find something in between."

"I don't want to be too rough with you," said Clete.

Greta wanted to say, "It's been seven years. I don't think it's possible for you to be too rough with me." But she said, "Don't let age beat you. Billy Conn didn't."

"You're telling me that Billy Conn is still tender with Mary Louise?"

"What're you talking about, Cletus?"

"You said that, didn't you? Somebody told me that. I thought it was you."

"I told you that he *was* tender with her," Greta said, touching her husband's chest. "Cletus, Billy Conn is dead. You know that."

"Dead?" said Clete. "Billy Conn? When?"

"You don't remember?"

Clete dabbed at his eyes. "No."

"You went to the funeral," Greta said, softly. "You spoke."

"I spoke at his funeral?"

"It was beautiful. So many people remembered you. They said, 'That's Clete Deauville. He was Billy's sparring partner.'"

"They did?"

"And people asked you for your autograph, but you didn't want to upstage Billy, so you waited until everyone was in the parking lot. Mary Louise said that she appreciated your humility."

"I wish I could remember," Clete cried. "God, I want to remember."

"Keep trying," said Greta. "Keep fighting."

"When did he die?"

"About ten years ago."

"Ten years ago?" said Clete. "Hell, we were tender a lot ten years ago. Weren't we?"

Greta wanted to say, I wouldn't say a lot, but instead said, "See? Billy Conn's got nothing on you."

"He doesn't, does he?" Clete said, his body relaxing.

Greta wanted to say, "Well, in fairness to him, he *is* dead," but she watched Clete's muscles softening, and she didn't want to anger him. But then, without a second thought, she said it. They looked at the surprise in one another's eyes. It was that that made them laugh. And even as they kissed, they laughed.

Clete felt a surge in his chest that was both familiar and frightening. When he was young, he equated it in some small measure with life. He had forgotten. It was easier to reinvent than to recall. He would try to remember this moment, when he learned that laughter was good for his blood flow.

At eighty-one, Greta learned that being herself had immeasurable rewards. She vowed to cherish her discovery. As her body responded to all that her husband remembered about her, she promised herself not to fear forgetting but rather to continue to recollect the lapses.

A Worthie Woman All Hir Live

by LindaAnn LoSchiavo

Of Alisoun, The Wife of Bath, Geoffrey Chaucer wrote:
'She was a worthie woman al hir live /
Husbands at churche door, she had five.'

Allison Bathfield, professor of Medieval Literature,
is fond of concocting homemade mead and tisanes,
infusions made from strange herbs, rare berries,
witchy flowers, leaves, and spices.

When a burglar breaks into her lonely hilltop house and claims to
have proof of her crimes, the newly widowed Allison Bathfield must decide
which is more prudent: trying to prove him wrong or silencing him.

"Just check if you have enough stamps for Special D. Don't pepper me with questions, Mona." Realizing her tone was shrewish, Allison gentled it with a playful Middle English phrase. *"She gan to grucche a me!"*

She taught Medieval Literature in the local college where Mona was a librarian. As she listened to her sister, she realized the drafty hillside house seemed colder.

"I thought this was a Leap Year February and I had an extra day. Yes, I still have last year's 1992 calendar up. Between the hospital, the funeral – – no, it's not an excuse. But it must be finished tonight. I can't miss that deadline." Allison paced the old-fashioned kitchen. "You've got extra stamps? Great!"

She reached for a black shawl draped on a towel rack. "Thanks, Mona. I'll coffee through an all-nighter and drive to your place by nine A.M. I want to mail it downtown before my first class. You're a lifesaver."

Trying to monitor the boiler's rubaiyat of rumbles, Allison pulled herself back to attention.

"What did you call me?"

Snuggling into the soft cashmere folds, Allison laughed merrily, quoting Chaucer again. "*I know the remedies for life's mischances.* But, Mona, I've got to go down to the cellar now, check on the boiler and the dryer. Call you later!"

She was reading a page still in her IBM Selectric when an interior door creaked.

"HELLO!," she shouted. "Is someone there?"

As she moved towards the hallway off the kitchen, the darkness was a surprise.

"Another lightbulb died – – and I forgot to buy replacements!," she chided herself. "Always one that outlasts the others. But... *No need just now to speak of that, forsooth.*" Even off campus, her interior monologues addressed her Fourteenth Century comrades, William Langland, Katherine of Sutton, the Pearl Poet, and Geoffrey Chaucer, in their language. They could be trusted to keep secrets. A low whistling sound caught her ears.

"What's *this*: a *restless soul?* Or winds jousting with my windows? May as well brew coffee, drink something hot." Allison recited from a page she'd typed earlier: "*She was a worthie woman all hir live – – husbands at churche door she had five.*"

From a cabinet, she automatically drew out two saucers and two cups, preoccupied and unaware of the man hiding on the other side of her kitchen door.

"TWO cups!" She shook her head. "As if you were here, Johnny." She inhaled. "I smell your after-shave." Allison decided she'd call Mona again, invite her to supper and ask her to bring the postage stamps. "Kill two birds... Oh, botheration!"

No dial tone. "May as well drive to Mona's, borrow some lightbulbs, get my..."

As she put the handset down, a stranger grabbed her from behind.

"Take your hands off me!" she screamed. It flashed on her that she could not call the police – – but did he know that? "Get out!" She turned her head to face him.

He gave her a shove. "Don't do anything silly and you won't get hurt."

"How did you get in here?"

The man moved his right hand menacingly inside his pea jacket. "Sit down."

Allison stared. Not a former student. Too young to have a kid in college. Who?

"You deaf? I said SIT DOWN."

"My husband will be home any second."

"Hubby's funeral was last month, ain't that so? Follow instructions and sit."

Allison slid the shawl over her shaking hands and sat. "Who are you? Do you – – did you know my husband?"

"Shut up. I'll ask the questions."

In a low voice, Allison intoned, *"She was a worthie woman all hir live."*

"Are you casting a spell? What did you say?"

"Just reciting a line from a poem I was working on before...before you interrupted my deadline."

"Lah-di-dah. So you fancy yourself a poet, eh?"

"I didn't write the poem. I'm working on a monograph about the poem." Allison softened her tone. "If you need money, I'm sorry for you because I don't have any."

He smirked. "You have time to go around monogramming poems."

"Monograph – – not monogram. I teach in college. Ever hear about 'publish or perish'?"

"I know a lot of people who died before their time, if that's what you mean."

"Please. I don't know why you selected our house but . . . "

"You left keys in the door. Like you wanted my company. Must get lonely – – no neighbors up on this hill. The closest house empty – – with a faded 'For Sale' sign flappin' at no one."

Keys in the door! A litany of mistakes chanted in her ears, no stamps, no lightbulbs! She had been a wheel turning without an axle, unsteady. "Prut!"

"What?" His voice sounded alarmed. "You got a cold?"

Can she scare him away? Invoke pity or terror? "Perhaps I'm coming down with influenza or the bubonic plague."

He laughed. "Maybe you can use one of your enchantments to get well."

"Enchantments?"

"Yeah, I've heard about these things of yours: potions – – abracadabra-ing weird shit. But I ain't afraid of you. I'm like a cat with nine lives."

"Obviously, you must have me mixed up with someone else."

"Naaaah. I got you pegged. Don't try none of your voodoo."

"There is no wizardry around here. What makes you think there is?"

"I heard about you."

"You were misinformed. I teach literature in a college – – for very low pay."

"Yeah, yeah. Don't get on my nerves, if you know what's good for you."

A tinny ping-ping sound startled them.

"Is that a burglar alarm?"

"No! That's the dryer. The cycle finished." The cellar had two half windows. How long would it take to escape? "Can I get my clothes? They get wrinkled if they stay cloistered in the hot machine."

"*Can I get my clothes?*" he imitated her. "You kidding me?"

Allison coughed loudly. "Can I get a glass of water then?"

"Don't be scheming, trying to grab a knife. G'ahead. I got my eye on you."

"Want a glass of water? There's not much in my refrigerator – – until payday."

He watched her, scanning the untidy counter. This one was no homemaker.

"What's the yellow stuff? Is that a bottle full of piss? Or some of your witches' brew?"

"This?" Allison held up a bottle. "This is mead. It's delicious. Want some?"

"What's mead?"

Allison kept up her cordial act. "It's wine made from honey. It's homemade."

"Is that how you killed your husband?"

"How dare you!" she shouted, losing control. "I didn't kill my husband!"

"Listen, girlie. You got your drink of water. Now sit down. Behave yourself."

"You really have some nerve – – breaking in here!"

"Ain't nobody broke in. I was invited like."

"Threatening me! Bullying me! Holding me against my will. Who are you?"

Ferociously, he scooped up papers. "Who are you? The whiff of bath?"

"That's part of my monograph on *The Wife of Bath*. Tonight I had to…"

His face was red with rage, his eyes crazy. "'*Whiff of bath*' is what you typed."

"You're right. I made a typo. I typed '*whiff*' instead of *wife*."

He was inches from her face now. "And what kind of a **WIFE** were you?"

"I was – – I am a good person. I don't like making people miserable."

He patted his pockets, looking for something. "Except when you were busy killing my sister-in-law."

"WHAT? I didn't kill anybody. I'm sure I do not even know your sister-in-law."

He took a photo from his jeans and shoved it her. "Here she is – – with her sex-machine Johnny-boy. Now they're both cold in the ground. Recognize her?"

"Yes." Many thoughts crossed her mind as she studied the picture. "I'm sorry for your loss. But I did not cause her death. It was known she had a heart condition."

"Yeah, yeah. Ol' Johnny-boy was her *'heart'* condition. My brother hasn't been the same since his wife died."

So that's who sent him, Dennis Perkins. He thinks he *knows the remedies for life's mischances.* Allison cleared her throat. "It is difficult to lose a spouse. But I had nothing to do with her...situation."

"Little birdie said Johnny was leaving you for her. Your black magic foxed her."

"No! She worked in the Bursar's Office at the college where I teach." Just a silly D-cup typist in a low-cut blouse. "She had a heart attack one evening."

"Maybe the cops bought that fairytale but we don't. I got evidence, girlie."

"I'm innocent. Honest." Missing teeth – – from barroom brawls?

He smiled, taking his time. "I got hard evidence – – more than a whiff of bath. I could bring proof to the police and the dean, Professor Allison Bathfield."

"I barely knew the woman. It's a pity she's dead but I don't know anything."

"I didn't expect a confession. You're a pro just like I'm good at what I do."

"What *is* your line of work? Home invasion? Assault and battery? Blackmail?"

"Johnny-boy used to like a brewski with supper. You got any beer left?"

Think! Get rid of him! "In the refrigerator."

As he opened the cold beer, she said sarcastically, "Sorry I can't offer you chips and onion dip."

"I wouldn't touch your food. Last meal she ate was a meat pie you brought her."

He raised the beer bottle in a toast. "You're a clever dame. Gotta hand it to you, professor. You almost escaped detection. *Almost.*"

Had you realized how clever, she thought, you would not have come. Aloud she said, "Next time you're robbing houses, keep in mind that college teachers struggle to pay the bills. Even my wedding band is plain. Today I was supposed to…"

"Nice try. But Johnny-boy was worth more dead than alive."

"All I have is a few dollars for my application fees and groceries. If I give you that, will you please leave? PLEASE! I really must get back to work."

"Okay, no problem." He held out a calloused palm. "That and your car keys."

"My car keys? You can barely get up or down this steep hill without a vehicle. How'd you get here?"

"Heh-heh-heh! Yeah, yeah, maybe I hitched a ride."

"My husband's car is in the garage. The blue sedan with the 'For Sale' sign on the side." She lowered her voice conspiratorially, so he had to come closer. "I was driving it last weekend, hoping to sell it. John's car is much newer than my jalopy."

"You wish to donate the better vehicle to my family. Touching. Yeah, riiight."

"Consider this. Neighbors recognize my rattle-trap. But if you were driving John's blue car, it would raise no suspicion. People would assume I sold it to you."

"Gimme the keys. And the money."

Allison went to her purse and put several tens in his hand and the keys.

"See ya tomorrow. We'll talk more – – on the way to your bank. Don't try nothing funny." He kissed her like a husband leaving for work and was gone.

Allison watched him from a window, then picked up the phone. "Botheration! I forgot – – there's no dial tone. He probably slashed my phone lines. I'll call Mona from a payphone." Reaching for a coat, she considered her options. "I'd better pack...just in case." The garage door slammed. "*I have the power durynge al my lyf.*"

Getting down the heaviest suitcase and gathering cash she had squirreled around the house took time. As she laid out clothes on the bed, the doorbell rang.

"Hello!" called a baritone voice. "I'm looking for a John Bath-field."

"Who's there?" The setting sun impeded her view.

"Police, ma'm. There's been a collision on Route 9. The license plate was linked to this address. Does John Bathfield...?"

Allison cracked open the door. "My husband is not here, officer. You mean to say a thief stole our sedan? Was there much damage?"

"I'm told it shot downhill like a bolt. Almost like it had no brakes at all."

"My husband kept saying he had to get the brakes fixed. How terrible."

"Sorry, m'am, but would you have any idea who was behind the wheel?"

"No name I can think of. Were there passengers? Was the driver injured?"

"Here's my card, ma'm. Call the station tomorrow. Off-the-record, it looks bad."

"Cars can be so unreliable. Always one that outlasts the others, though."

"Have a good night, Mrs. Bathfield."

"*She was a worthie woman all hir live. Husbands at churche door she had five.*"

Allison sat down at her IBM Selectric, amused at the Perkins brother with his bar-bashed teeth and his entirely unfounded sense of optimism.

Background:

"A Worthie Woman All Hir Live" first met its audience as a stage play. It was produced by an indie theatre company in San Francisco.

It was revised as an 11-minute radio drama. Since the title is a quote from Chaucer's "Canterbury Tales," Columbia University's radio station broadcast it once during April, the month the pilgrims begin their journey.

Now it's been revamped as a short story.

Motta

by Anthony Michael Malara

Anthony always had a yearning to know about the family history.
He knew the family was from southern Italy, but where? Through research
and tenacity he locates where the family originated, and so much more.

Standing on the terrace that doubled as the roof, he looked out towards the Ionian Sea, or was it the Straight of Messina? He made a mental note to review a map to know for sure. The view was spectacular, a green valley below stretched all the way, it seemed, to the sea. Directly to the left was a ruin of a house, dating back hundreds of years. Now four crumbling walls, it housed a plethora of plants including palms, flowers and what seemed to be a small olive tree. It was easy to see as where a window in the ruin house was once; it was now open two stories below from the terrace where Antonio stood. The sky was a shade of blue that was unknown to him. Some wispy white clouds seemed to be painted on this canvas that was the sky here in Calabria. Having lived in Orange, California for the last 35 years, a transplant from Chicago, this was amazing to him. So vivid, almost as if someone placed a color filter; it was so surreal.

Still in a daze, between the twelve-hour flight to Rome then another one-hour flight to Reggio Calabria and additional one-hour drive, there he was, with his cousin Giuseppe, who lived in Pellaro, just outside the city of Reggio Calabria. But this is not quite where it all began.

So, the story begins ten years earlier. Antonio was always interested in history, all history. He now became focused on finding his family history. Through the years, knowing his family was from Italy, the tales told have always interested him. When he was young, his grandfather Antonio, aka "Big Tony," told stories, lots of stories. At the same time, some questions were never answered. As Antonio grew older more of his questions were answered with a stern, "I don't want to talk about it" from Big Tony. The questions in Antonio's head, though, never went away.

Over the next years Antonio's grandfather died as did his grandmother. The house was sold, all his aunts and uncles that lived all within blocks of each other, soon moved to different cities and states. He too had moved to California. The family as it once was, was distanced and disenfranchised. Antonio did keep in touch with his aunt Jeanette. She had now become the family historian, the keeper of records and stories. He asked questions and from what she remembered or the stories she was told, she answered. But Antonio was still unsettled; some things just didn't make sense. Like why didn't any of grandpa's sisters or brothers visit? That was of course with the exception of aunt Virgilia. She was Big Tony's sister. Aunt Virginia, as she was known, always made appearances when there was a wedding, baptism or funeral. She also liked to have her wine, and when Aunt Virginia had her wine, it almost acted like truth serum. It was during one of those conversations where Antonio learned that his great grandfather was not his "blood" great-grandfather but a step great-grandfather.

As Big Tony often had answered questions with "I don't want to talk about it," Antonio would then ask his grandmother, who after being Big Tony's wife for over 45 years would simply answer, "Oh, Antonio, I don't know, if grandpa doesn't want to talk about it, then it's not going to be talked about." Antonio's father "Tony" also kept the information quiet. His response was pretty much the same, or it could be glorified with, "the past is the past, you don't need to know about it." So that was it. Limited information on the family. To Antonio though, he needed to know what a "story" was and what was the truth.

So, after years of wondering he hired a genealogist. For his forty-fifth birthday, the gift he gave himself was hiring a genealogist.

He searched through Google. Then it came up, a company that specialized in Italian ancestry. Antonio had saved knowing that these researches could be expensive and time consuming. So, prior to contacting the genealogist, he spoke with his aunt Jeanette. She welcomed the idea and then began to go through the boxes that she joked about and called it the family archives. Antonio and his aunt were close. He was the oldest, and when he was young, his aunt and her boyfriend, then husband, Danny would take him to the zoo. He felt special getting to be with them and spoiled with trips to the zoo and helping Uncle Danny wash his red convertible.

Then the photographs and documents began being sent through email from his aunt. First, his grandfathers baptismal record, his grandparent's marriage license and many other photographs Antonio had not seen before. One photograph was his grandfather, "Big Tony," in the center of a group of men. He was dapper in his suit as were all the men. On the back in cursive writing it read "The Outfit 1938."

Antonio spoke with the genealogist and was specific about what he was looking to achieve as well as budget. Aliza, the owner of the research firm, was very honest, the budget was pretty limiting since he was unsure of so many things related to where the family came from, and most importantly the family name. So, he sent his limited documentation to the firm and hoped for the best. Months went by and he would send an occasional email checking to see how progress was, not trying to be pressing, but it was met by the return of an email that said it was still being researched. Finally, after eight months an email was sent from the research firm, and they had information, plenty of information.

He called and set the appointment with the firm to have it all explained and reviewed. His excitement was also tempered with skepticism. Could this information be reliable? Is it just all made up? He would have to wait and weigh it all for himself.

The time came and the conference call was done in conjunction with the email showing copy after copy of records from the U.S. Census and records from Italy. He learned that the best records were kept in Italy. The church was a treasure trove of information. Aliza from the research firm began with the location of where the family seemed to have lived for over a century, Motta San Giovanni. After going through the family tree with birth records and death records, she said that his great grandfather was the only one of the four brothers to immigrate from Italy to New York. The year of his departure was 1900, sailing from Palermo to New York, and then on to Pennsylvania, and Ohio, where he died in 1918 at the age of 28 of the Spanish Flu, leaving behind a wife and three children, one of them Antonio's grandfather, Big Tony.

Excited about the information, he could not wait to share it with his Aunt Jeanette, who happened to celebrate her 75th birthday. Explaining to her the family tree, the various dates and all the geological information of where the family had come from, made Jeanette so happy. She told Antonio it was the best birthday present she could have received, and now there was closure, the last name of the family being Malara, not Miller as it had been since his grandfather, who chose the name when he ran away from home at 14.

So now what? Antonio had the information of where the family was from, would there be any relatives still there? How could he locate these family members, and would they believe him and this story?

As time went on, he looked at the map of the southern Italy, specifically the town of Motta San Giovanni. Using Google maps, he could tour the city from the comfort of his home computer. How amazing it looked, by choosing the road that began at E90, it was the single road up the hill, Via Provinciale Motta San Giovanni. He took this tour via Google and it was even more amazing: the terrain, the patchwork of farmhouses, the small roadside pull offs so larger vehicles could pass.

He thought back as to how this must have been a dirt road that was a day long trip just to get from the town, down to the sea. Using the features, Antonio was able to see the town was not large. It had a few bars, restaurants, and the like. He even saw the tiny street where his family once called home. The house long since a ruin, was located on Via Del Carmine. Looking at the former two-story building, the walls still showing the various colors of plaster that had faded over time. Shrubs long since overgrown, dominated the hillside and the small Juliet balcony, slowly rotting, had long trail of geraniums. Had they survived all these years unattended?

While having dinner with friends and giving the news about his family, one of them suggested searching via Facebook.

Antonio looked at him and then said, "You know, I don't have Facebook."

The look of astonishment covered everyone's faces, followed by the offers of help to build his page, but he just smiled and then replied, "I'll build it myself."

The coming days were spent with Antonio joining the millions of people that had Facebook. For him, it was quite the process, it just seemed to ask so many questions; did he want to give out that much information? Then he thought, *how am I going find any relatives in this area of Reggio Calabria?* First and foremost, Antonio spoke no Italian; would anyone even review this new page on Facebook?

After several days of building this new "Facebook page", he launched it. In doing so, he knew that additional steps needed to be taken. For one, according to the genealogist, there were approximately 242 family members in the areas of Reggio Calabria and Sicily. So, the task began by typing in the search page the last name Malara and Calabria. Within seconds, the names of hundreds, if not thousands, bearing the same last name appeared. So, additional research would be required, narrowing the location to the southern areas or communes in Reggio Calabria.

The next day, Antonio went to Barnes and Noble to buy a map of Italy. Yes, a big fold up paper map, that had every small town and side road. Once home he unfurled the map on the floor. Southern Italy, specifically, the areas around Reggio Calabria have several towns and villages. Writing several of them down, he then went to Facebook and continued research. Everyday he sent messages to anyone that had the last name Malara. Utilizing Google translate, he used the same message with a brief overview of his great grandparents, the area they lived and various names of his great-grandfather's brothers. This went on for several weeks. Some of the respondents were very consolatory stating they were not related but wished him luck in his adventure. Then, one day, a message came back from Paolo Malara; he stated that his father, whose name was Giuseppe, was the brother of Vincenzo, Antonio's paternal great-grandfather.

Reading the message from Paolo, he could not believe that he had located a relative! Then a wave of cynicism went through his head. What if this was all just a scam? What if this person was just looking to make contact, then want money? He had to check the documents that the genealogist sent and ask some questions that only a true family member would know.

A quick Google of Paolo Malara indicated that he lived in Pellaro, one of the farthest southern areas in the Reggio Calabria's province. He owned a bakery, a successful bakery. The reviews and photos that were on several online sites, praised the great breads, specialty cakes and coffees. This gave pause to Antonio's thought that this person was a grifter. So, the next message was full of questions. They were extremely specific and questions that only a family member would be able to answer. Once Paolo replied with all spot-on answers, Antonio knew that this man was his cousin.

So, for the next several months, Antonio had conversations with Paolo, and they exchanged photographs and stories about the family here in United States, and in Italy. Some of the stories shared were sad, some of them happy. One of the saddest that he shared with his cousin Paolo, was how his uncle, Antonio's great grandfather died. The genealogist located him through census records, and since arriving to United States in 1900, he had held several jobs and lived in three states.

Spending a brief time in New York, he moved to Pennsylvania where he worked in the coal mines. Saving enough money, he sent for his wife Maria Lucia Cocco. When she arrived, in 1904, they quickly began the family. By 1906 one daughter, then another in 1908. They had a son in 1912. They named him Antonio after Vincenzo's father. In 1916 they moved to Ohio. Lots of Italians were relocating to work at the concrete factories. Vincenzo went to make a better wage for his growing family. They had a small company house located in Cambria County, Ohio. He continued to work at the factory providing for his family until the fall of 1918, when he fell ill and died on November 24, 1918 at the age of 30 of the Spanish Influenza.

Then Antonio decided to visit the country from where his great grandfather departed so many years earlier. The planning began. Currently living outside Los Angeles, flights were abundant to Rome and Milan, however, in reviewing the map, the area that he would be visiting, Reggio Calabria, was all the way at the bottom of Italy. So, the dates in mid-September were selected and the local B&B was booked. Antonio was anxious, yet cautious about meeting his new "famiglia" in Italy. He checked all the places to visit that would be nearby, Tropea, Scalea, Bianco and of course a day or two in Sicily.

After a few days in the rental car and seeing all sorts of villages in southern Italy, including the one that was the birthplace of his great-great-grandfather, just up the hill from Pellaro, Motta San Giovanni. Antonio made it a day trip, so he left the B&B and travelled the 60 minutes to the small village; climbing the steep hill on a very winding road in a Fiat 500, he took in the beauty. The terrain was sparse with cactus and sage. As he continued up the hill, more greenery appeared; grasses and trees were strewn through the landscape. Once he arrived at the small village, he walked around snapping photographs on his phone, wondering exactly where the family had lived. Several of the homes were either a ruin or in a terrible state with imploded roofs. Then he came upon a monument in the square, which appeared to have several names. One of those names was Antonio Malara. The monument very weathered and in Italian held some type of significance, but he had no idea what it was for. He smiled and ran his hand over the name of his great-great-grandfather and knew that it was time to meet his family that now had relocated down the hill to Pellaro.

The next morning, after breakfast and a walk along the shore, Antonio reviewed his cell phone for directions to the bakery that his cousin Paolo owned. He made a note of the exit off E90 that was Via delle Rimembranze and then on the corner of Via Nazionale. So, he set off to meet the famiglia he had been corresponding with on Facebook.

Once he parked, he noticed how big the bakery was, almost the entire first floor of the building. Above was a four-story apartment building. Bright yellow awnings projected from the building and were lettered with "Forno Malara." Antonio opened the large doubled wood doors. To the left was the entrance to the bakery; before going through, he took in the smell of freshly baked bread, pastry, and coffee. This made him smile, thinking back to visiting the bakery in Chicago. His mom would take him and his brother almost daily to pick bread. The ladies that worked there all had bright white uniforms and could not resist giving them both a pastry or a cookie. He suddenly felt transported back to that moment in time. He walked in and in the corner was a face he recognized from Facebook; it was Paolo. He immediately saw Antonio and yelled "Antonio Malara," and quickly left the cash register to meet him. After a bear hug and kiss on each check he clapped his hands and yelled in Italian, opening the double swinging doors to what must have been the kitchen. Almost immediately, two young men appeared. They were introduced as Simone and Giuseppe, both his sons. Another round of hugs and kisses were exchanged and then Paolo moved to a white push button phone on the wall and within minutes another young man appeared and was introduced as Giuseppe. This cousin spoke English, though. After the greeting he spoke in fluent English and acted as the translator for Antonio and Paolo. By now the customers were being introduced and it had become a family reunion! A short time later, Paolo's wife Fernanda was in the lobby area as well. Giuseppe was doing his best to translate all the conversations back and forth. Then Fernanda spoke to Paolo directly and she said in English, "You come to our house for dinner on Thursday at 8:00pm."

Giuseppe then confirmed the invitation and said that other family would be attending as well. At that exact moment, Fernanda emerged with a shopping bag with "Forno Malara" emblazoned on it. She handed it to Antonio, then said in English, "Here are some things to eat from the bakery; enjoy."

As Antonio took the bag, he could not help but realize how heavy it was! He kissed everyone goodbye and walked out with Giuseppe to the sidewalk outside the bakery. Antonio was told to be sure not to eat on Thursday, as Fernanda would be cooking a feast in his honor.

When returning to the B&B, he unloaded the bag and was shocked by all it contained. Arancini balls, still warm in their container. Breads, pastries, and cannoli. If this were an indication of dinner Thursday, he would need to stop eating for more than just Thursday.

Prior to dinner Thursday, Antonio sought out a florist and bought some beautiful potted blooming flowers. The clerk put some beautiful fabric on the outside and then a matching ribbon. Carefully placing them in the shopping bag, he was ready for the dinner to come.

The owner of the B&B assisted him with getting him a taxi as he was not comfortable driving at night in a city where he was unfamiliar. He also knew that there would be wine with dinner, so why chance an accident or a run in with the local "polizia".

The taxi dropped him off in front of the bakery right at 8:00pm. As soon as he exited, Paola and Giuseppe greeted him. They then climbed the stairs to the fourth floor. As they climbed, Giuseppe explained that Paolo owned the building and that his brother Consolato and his wife Francesca, who were his parents, lived there. Additionally, he reserved one of the apartments as rental or for guests when they wished to stay. It was then that Paolo told Giuseppe that he must stay here with the family on the next visit.

As they entered the apartment, he was greeted by Fernanda wiping her hands on her apron. Anthony handed the bag of potted flowers to Fernanda, thanking her for the invitation and the dinner. Then introductions were made to his cousin Consolato and Francesca, who greeted him in English. Antonio's immediate thought was it must a relief to Giuseppe, at least he would have assistance in translating from his mother Francesca. Shorty after they all sat at the table. Directly behind Antonio was a buffet that was filled with pastries and cakes. Wine was poured and the conversation began. It was also during that time that food began to emerge from kitchen. First the appetizers, one of bruschetta topped with fresh grilled sardines, then bread with pesto. More wine was poured, and the pasta course was a homemade ravioli stuffed with a smoked swordfish. Soon more fish was brought on platters, more pasta and a huge wooden bowl filled with various greens for the salad. More wine was poured, and the conversation was now being translated by both Francesca and Giuseppe. It was during all the conversation that Antonio learned about his family. His great grandfather was the only member of the family to migrate to the United States. Antonio's great grandfather Vincenzo's brother, Giuseppe, was Paolo and Consolato's father. The evening was one of enlightenment and answers to many questions. Antonio shared photos of his family and it was amazing to compare the photographs and the family resemblance. Soon the dishes were cleared, and more plates were handed around to begin the dessert course, which included gelato formed in several sea shapes like shells, sea horses and the like. Then, Paolo got up and went to a corner where several bottles of liquor were stored on the shelves. He selected one that had an amber color, and announced we were all having a 40-year-old Grappa. He poured and filled the cordials that were then passed around the table. Each person grasped their glasses as Paolo stood at that head of the table and said, "Welcome to the family, Antonio." Tearing up, Antonio thanked everyone and knew that his journey of finding family in Italy had been realized.

The evening ended with Giuseppe driving Antonio back to the B&B. They chatted along the way with him telling his cousin to visit Los Angeles and to see all the places that tourists like to see. They embraced and promised to be in touch and as the car door closed and a mutual

"Ciao" closed the evening, Antonio knew that one evening had changed his life. That all the years of silence from his grandfather not discussing the family no longer mattered. He found the truth and now knew where he was from and the family that was his family after all these years.

• • • • • • • • • • • • • • • • •

During the next year, Antonio kept in touch with the family. Celebrating birthdays electronically, via ZOOM or Facebook. He loved the connection and warmth, even learning some Italian. In late August, Antonio began planning to return to Italy in late September. He checked the dates with his family there, and they insisted that he stay there in the apartment they maintained for family or guests. He agreed and as the date approached, he started to pack a suitcase with all sorts of t-shirts and like from the tourist attractions in Los Angeles. He knew his family would like these trinkets and both be amused and grateful for the thoughtfulness.

It was decided that Giuseppe would meet Antonio at the airport in Reggio Calabria, which he did. Putting the pieces of luggage into the car they began the journey to Pellaro. They exchanged the usual conversation regarding the flight etc. Giuseppe had just graduated law school and talked about going back to Rome, where his mother Francesca was from, to practice. His brother Salvatore had already relocated to Milan with his fiancé to work as an architect. He explained how his family would be disappointed, but this was his wish. They continued to travel down the E90 but instead of taking the exit Via delle Rimembranze, he passed it. Antonio thought that perhaps all of their talking distracted Giuseppe, so he let him know they just passed the exit. Unfazed, Giuseppe simply said they were meeting the family in Motta San Giovanni first. Thinking that perhaps there was more family to meet or a special restaurant, they continued talking as they climbed the winding road up the hill.

Once there, Giuseppe parked the car and motioned to Antonio to follow him down a pathway to a house perched at the end of the hill.

The area looked very familiar. Then Antonio remembered, the house next door was the ruin he had seen while touring on Google and the birthplace of his great great grandfather. He then saw his family on the roof top terrace. They both climbed the cement steps reaching the top. He looked around, surprised to see the entire family was there. Several tables had been set up with a large buffet of food and drink. Antonio was greeted with kisses and hugs from the family. Then Paolo and Consolato motioned for everyone to give their attention. Giuseppe then left his seat to join them. He carried a large legal-size envelope with him that was very weathered. Once everyone was quiet, Paolo spoke in Italian, then paused so Giuseppe could interpret to Antonio. Paolo said, "Antonio has travelled a far way to learn of his family here in Italy; he is now part of this family. He always has a place at our table; he must too have his place here in Italy."

Antonio was a bit confused and thought he had lost part of the translation from Giuseppe. Then Giuseppe handed him the envelope and Paolo and Consolato motioned to open it. He reached inside and found paperwork, all in Italian, and an incredibly large old key. As Antonio was still confused, Giuseppe explained that the house directly below them was now his. At that, Antonio stood there in complete shock as everyone began clapping. How could this be? He then began to sob and Paolo, Fernanda, Consolato and Francesca all gave him a group hug. Francesca then said that the house needed work; it had not been lived in for at least thirty years. It originally was owned by Vincenzo's father, named Antonio. It had passed through various family members, and now it should be given a new life to a direct descendant, Antonio. Francesca told him that the family would help to make this his home. Antonio then looked at the family, thanked them, then said, "Ora sono a casa," or in English, "Now I am home."

A Christmas Story Allegory: The Fire and The Trust

by Maria Massimi

Have you ever felt a terrible heartache, and tried every cure? Sometimes only the mystery of a miracle will do, as happened on this Christmas Eve!

This is a simple tale, told by a wise and wizened wanderer, alone on the road he is destined to follow. Along its many trails that weave in and out of life, he meets those who believe, and those who cannot, those who try, and those for whom such stories can only remain a legend. It is a tale, however, that he cannot forget, nor discount. For on a special night once a year when the stars twinkle in a special way, he hears a baby's cry that calls to him, that whispers in his ear, "It will be all right."

It was the morn of Christmas Eve, when all was bright with expectation. The church bells would be ringing later that night, to mark a new birth that is ever recurrent. But now alone, she bent down when she saw something still moving, still breathing, still showing signs of life beneath the charred ashes that covered the earth around her. It was still moving despite all that had transpired, despite all that it had endured in this uncertain life. Quiet fires had been raging for months now, as the seasons came and went, as seasons miraculously do. And now what remained in its wake, were the still smoldering, grey, smoking cinders. She saw it still beating in the cinders, still alive, but barely so. It was her heart, troubled and powerless, yet hopeful that it still had the strength to survive, to overcome, desperate to resume its life no matter what. She bent down and picked it up among the flickers of a fiery furnace, fiercely fuming around her feet.

Holding that delicate organ in her hand, she did not know what to do with it. But coming undone, she knew she must act quickly to restore it, to find the inner peace that had been rattled. It had become separated from her soul, where it could not long survive. Still holding it tightly in her hand, she brought it to a man of medicine, for surely a man in a white coat would be able to help. Is it not he to whom we go in times of need? At first she could not let go of it. Faced with confronting the depths of despair, she nevertheless found it difficult to relinquish the source of the pain, to expose her troubled heart. And then, in an instant, propelled by a force she did not think she had, that she did not quite understand, she was able to finally open her hand and reveal that part of her that was now failing faster than ever. There it was, laying quietly and vulnerable. In an attempt to restore it to life, he tried to tell her everything that he had learned to make things right again, to give her what might help a heart in need.

Losing hope, she had come to him as a last resort for healing, and yet, deep down she knew no prescription, bandages, medicine, or combination of words from a medical journal would have any effect, so deep was the suffering that wrenched her very soul. She was succumbing to the belief that there was nothing in this world to make it right again. Desperate to prevail, to restore her peace once again, with nowhere else to go, something in these tired months had now led her there. Would she really find relief for what felt like a supernatural explosion of distress?

As it remained in her hand, it grew more lifeless. "Strong," had he said? Did he really think she had the strength to see this through? Did he not know that she had nothing of what it would take? Fragile and weak is all she felt, life leaving her body. And instead of persevering in her usual determined way, she was losing all energy with no choice left but to succumb to a morbid surrender of the life she once knew. What kind of intervention was needed, she did not know. The mystery of it all still puzzled her, the mystery of who or what would put this heart back on its course. This was a greater challenge than anything she had previously experienced, and powerless to pull herself out of this unhappiness which was swiftly setting in, she felt a depression borne of hopelessness. "When had it originated? What was its meaning? How would it conclude?" she thought.

With fear and distress tearing at her, she again closed it within her hand, ready to take it away, to abandon it somewhere and just be done! Then somehow, quite unexpectedly, this man in the white coat uttered his wish aloud, barely aware of it himself. However faintly beneath his breath it was, his words could be gleaned, "It will be all right." Then, instantaneously, and without any warning...

...an angel heard the plea, however vague, and the need crystallized. At that same moment, dazed, she was preparing to leave, sure that here nothing further could be done. She had experienced the dark depths of the human condition as never before. It was a black cavern into which she had fallen so deeply, a chasm that seemed to have no exit. She had always known of others who had terrifying experiences in life, or those who lived a tragedy, illness, or loss, those to whom great harm had been done, who had been gravely misunderstood or even worse, those whom love had overlooked. These victims seemed to pass through life, scorched, fragmented, immune or hardened to the sufferings and trials of life, until the day when they would return to the earth once again. How had they all survived, learned the secrets that would keep them going, which now eluded her? Focused on her fears, she did not realize that an old Friend had been summoned by the angel. That Friend arrived in less than seconds, and quite unexpectedly as well. He came to get her, and stunned, she recognized Him immediately. She then heard the familiar words, "Do not let your heart be troubled. My peace I give to you." And in His reassuring quiet voice she heard Him whisper, "Don't you know I am always this close to you"? Was it the magic of that special eve that brought about His arrival? A special magic that some say occurs once a year, and which would now bring about a sudden transformation?

This old time Friend loved her, and had not forgotten her. She had always held Him in her heart, and now He hoped she would be courageous enough to surrender totally to His care, to His trust. She knew He was her best friend, always present in Her darkest hours, and so it was that now she placed her entire trust in Him and in Him alone, giving body, mind and soul totally to His care. It was not an easy act. But in an instant she at once felt miraculously re-created. With one hand He took her arm and as He reached for the door with the other, opened it. She stepped out into the clear day and for the first time in months, she saw the sun shining brightly. She felt whole and new again, having left the dark menacing shadows that had clouded her life, behind.

A peace transformed her, swelled her heart, lifted her soul. She looked up and smiled, as He shared His strength with her. She saw the sun, yes, for the first time in many months, that same sun that had been there all the while. It was the sun which would give way that evening to stars that would dress the sky, to shine their brightest, in celebration of a baby's birth, a baby who was to come to be a Savior on that special night. It was the night of miracles. And somehow she knew then that she would never look up at the stars in the sky quite the same way again.

With her Friend walking with her like a shield, His shoulder touching hers, she could walk with the confidence knowing that her best friend was by her side, omnipotent. He knew her pain, and shared it like His own. Finally sure and strong and safe, she would fear nothing. She could not understand the mystery of it all, but had learned one thing, that an everlasting peace could be forever. It was the mystery of Trust.

That day she left with her heart intact once again, to live, to love, and to laugh. She knew she would see Him later, for He would be waiting at Christmas Mass for her and for all those who could be brave enough to trust and to surrender totally, body, mind and soul, to

Him. He, who showed her the sun that day, would lead her by a star at night. It is said that on that special eve, a star is picked among many, to be the one special star, destined to outshine all the others, to shine the brightest in the darkest sky, the one to guide, to lead the way through the murkiest path, to summon an angel who would bring the good news that a Savior has come.

* * * Epilogue * * *

She had once told the man in white that her life was in his hands. She did not know how or why or when, but she knew it was so. His earnestness was recognized, and played a role in "saving" her at a very terrible moment. He had no idea what the wish would bring, that it would be heard by an angel who would deliver it to One who could help, who would render permanent mercy and peace. It could not be explained, but perhaps our wishes are really soft prayers, heard by an angel. He could not anticipate the role that he was to play, nor understand it fully. But one thing is certain. Her heart was broken, overcome by fear and the sadness of separation. Her world had become completely dark. And then, unexpectedly, very unexpectedly, he was instrumental in bringing about the One who would alleviate her worry, contain her fear, restore her heart, and bring her peace. It was a special star that shone for her that day, which guided her through that murky path.

The old wizened traveler might say that maybe we are all picked at one time or another to be the shiny star for someone, even when we least suspect it. Great things happen in the littlest ways, in the quietest of times, times like the night a baby was born in a grotto, in the magic of Christmas Eve.

Four Hands

by Steve Piacente

An orchestra conductor's reputation is at stake when his
young daughters' piano teacher assigns a recital piece that forces
the girls to put aside their differences and play together.

It takes 12 minutes, 35 seconds and twenty fingers to get through
Christophe Friedheim's "Sonatina for Two." This is not hyperbole; the
piece was written for four hands, but meant to be played on one piano.
Why? Good question. I've asked myself the same thing more than once,
and I'm a symphony conductor. Why not write for piano and violin, or
maybe two pianos? Maybe Friedheim wanted to push the abilities of a
singular pianist and wound up going too far, for this is no ordinary duet.
I imagine him late at night in a tiny music studio that is dark except for
a small brass lamp and the glow of his cigarette. He is hunched over an
old, beat-up Steinway with his left hand fiddling in the lowest register
and his right due east among the upper octaves. Some of the white keys
have dreadful scars; he is not a careful smoker.

As he hunts for the notes in his mind, Friedheim's arms are
stretched so wide, he looks like he's embracing the piano, not playing it.
Solution? Two more hands.

No such thoughts occur to Steffie and Bette as they labor through the opening movement that must be played *allegro moderato.* I see Steffie has forgotten the moderate part and is racing as if on deadline; Bette is stuck in the sludge of a rapid bass line riddled with accidentals.

The music stops, the black metronome continues. It is merciless and never wrong.

"You're off."

"No, you're off."

Click, click, click.

"Shut that thing!"

It doesn't matter who is speaking. They say the same things to each other again and again until the heat and pressure rise and one blasts off the piano bench.

"Call me after you learn your part."

"Right."

My impulse is to tell them to quit it and get back to work, but here I am the father, not the conductor. Paying for lessons does not entitle me to wave my baton.

Today it is Bette who stays at the Yamaha, which has had a sticky lower D since it was delivered to our living room nearly ten years ago. Bette is twelve, a smallish, wavy-haired child with what her fourth-grade teacher calls an "artist's personality."

What is a parent supposed to make of such a remark, that she's deep? Creative? Impulsive?

Hopefully it does not mean distracted or unfocused. When pressed, the teacher did not have the words to adequately explain. Maybe she, too, had an artist's personality.

When the girls practice, they improve. That is why we practice, after all. Too bad the same principle applies to wounding each other.

Once I thought I could order peace. By stepping in, however, I became not a peacemaker, but a third combatant. The yelling shook the windows. So now I shut up and hope they will not embarrass the great conductor at their next recital.

One-and-two-and, Da! Da! Da! Da! Da-Da-Da.

This day Bette, who plays *Secondo* to Steffie's *Primo*, presses on like a Marine wading through thick muck. Even when played properly, her part sounds dull and naked, like a tuba solo. She needs trumpets, flutes and clarinets to sound complete. That's Steffie's part.

The piano teacher warned up front that the Friedheim would be a little tough for Bette and a little easy for Steffie. Steffie, two months from fifteen, has more of what the classical music crowd calls *facility*. Most would call it skill, poise, or maybe technical proficiency. Her fingers, which of course have been around longer, are also stronger and cleverer, at least for now.

Bette has always been chasing Steffie, who would shoot ahead in piano, tennis, schoolwork, you name it. I'm not even sure the chase is conscious. In the Friedheim, Bette's part sometimes rises an octave or more. By necessity, the upper player's hands move to the highest notes, the china cabinet. Naturally there is a moment when Bette's right hand accidentally brushes Steffie's left hand and the sniping starts up again.

"Sorry."

"Be careful."

"Click, click, click."

"And over here—that's cre-scen-do," Steffie says, as if speaking to a child new to both music and English.

"Do you know what a crescendo is?"

"Yes, I know what a crescendo is," Bette answers, though she has ignored the symbol on the score.

"Well, if you know, play it that way."

"Shut up."

"No, you shut up."

I put two fingers to my forehead. "*Mannaggia.*"

Thing is, for all her facility, Steffie cannot handle the piece alone. Trumpets and flutes are like the top floor of a skyscraper. They need a bottom, a solid foundation. Imagine the best trumpeter in the world, say Wynton Marsalis. How long could you listen to him play solo before reaching for an aspirin?

The recital is six weeks off. By then, Israel and Palestine must put aside their differences and work to achieve harmony, to say nothing of tempo, rhythm and dynamics. For all the turmoil Friedheim's composition has wrought in my home, Steffie and Bette would rather shave their heads than mess up a performance.

It happened once when she was eleven. A piece by Beethoven in A. All those sharps got jumbled in her mind and she just lost track. At first, she tried to bluff her way through—she knows audiences are full of dopey parents who don't have a clue. But the further she traveled, the more lost she became. When you play from memory, your mind is always a little ahead of your fingers. There are mental checkpoints and musical landmarks. You reach them and your fingers automatically strike the notes that comprise the passage. Then it's on to the next segment. When you lose it, something feels wrong, like when you fasten each shirt button, reach the collar, and realize you started at the wrong button.

Steffie had her long brown hair swept up that day—and a glint of panic in her eyes. Her braces glistened and the taut little rubber bands that connected top to bottom seemed more constrictive than usual. Eventually she stopped altogether. Such loud silence. All of us waited, leaning in, willing her to keep going. She did. She took a deep breath and started from the midpoint. She got through it and was applauded for the effort. Afterward, she cried.

I held her for a moment and suffered a stab of guilt. Steffie works so little and does so well. Think what she could do if she really worked hard. When she was preparing for this recital, I wondered—not hoped, mind you, just wondered—if a flawed outing might not be the lesson she needed. How quickly my mind changed as she cried quietly in my arms. Had I really wished this upon her?

Search engines, instant messaging and cruise control were invented for people like Steffie. Her room is a mess, but her life is ruthlessly efficient. When you complain about piles of books, papers and clothes all over the floor, she replies, "I know where everything is." And she does. She has had nothing but As and Bs since her first report card. Mostly As.

The second movement, which is played *allegretto,* a bit faster than the opening section, is my favorite. Friedheim was ingenious here, visually as well as musically. Instead of one pair of hands chasing the other, the notes flow from top to bottom and bottom to top. In profile, you can see Bette's fingers struggling to make a run of sixteenth notes that end around middle C. Her face is tense in concentration, she does not want to be the one to slip. Steffie's part ends up at the same place, but she starts in the china cabinet. She makes the runs like a delivery man who's had the same route forever. The passages then repeat with slight variations. But the effect is the same: two pairs of hands starting at opposite ends of the piano, converging in the middle, then returning to the original starting point. Performed properly, it is delightful, like a fast-moving river or log flume ride with one chilling turn after another and no straightaway until the very end.

Bette and Steffie are paddling hard but canoeing slowly. They keep crunching into big rocks just below the surface and looking at each other with what appears to be naked hatred. It is not, I am assured by my unflappable wife. "They're sisters," she says. "Didn't you fight with your sister? Well?"

The second movement starts fast but must be played softly, no easy trick, particularly for Bette. The instinct when you go fast is to go hard; just think about running. After much practice alone, Bette has found the notes, but can't keep from banging.

"You're drowning me out," Steffie complains. "This is supposed to be played lightly." She has developed a habit of stopping and lifting Bette's right hand off the piano as the younger girl plays on. Steffie points to the *pp* at the top of page seven.

"Know what that means?"

"Don't touch me."

"Play softer."

"I'm trying."

"Try harder."

I believe if they had weapons, there might be bloodshed.

At one point in this section, the devious Friedheim has set a trap.

Bette, while punching out a two-note bass line with her left hand, must stretch way up and also play the melody with her right. The sheet music even says, "Prepare for right hand to go high on the keyboard." Steffie's right hand at this point takes a rest for about eight measures, but her left must cross under Bette's right hand and play counterpoint to the melody. This involves some touching and thus, unpleasantness. *Friedheim, I think, you dog.* He has even sent Steffie an instruction: "Left hand down in lap out of Secondo's way."

Right.

The third and final movement is the rondo, which must be lively and vivacious, *vivace.* All four hands are moving fast, there is not a finger to spare. We are four weeks in with two to go before the recital, which is to be held nearby at St. Paul's Church. The first two movements are nearly ready; the third is another story. When mistakes occur, Bette wants to go back and do it over until they get it right. Steffie would rather plow through to the end, then go back. So, Bette stops and Steffie continues. She wants Bette to find her place and jump back in. Instead, Bette clears her throat.

"You're playing alone, Primo. You and the metronome. Sounds great."

"Why do you stop? Don't stop. Keep going."

"I stopped because we weren't playing it right."

"God, you're so annoying."

"Start at measure seventeen. One-two-ready-go."

Another week and it will be good enough for dress rehearsal. The girls are putting in an hour a day except for Fridays and Saturdays, when social life takes over.

Steffie runs with a core group of seven girls and five boys. They are all brilliant, beautiful clones of one another. The girls have straight, shoulder-length hair, two small earrings per lobe, and an affinity bordering on the unhealthy, in my view, for Instagram, Tik Tok and WhatsApp. Almost as beloved is the word "whatever."

"You look great today."

"Whatever."

"You look like hell today."

"Whatever."

"Let's go to the mall."

"Whatever."

I look to my wife for help when such exchanges occur within earshot.

"Listen," she says, taking my hands in hers. "Sit down and talk to Steffie's friends. They're all involved in extracurriculars. They all get good grades. And they know how to conduct a normal conversation. There's nothing to worry about."

Squeeze the circle of friends down to one and you've got Bette's social agenda.

She and Josephine have been inseparable since kindergarten. They play softball, rollerblade, work on school projects, and snicker when Steffie tries to pull rank and commandeer the TV or the last doughnut. If Steffie and her friends use verbal shorthand, Bette and Josephine seem at times to communicate telepathically. They could be sitting quietly on the couch reading "Seventeen." One will look at the other and off they'll go, laughing like lunatics.

When Steffie and Bette practice, I silence their phones. I know it's low, but the things go off non-stop. How would they ever get any work done?

Indeed, now they have reached the middle of the rondo, crisply, no mistakes, no dirty looks, timing so good the metronome has been ticking along almost unnoticed.

Backs are straight, elbows level, fingers poised like little trip-hammers. But things begin coming apart at measure 37 when Bette must navigate a series of right- and left-handed melody runs against Steffie's chords. The first mistake goes by and Bette rights herself. The second error is more jarring. Steffie stops and lifts her sister's right hand off the keys.

"Don't do that."

"You're totally off."

"I know I'm off. I don't need you to tell me I'm off. Just play the chords."

For once Steffie lets Bette have the last word. They start again. The recital is in six days. I am a little worried but keep it to myself.

. . . .

St. Paul's has stained-glass windows, a high ceiling with natural wooden rafters, a large painting of Mary and the baby Jesus, and a huge wooden likeness of Christ on the cross. There is room for 180 worshipers in the long line of pews that lead up to a four-foot stage where the priest usually performs his service. There is no priest today. There is a black grand piano that will soon, according to the program in my hand, fill the room with the work of Bach, Haydn, Beethoven and some lesser-known composers like my new friend Friedheim. The first few rows are taken by nineteen of Lydia Kupchak's piano students ages nine to fifteen, who have traded their usual T-shirts and jeans for suits and dresses. Steffie has chosen an elegant black dress and shiny black flats for the recital; Bette has a black skirt and pearl top. Both wear small gold chains around their necks and wrists, and small gold hoop earrings. The sisters will go last.

Most of the students have prepared well and knock off their pieces with no trouble. Dr. Kupchak has a mix of new, experienced and a few advanced students, but will not allow anyone to perform who is not ready. I watch her as she watches each child. She is seated close behind the piano, very serious, trying to remain composed.

The only hint of nervousness is her right hand, which keeps time in small, chopping downward strokes. She has taken the place of the metronome.

Bette and Steffie are paying just enough attention. They don't want to confuse themselves by thinking too much about the other selections. Bette at moments closes her eyes. I know she is visualizing her part, seeing the music in her mind. Her fingers tap out the notes on her knees. Steffie yawns.

The students pour four months of study into performances that last but a few minutes. Some are quite good and clearly cherish their moment on stage. Others can't wait to finish. My guess is they see their dress clothes as prison uniforms, and the recital as the last act of penance before they are free once more.

The end draws near. I look up. Mrs. Kupchak says, "We conclude our program today with something a little different—a duet that will be performed by Steffie and Bette Spencer.

A few of the adults look at me. Their eyes ask: How will the children of the bigshot conductor do today? How well have they prepared?

The girls rise and move to the piano, remembering to adjust the bench.

Steffie whispers one-two-three-four, and they begin. Please, God, I pray.

Most parents are bored and distracted by the end of a recital. Today is different. As the girls rip through the opening movement, all fidgeting stops. Programs are held still. People have been caught and are now on board as Bette and Steffie dash through each musical turn. Dr. Kupchak's hand is moving as furiously as if she were banging a tambourine. The end of the first section comes with a resounding A minor chord. Still no one stirs.

The girls pause, then launch into the second movement, again both smooth and dangerous. They perform efficiently, with no unnecessary flourishes. When the four hands start racing toward the middle and then out, calling and answering, calling and answering, I notice a woman whisper to her husband. Another man who told me earlier he'd rather be home watching football now has an expression that says, *Hey, this is okay.*

No one sees the crash coming but me. It is toward the end of the movement. Steffie begins a passage that should start on E flat with D flat. The mistake corrupts each note that follows, and soon they must stop. I remember the look of panic that hit Steffie that black day she botched the Beethoven; it has seized her face again. What should they do? Everyone is looking. Tension rises. Parents and students start to shift uncomfortably. The sound of the last sour note has risen, bounced off the rafters and faded into memory. Now there is silence. Mrs. Kupchak begins to rise but stops when she sees Bette put her hand firmly on Steffie's knee.

I cannot hear, but I read the younger girl's lips: "From 28. One-two-ready-and..."

They begin again, finish the section, and eat up the rondo like dessert. Applause rings out; I make a move to rise. Not to applaud, but to be applauded. In the instant my toes push down on the floor, something stops me. I cannot quite make out the voice, but I get the message: The ovation is for them, stupid, not you.

Instead, I shift in my seat and clap with the crowd. My wife puts her arm around me. It occurs to me that Friedheim would be pleased.

On stage, Dr. Kupchak places a loving hand on each girl's shoulder. B for performance, A for effort. As our daughters take their customary bow, their eyes lock and a quick smile passes between them.

The Tour Guide

by Paul Salsini

With the loss of clients because of the pandemic, a tour guide in Florence finds a new look on life in an unlikely source in a Tuscan village.

ANOTHER NIGHT. Yet another night. Again with no sleep. Tommaso turned over on his left side, then his back, then his right side, then his stomach.

"Tommaso," his wife said, "what are you doing?"

"Trying to get some sleep."

"Well, you're keeping me awake."

"OK, OK."

Tommaso slipped out of bed, grabbed a robe and went down the hall. The balcony was cool and quiet this early in the morning. Stars and a crescent moon would soon give way to the slowly brightening horizon in the east. Lights were beginning to shine in the homes down below, and far in the distance the skyline of Florence twinkled.

Adjusting the cushions on the lounge, Tommaso leaned back and closed his eyes although he knew he would not fall asleep.

When is this ever going to end? When will there be relief?

"Tommaso? What are you doing?" His wife was in the doorway.

"Couldn't sleep. Just getting some fresh air."

"Well, you woke me and now I can't sleep." She went into the kitchen and turned the cappuccino maker on.

Oh my, Tommaso thought, *it's going to be a long day.*

He knew he shouldn't, but whenever he was depressed like this he thought back to the good times he'd had last year. It was an exceptional year for tourists—the government said 62 million—and as one of the most popular tour guides in Florence and elsewhere in Italy, he was completely booked from April until November.

Tommaso Tomaselli Tours was known far beyond Italy, and he could have taken on even more clients. There was a time in April and another in October when he actually had to refer a few to another tour guide. He didn't like to do that because he knew that Nico gouged people right and left, adding generous tips for himself to the bills for dinners and rooms.

Perhaps he was popular because he was so attentive to his clients' needs. Since he knew a smattering of languages, he was able to have good conversations and make a point of finding out personal information like family origins and educations and occupations. He went out of his way to find the best hotels at the most reasonable prices, restaurants that would serve memorable meals and visits to unknown places far away from the Michelangelos and daVincis.

Sometimes, he later regretted voicing his strong opinions about the Vatican banking scandals, corrupt politicians and the influx of refugees from Africa. His clients usually didn't know what he was talking about.

Anita came in with a cup of coffee and toast, put it on the table near him, and turned and left.

"Thank you," he said.

Tommaso sighed and nibbled his toast. He had hoped this year would be a good one, too. There had been no reason it wouldn't be.

Then the coronavirus struck. Italy was one of the first hit and the hardest. Rome declared a strict quarantine and then a lockdown. Travel to the country was banned, which meant that he had no customers.

He and Anita stayed in their home, or at least he stayed on the balcony and she in the living room knitting with her three cats at her side. They didn't talk much.

When Italy opened its doors to other European countries on June 3, he did have a few clients, a French teacher and a Spanish writer, but both wanted only a day tour of Florence. It was now the end of June and he was still waiting, and not sleeping.

"Why don't you try to find some other work, even part time?" Anita frequently asked.

"I think business will pick up soon," he would say.

"When?"

"I don't know."

Tommaso had been a teacher before he became a tour guide and he knew, at fifty-four, that he couldn't go back to that. He seemed to have no other options.

What he really looked forward to were the Americans. They would surely come now. Once more, Tommaso would have an income and he and Anita would not have to depend on the little money she got cleaning neighbors' apartments.

The sun had now risen and from this view in Fiesole, the dome of Florence's famous Duomo seemed to glow. Anita brought out today's *La Stampa* and Tommaso hoped there would be good news. Yes! A main headline read: "E.U. Sets New List of Approved Travel Partners."

Tommaso had been eagerly awaiting this announcement because he knew that only visitors from countries that had controlled the coronavirus pandemic would be allowed to enter European countries. Surely the United States would be on the list.

He read the list of countries that were allowed: Australia, Canada, Georgia, Japan…

"Where is the United States?"

Then he read the list of countries that were not allowed: Brazil, Russia, United States.

"The United States? No Americans? Oh my God."

THE NEWS set Tommaso off for the day. He snapped at Anita, kicked at one of the cats and slammed the door behind him when he left to have coffee with his longtime friend Luigi. Since the lockdown had been lifted they had resumed their almost daily morning get-togethers at their favorite *bar*, Franco's, just off Piazza Mino.

"I heard the news," Luigi said. "I'm sorry."

"Damn E.U," Tommaso said.

"Well, they wouldn't want people with the infections to come, right? We're not completely over this ourselves."

"We're almost over it."

"Better not take chances," Luigi said.

"Damn E.U."

As always, Luigi was optimistic. "Maybe the ban will be lifted when they review it in two weeks. That's not too long to wait."

"Damn E.U."

"Let's look at the papers."

Tommaso had brought his *La Stampa* and Luigi brought *la Repubblica* and they liked to go through them together.

"Here's an interesting story," Luigi said. "An Italian village is selling homes for just one euro."

"Must be a catch."

"It says the town of Cinquefrondi in Calabria hopes to attract new residents with this low price. It says it has lost many young people to cities to find work."

"I see the Calabrians on the streets all the time," Tommaso said. "They try to take the jobs northerners have."

"It says the homes have been abandoned."

"They're probably falling down and not even worth a euro. Damn E.U."

Luigi sighed. "Tommaso, why don't you find a story?"

Tommaso turned page after page trying to find something that interested him.

"OK, here's one from London."

He began to read. "'Thousands of demonstrators gathered in

London on Saturday in a largely peaceful protest against the death of George Floyd and of systemic racism in the United States and around the world.

"'Activists braved bad weather to fill Parliament Square during the day, but more heated scenes unfolded in the evening when protesters clashed with police outside Downing Street, the official residence of Prime Minister Boris Johnson.

"'Meanwhile, sizable crowds chanted Floyd's name and 'Black Lives Matter,' at one point all taking a knee in unison outside Parliament.

"'One protester said, 'It's a worldwide issue, no matter where you are. It's an issue everywhere; we all need to rise up.'"

"Good God," Tommaso said. "Now this thing is spreading around the world. Why? Why should we care what happened in some town in Minnesota?"

"It's not just Minnesota, Tommaso. This Black guy was choked by a white cop for more than eight minutes. Eight minutes! It just an example of how Blacks are treated. So this has raised consciousness everywhere. Even in Italy."

"We treat Blacks very nice," Tommaso said. "I see them in Florence all the time. If they don't bother me, I don't bother them."

Tommaso and Luigi had had this argument many times and Luigi knew he couldn't win.

"Find another story, Tommaso."

Tommaso turned to the international news.

"Damn. Listen to this," he said. "It says that Columbus, Ohio, has removed a statue of its namesake, Christopher Columbus, from City Hall as part of a nationwide call to replace statues of colonizers, slave owners and other controversial historical figures. What? Columbus? Christopher Columbus?"

"Read some more, Tommaso."

"It says the mayor declared that the statue does not reflect the city and represents patriarchy, oppression and divisiveness. Oh my God!"

"I've read," Luigi said, "that Columbus was actually a slave trader and that he treated Native Americans brutally. I guess people are starting to look at his whole life, not just his voyages."

Tommaso slammed the paper down.

"Christopher Columbus! They're ignoring what Columbus did! That's...that's...a sacrilege! He discovered America! Where would all Americans be if it wasn't for him?"

Luigi tried to make light of it. "In Spain?"

"I think I'll go for a walk," Tommaso said. "See you in a couple of days."

THREE DAYS LATER, Tommaso had calmed down when he met Luigi for coffee. He had resigned himself to the lack of business and had taken a part-time job at Anita's church. Now that Masses had resumed, the place needed a janitor.

"Only ten more days and the E.U. will review its ban on United States visitors," Luigi said as they stirred more sugar into their little cups. "I bet there won't be a problem this time."

"No, I think there will be."

"Why?"

"I got an email from a former client in Michigan. He said things are getting worse in the United States, not better. There are now more than 2,700,000 cases and about 130,000 deaths."

"That's terrible!"

"And there are new hot spots. California, Texas, Florida."

"What the hell happened?"

"Their president let the states have control and some of them opened too early and people were tired of the lockdown so they took chances. Didn't wear masks, didn't stay apart. Of course more people got infected."

"Why did the president do that?"

"Who knows? I don't understand American politics, not under this president."

"Sick, sick, sick. So you think you won't get any American customers for a while?"

"Not for a very long while, Luigi. Maybe there'll be some from Spain, France, England. Not from Germany. They drive so they don't need me."

"Let's read the papers."

They put their coffee cups aside and opened *La Stampa* and *la Repubblica.*

"Well," Luigi said, "you'll enjoy this story."

"What?"

Luigi put on his glasses. "Sardinia Blocks Americans Who Land in Private Jet."

"Really?" Tommaso said. "Read the story."

"OK. It says that officials on the island of Sardinia prevented a group of Americans who arrived in a private plane from Colorado from going to their summer house because the European Union has banned travel from the United States."

"Ha! So they tried to sneak in and got caught," Tommaso said.

"Let me go on. It says that the group of about ten people landed at the Sardinia airport on Wednesday and after several hours they were ordered to go back on the plane. They flew back to the U.S."

Luigi put the paper down. "Well, we know one thing. Italy is enforcing the travel ban."

"Damn E.U. I'm never going to get any Americans."

"You will," Luigi said. "It'll just take time. Let me find another story. Oh, here's one. 'Italy OK's Rescue of 180 Migrants from Mediterranean.'"

"What?"

Luigi began to read. "It says that Italy has authorized the charity vessel Ocean Viking to transfer 180 migrants rescued in the Mediterranean to a ship in Sicily for quarantine.

"It says that those on board exploded with joy at the announcement that their ordeal amid the cramped conditions on the ship would soon be over. It says the migrants, who include Pakistanis,

North Africans, Eritreans, Nigerians and others, were picked up after fleeing Libya in four separate rescues. The migrants include twenty-five children."

Luigi put down the paper. "That makes me feel good. Italy did something right about the migrants for once."

Tommaso didn't say anything.

"OK," Luigi said, "here's another. 'Italy to Grant Amnesty to 600,000 Illegal Migrants.'"

"That's insane!" Tommao said.

"It's true. It says that Teresa Bellanova, Italy's pro-mass-migration agriculture minister, signed the bill that grants six-month residency permits to illegal migrants working in the agricultural and domestic sectors. It said she cried tears of joy."

"Well," Tommaso interrupted, "millions of Italians are going to be crying, but not in joy."

Luigi continued. "Here's a quote from Matteo Salvini. You know, the right-wing former deputy prime minister. He said, 'Minister Bellanova's tears for the poor immigrants, with no reference to the millions of unemployed Italians, do not move anyone.'"

"He's right," Tommaso said.

Over the years, Tommaso and Luigi had frequent discussions—some would say arguments, others would say battles—over the migrant issue. Thousands of migrants from Libya, Eritrea, Somalia, Nigeria, Ghana and elsewhere had died trying to enter Italy, and scenes of migrants in overcrowded, ill-equipped boats had horrified people around the world.

Tommaso at first was sympathetic, especially when 250 migrants drowned off the coast of Lampedusa on March 27, 2009.

But as the number of migrants in Italy swelled to more than a million, he and many others began to resent their presence. They were, the opponents said, costing Italy too much to take care of them and they were also taking jobs away from Italians. A poll found that seventy-one percent of Italians wanted fewer immigrants to be allowed in the country.

"Listen," Tommaso said, "we've lost so many jobs during the lockdown and now we're going to let more of these people in?"

"'These people,'" Luigi said, "are human beings. Remember what Jesus said, 'Whatever you did for one of the least of these brothers and sisters, you did for me.'"

"Yeah, yeah. He didn't have to look for a job. Now I'm a part-time janitor."

"Tommaso, you always talk like the migrants are one big mob. These are individual people who are escaping terrible conditions in their own countries. Do you know any migrants?"

Tommaso couldn't offer any response to that, and they soon finished their coffee for the day.

"See you when I see you," Tommaso said.

AT HOME, Tommaso watered the cats, trimmed weeds in his garden and picked up a book. Back on the balcony, he tried to analyze his opinions about migrants. He really resented them taking jobs from Italians, especially now when the unemployment rate was so high. But maybe Luigi was right. Maybe he should think about migrants as individuals, not as a horde.

He had to admit that he didn't know any. There was a young sad-eyed woman with a baby begging every day on the steps of Chiesa di Santa Maria Assunta in Fiesole. Everyone said he shouldn't put coins in her plate, and so he always walked on and soon forgot about her.

"The migrants probably planted her there," he thought.

Unable to resolve the issue, he decided to check his emails, not that anyone wrote to him anymore.

Someone did!

"Tommaso Tomaselli Tours: You have been recommended to me by a colleague who was impressed with your services when you took him to the graves of Keats and Shelley in Rome. You may remember him."

"What? Of course, I remember him. That professor who didn't want to go to the Vatican and was such a pain in the ass? He recommended me?"

"I am a professor of anthropology at Oxford and would like to go to the village of Sant'Angelo as part of my research on the SPRAR project there. You may know the project as the Protection System for Refugees and Asylum Seekers.

"I would like to arrive on the fifteenth of this month and spend three weeks there. It will be necessary that you accompany me throughout this time because of my limited knowledge of Italian. Accommodations are provided and I have a grant to take care of all your expenses.

"Please let me know at your earliest convenience if this is acceptable.

Sincerely,
K.L. Anderson, Ph.D

Tommaso read the email again. And a third and fourth time. This was incredible. He had a job! Three weeks! All expenses paid! This would be enough for him and Anita to get by for several months. He wouldn't have to be a janitor any more. And maybe by then Americans would be able to fly to Italy.

He quickly Googled "Protection System for Refugees and Asylum Seekers." He'd never heard of it.

The SPRAR project (Protection System for Refugees and Asylum Seekers) is financed by the Ministry for the Interior through the National Fund for Asylum Policy and Services. Its aim is to support and protect asylum seekers, refugees and immigrants who fall under other forms of humanitarian protection.

SPRAR works in the villages of Vaiano, Carmignano, Poggio a Caiano, Montemurlo, Bagno a Ripoli, Sant'Angelo and S. Casciano Val di Pesa. Each can offer support to a maximum number of 50 people. There is a waiting list.

The services consist of: accommodation in a small house; supply of food vouchers for board; orientation in relation to local services; support of a linguistic mediator, assistance in procedures to access social, health and educational services (Italian language courses for adults, enrolment in school for minors).

Tommaso read the entry again and again. So this was a government service that places refugees into little villages and supplies them with food and board, teaches them Italian and gives them support to start new lives. Hmmm. There must be a catch. He'd be living with migrants? Well, he needed the job. He would reply to this Professor Anderson and tell him he would accept.

ANITA WAS, of course, pleased that Tommaso had a job. Three weeks would provide a good income for a while, not to mention that he would be out from under foot. They both knew they needed some time apart.

"Have fun!" She gave him a peck on the cheek and he loaded the Fiat Panda with three suitcases. For some reason, he always packed as if he was going to be away for three months.

In a subsequent email Dr. Anderson had said that the British Airways flight would arrive at Amerigo Vespucci Airport in Florence at 3:20 p.m., and Tommaso, as always, was right on time.

The plane didn't land until 3:42 and by that time Tommaso had become more and more worried as the passengers retrieved their bags and left the terminal. He kept looking for what he assumed would be a tall, professorial-looking gentleman, perhaps with white hair and a beard, but no one matched that description.

At last, only one person was waiting, a very short, 30-something woman wearing a dark blue pantsuit and carrying a large tote bag. Her blond hair stretched in a long braid down her back. She saw Tommaso first.

"Signor Tomaselli? From Tommaso Tomaselli Tours?"

"Yes?"

"I'm Karen Anderson. So pleased to meet you."

"But...but..."

"You thought I'd be taller."

"No... no, I just thought..."

"I should have used my full name. So sorry. Shall we go? I can't wait to see Sant'Angelo."

Karen Anderson had only one suitcase plus her tote bag and they were soon on their way. They drove northwest, going through Prato, Pistoia and Lucca before entering the rugged part of Tuscany called the Garfagnana.

Tommaso pointed out the snow-capped mountains, the little streams, the small villages.

"This is gorgeous!" his passenger said. "I've never been in this part of Italy."

"It's my favorite part, Dr. Anderson."

"Please, call me Karen."

"Karen it is."

Along the way, Karen told Tommaso that she was born in Leeds, the only child of a medical doctor and a nurse practitioner. When she was young, under ten, her parents went to Zambia where her parents helped operate a clinic.

"Fortunately, the main language was English, but I did learn a little of the native languages, Nyanja and Bemba. I don't know if I remember any of that now. But I did learn to love the people so much!"

Living with the natives, she said, aroused a lifelong desire to work with the peoples of Africa, and she received a doctorate in African Studies at Oxford. She was fortunate to join the faculty after that and was now an assistant professor.

"I hope my research here at Sant'Angelo will be the last thing I need to get a promotion," she said. "And you, Signor Tomasselli? Tell me about your life."

"Call me Tommaso, please. Not much to tell. I'm from a little town near here. I was a schoolteacher for many years but then I couldn't take the kids anymore and a friend asked me to join him in the tourist business. I did, and eventually bought him out. My first wife died sixteen years ago and I married Anita ten years ago."

"How lovely! To find love again!"

"Yes. And you?"

"No, no. A few relationships but nothing that lasted."

They were now winding through the town of Castelnuovo di Garfagnana, and Tommaso pointed out the castle ("Twelfth century"), the Duomo ("Sixteenth century"), the fortress ("late Sixteenth century").

"Oh my," Karen said. "I wish I could have lived back then."

"If you lived in the Fourteenth century, you might have died in the Black Death. Of course, we just lived through Covid-19."

"Knock on wood."

A few miles north of Castelnuovo di Garfagnana, they were on the outskirts of Sant'Angelo and then, because it was so small, they were in the middle of it.

"Oh my," Karen said. "Oh my, Oh, my, Oh, my."

"Beautiful, right?"

Sant'Angelo looked like other towns in the Garfagnana. Small stone houses with red-tiled roofs flanked the narrow main street. A few shops displayed vegetables and fruits outside. At the center, a church, a two-story municipal building, a tall tower and what might be called a palace surrounded a small piazza.

Unlike other villages, however, not all of the people who filled the streets talking and shouting looked like typical Italians. Some wore very bright clothes.

"From what I've read," Karen said, "the people are from all over, Eritrea, Nigeria, Somalia, Sudan, Syria, Gambia, Bangladesh, Liberia, Ghana. A lovely mix."

Tommaso was startled when he saw a very black hand knocking on his window. He rolled it down. The man, well over six feet and very thin, wore a dazzling red shirt emblazoned with yellow suns. When he smiled, his white teeth contrasted sharply with his dark skin.

He reached out a hand. "Hello. I am Maduka. Welcome to Sant' Angelo."

TOMMASO AND KAREN were assigned rooms on the second floor of the municipal building, now converted into a bread and breakfast. The rooms were small but adequate, nothing like the luxurious hotels where Tommaso had stayed in Rome or Milan. They were told that dinner would be served shortly in the restaurant.

The Ras Dashen Canteen, remodeled from its previous life as a convent, was a blast of colors with abstract murals on the walls and bright tablecloths. The tables were set safely apart even though Sant'Angelo had welcomed few visitors during the pandemic and had, miraculously, not had a single case of Covid-19.

Tommaso and Karen were seated with their greeter, Maduka, who said he was from Nigeria, plus Father Aloysius, whose parish helped to sponsor the program, and Gamal, a teenager from Syria.

They had just finished the introductions when Amukusana, a striking middle-aged woman in a long flowered dress, began serving their meal.

"This is what we call *nshima.* We eat it all the time in Zambia. It is made from corn that is processed into a fine white powder called 'mealie meal.' It is basically a very thick porridge and as you can see, it is served in lumps. And, oh yes, it should be eaten with your hands."

While the others proceeded to dig in, Tommaso stared at the concoction in front of him. He had never seen anything like it before. He had never eaten with his hands before. And yet it smelled awfully good.

Watching to see how it was done, he grabbed a portion and rolled it into sort of a ball, and then took a bite.

It tasted nothing like the pasta he was used to. It was delicious.

The others talked about what they did that day, but Tommaso was too absorbed in a second helping and heard only parts of the conversation.

Father Aloysius was forming a new choir with immigrants,

Maduka was finishing a table in a wood-working class, and Gamal said he met a girl from Syria and they were going to watch the outdoor movie in the piazza that night.

An hour later, Karen nudged Tommaso. "I'm beat. Want to call it a night?"

He did.

AFTER SLEEPING straight through for the first time in months, Tommaso joined Karen for a briefing from Father Aloysius and Maduka. The project, the priest said, had begun five years ago and usually involved thirty-five families on a rotating basis. They learned trades, the Italian language, reading, writing and simply how to get along better in a foreign country.

"What we want to do here," the priest said, "is to help these people live a normal life. They've been through so many traumas in their own countries. You can't even imagine it. And then the terrible sea crossing in which so many died, many of them family members. We try to help them find the right path, the way they want, not the one we want for them."

The priest showed them photos of migrants studying, cooking, and working in a farm field.

"There is no question," he said, "that the anti-immigrant prejudice has grown. It says all migrants are bad and dirty and stealing jobs, which isn't true. If all our immigrants left Italy tomorrow, the country would descend into chaos."

Tommaso could feel his face getting red.

After going through scrapbooks and ledgers, Karen went off to talk to others, and Maduka offered to give Tommaso a tour of the village.

They stopped first in the kitchen of the Ras Dashen Canteen where a dozen women, ranging from Italian grandmothers to migrant teenagers, were at oversize stoves stirring pots that gave off delectable aromas.

"We teach," one of the women explained, "migrant women how to adapt their cooking to Italian patrons. Then they can get jobs in restaurants and in catering businesses in the nearby towns."

A woman offered Tommaso a spoonful of what was in a pot.

"We are serving this tonight," she said. "It's called *kubbah safar-jalīyah*. It is from Syria. It consists of stuffed meatballs cooked with a quince-based soup."

After swallowing, Tommaso couldn't wait until dinner.

Maduka led the way to an old villa behind the restaurant.

"They say this was built in the Fourteenth century," a receptionist at the entrance said, "but now it is used as a clinic. There are classes in meditation and stress relief, but we also have two psychiatrists. We all know that many migrants have suffered severe trauma. Some are suicidal. A young woman took her life last year. She had been raped and tortured in Libya."

Tommaso winced.

From there, they went to what was once a barn where women were sewing aprons, men were making little bookcases and men and women formed necklaces from brightly colored stones. Maduka explained that the items would be sold at a shop in Florence.

Tommaso saw a young man finishing a necklace.

"That's beautiful! My wife would like one of those. I wonder... I wonder if I might come here and make something like that."

"Of course," Maduka said. "Start tomorrow."

At another ancient building, Maduka explained that this was used as a classroom where the Italian language was taught.

As they returned to the piazza, Tommaso was overwhelmed by the sights and sounds. Men, women and children in brilliant African clothing talked and shouted in their native languages and in Italian. Smartphones blared hit tunes from Syria, Nigeria, Ethiopia. Exotic cooking smells filled the air.

"I've been to many Italian villages," he told Karen later, "but nothing like this."

TOMMASO HAD BROUGHT a bagful of books along, thinking that he would read when Karen didn't need him for translations. Instead, he could hardly wait to get out every morning to meet people, listen to their music and learn a little of their languages. In between, he began making the necklace for Anita.

From his work translating the migrants' hesitant Italian to Karen, he met Shadi, who had escaped kidnapping during the civil war in Syria. He met Asida, a Rohingya Muslim woman who had been raped in Bangladesh. He met Mustafa, who had fled the revolution in Tunisia and landed on the island of Lampedusa.

Makin, a teenager from Syria, said he was on a boat with 200 migrants that capsized when people moved to one side of the vessel. Fifty-six survivors were taken to Italy.

"My brother...my brother. I hold on to his shirt. He told me to let go, to go back. But he got away. He went into sea. Now I am alone."

Everyone had a story and every story was heart-breaking.

Every night there was a new adventure in dining. The stuffed vine leaves called *dolma* from Syria. The raw marinated meat called *kitfo* from Ethiopia. The medley of beans and rice called *waakye* from Ghana. The soft cake called *doolshe buuro* from Somalia. Tommaso wondered if could make these things if he got the recipes, but decided against it.

Maduka had become his good friend. They walked together each night in a sort of international version of a *passeggiata* and then sat on a bench and talked. Maduka wanted to know all about Tommaso's tourist adventures and he told him stories about his customers.

The American couple who clearly didn't understand papal protocol and wrote: "We are arriving on the Nineteenth. Please arrange a private meeting with the pope at 2 p.m. on the Twentieth."

The Parisian man who countered anything Italian with something better in France. Viewing daVinci's "Last Supper" in Milan, he had said, "But we have the Mona Lisa in the Louvre."

All the sulking teenagers who refused to eat anywhere but McDonald's.

But also all the friends he'd made, so many of them American. The grandmother and her family who were enchanted in Florence by the armor collection at the Stibbert Museum, the perfumes in the Santa Maria Novella Pharmacy, the flea market in Piazza dei Ciompi.

The elderly rabbi from New Rochelle who needed help researching his relatives killed in the Ardeatine massacre in Rome in World War II.

The Wisconsin author who wrote a series of novels set in Tuscany and who came back again and again for what he called "research."

The young family from Delaware that had promised the kids they'd see Rome at Christmas.

Individuals and groups, school classes and senior citizens, he'd had so many over the years.

Maduka was fascinated, but changed the subject every time Tommaso asked about his own life.

Each night, Tommaso met with Karen, who reported that her interviews filled forty-three files in her laptop. She was exhausted but exhilarated.

"This has been wonderful," she said on the Friday of their last week, "but I'm ready to go home."

"I don't want to, but I guess we have to."

First, they met with Father Aloysius and told him how grateful they were to have received such a warm welcome from everyone in Sant'Angelo. The priest noted that the Protection System for Refugees and Asylum Seekers was planning a similar project just north of Florence in the village of San Domenico and was seeking applicants.

Tommaso immediately thought of someone.

"There's a young woman in front of Chiesa di Santa Maria Assunta in Fiesole every day. I'll tell her."

"You might also be interested in knowing this," the priest said. "They're looking for people to teach and do other things. It doesn't pay much, but enough. Would you know of anyone?"

"Really?" Tommaso said. His thoughts tumbled. He wouldn't have to worry about the lack of American tourists. Maybe Anita could join him. It would be a short drive. And he'd be working with migrants. He would call next week.

After loading the Fiat, Tommaso said he wanted to talk to Maduka one more time.

They sat on their bench and after hesitating, Tommaso said, "Maduka, I have spent a lot of time talking about my life but you haven't told me anything about yours. If you don't want to talk about it, that's fine. But I'm your friend. I'm interested."

Maduka looked into the distance, then leaned his long body forward and held his shaking hands.

"Is not a good story."

"I understand."

He paused.

"You know of Boko Haram?"

"A little. Terrorist organization in Nigeria."

"Terrible. Terrible. Murderers. Rapists. Suicide bombings by young girls. Terrible. Terrible."

"I've read some," Tommaso said.

"You know what happened in 2014?"

"Yes. I remember. Terrible."

Maduka took a deep breath and continued.

"They kidnapped 276 girls."

"From a school, right?"

"The Secondary School in the town of Chibok."

"Yes."

"To become sex slaves."

Maduka took another deep breath.

"My daughter...my daughter...Ginika..."

"Go slow, Maduka, go slow."

"She was one."

"Oh my God."

It was another five minutes before he could continue. His whole body shook, and sweat poured down his face. Tommaso put his hand on Maduka's shoulder.

"My wife. My wife, she go crazy. Cry all the time. Hysterical. Hide under covers. I could do nothing. Nothing."

"Oh, Maduka. My friend."

"One night, I couldn't find her. I look everywhere. I go all over village. I go down to river. I find her body in the...in the water."

Maduka let his tears fall. Tommaso stroked his back and they sat silently for a long time.

When he had gained composure, Maduka said that he learned later that their daughter had died soon after her arrival in the Boko Haram camp, and he was actually grateful.

"No sex slave. She is in heaven. With her mother."

"And you?" Tommaso asked.

"I run away. Fast as I can."

Maduka got up and walked aimlessly around, toward the church, toward the tower, toward the palace, and sat down again.

"You married, Tommaso?"

"Yes."

"Children?"

"No, no children."

"Love your wife, Tommaso. Love your wife."

Maduka dug into his pocket and brought out a small gold piece.

"See the picture of the tortoise, Tommaso? In Nigeria, the tortoise brings good luck. You give this to your wife and she will be happy and you will be happy. You will have good luck."

They stood up. The tall man from a foreign country and the short, stocky Italian. Color didn't matter. Where they came from didn't matter. They hugged.

Evil Spirits

by Marylouise Serrato

Poverty and superstition infuse the life of the Borgo family and life events appear to young Luigia to be forever dictated by illusive evil spirits.

Luigia had limped for as long as she could remember. Her parents said that it was because of an accident she had as a child. However, sometimes Luigia heard her aunts say that her mother had been visited by an evil spirit during her pregnancy and that this was the real reason for her deformity. Luigia contemplated this as she looked down from the side of her bed at her right foot dangling inches away from the floor as her left foot rubbed against the roughness of the wood planks. She stretched her arms skyward and spied her younger sister Erica still sleeping in the bed across the room.

Luigia could hear her mother Beatrice downstairs in the kitchen, the dint of pots knocking against one another and the slow slamming of the door back and forth echoing her footsteps. The only time Beatrice had ever stopped working the Borgo farm was to give birth to her five children and while she was desperately trying to save baby Carlo from dying of fever. Carlo has always seemed sickly but Luigia's grandmother said that Beatrice had been to blame for Carlo's death. Beatrice had been visited by an evil spirit just like she had when she was pregnant with Luigia. Luigia often wondered what her mother had done to deserve having the evil spirit visit her so often. Once, during confession, Luigia asked Father Matteo about the evil spirit but he told her never to speak of such things and to say a full rosary as penance for even having such a thought.

Beatrice's face was dark and weathered like a chestnut and her hands were calloused and rough to the touch. Beatrice did not look at all like Signora Silvestri, who lived in the large house off the *piazza* in the center of town. Signora Silvestri's face was round and pink and her hands were smooth with pearly oval nails. Signora Silvestri was married to "*il magistrato*," Signor Silvestri. They had been married many years but had never had any children. Some people rumored that an evil spirit was responsible for this because Judge Silvestri sometimes passed sentences that seemed unfair, like when he made Francesco Forte pay a fine for stealing a goat from his neighbor to feed his family during a particularly difficult winter.

Generations of the Borgo family had provided the Silvestri family with their vegetables and eggs. From her great-great grandparents on down, it was now up to Luigia to make the twice weekly deliveries to the Silvestri house. Luigia finished dressing and hobbled down the stairs to the kitchen. Sitting at the weathered pinewood table while her mother cooked quietly at the stove, Luigia dunked the hard end of last night's bread into the dark bowl of aromatic coffee.

"I'm off," said Luigia, as she picked up the basket of provisions her mother had prepared for the Silvestri family.

Her mother glanced over her shoulder, her head covered in her bandana, eyes weary, "Don't forget to add some extra eggs to the basket on your way out."

Luigia held her breath as she pushed the slatted wooden door into the chicken coup and waved away the errant feathers that floated down around her. Tucking her hand under the warm bottom of the hens, she picked up four more eggs and gently laid them in the basket next to the radicchio. On the long walk into town, Luigia passed in front of the farms of her neighbors as they greeted her. Although they were always polite and friendly, Luigia knew that her neighbors felt sorry for her and her family. Everyone knew that it was only the women who were left to tend the Borgo farm. Sometimes, when she bartered with them for goods, they would offer her some extra meat to bring home to her mother. Often she heard them under their breath say what a shame it was that the evil spirit had made Luigia a cripple because no one was ever going to marry her.

As she approached the main *piazza*, life around it was slowly waking up. Storefronts were rolling up their *tapparelle*, men were sitting at the outdoor tables fortifying themselves with *caffé corretto* and women were lining up with their copper buckets to collect water. Luigia stopped for a moment in front of Saint Ambrose's church, crossed herself and then turned up the street that led to the long poplar lined pathway of the Silvestri house. Luigia always entered the house from the back, through the kitchen where Teresina, the cook, was a permanent fixture. But she liked to stop for a bit in the front the house and imagine what it would be like to enter from the front door that lay beyond the terrace lined with pots of oleanders and encircled by the carved white balustrade. She imagined that the inside must be as opulent and grand as the inside of St. Ambrose's church. Luigia had never stepped inside anything as grand as St. Ambrose.

Usually, Luigia would only see Teresina during her visits but sometimes Signora Silvestri would be in the kitchen checking on meal preparations. Signora Silvestri was always kind to Luigia–occasionally slipping her an extra *scudo* in her pocket. Once, she asked Luigia to sit and drink a glass of lemon-water with her. It had happened during a hot summer day, Signora Silvestri was fanning herself at the kitchen table when Luigia entered laden with her basket and her hair matted from the heat. She invited Luigia to sit down to join her as she poured out two glasses of lemon water with her perfectly manicured hands, her slim gold wedding band clinking against the glass pitcher. Signora Silvestri knew all about Luigia's family and would often ask after her sisters and her brother, Alberto, a priest in Bergamo. Sometimes she even inquired about her father Guido—which for most everyone else was a subject to be avoided.

Luigia's father Guido had given up on working the farm shortly before Alberto had left for the seminary. One day, Guido came in from the fields, took to his bed and stayed there for three months. When he finally came down from the small room in the attic, he took a rucksack and a bottle of wine and left. Occasionally Guido would return with a few *lire* in his pocket and lots of alcohol on his breath. The last time Guido had come home, Beatrice asked him how long he would be staying and he answered her with the raised palm of his hand. That was years ago, it seemed, as Luigia can no longer remember a time when her father was standing behind the plow instead of her mother.

Alberto leaving for the priesthood only added to the Borgo family upheaval. The day Alberto announced he was entering the seminary, Beatrice threw three dishes and a water pitcher against the wall in despair. Alberto said he felt the calling to spread God's message and heal those in spiritual pain.

"Who is God going to send to us to help keep us physically alive while you go tending to the spiritual health of strangers?" Beatrice asked sarcastically.

Without her husband and son to help and unable to pay for hired help, Beatrice was forced to sell off a small parcel of her land and to the church no less. Looking to build a convent for the nuns with land to cultivate, the Borgo track suited perfectly except now she had several focal points for her ire, her husband, her son and the neighboring nuns.

Years later, Alberto returned to be ordained in St. Ambrose's. After his ordination, Beatrice, Luigia and her sisters, along with Father Matteo, sat through a melancholy luncheon at the local osteria before heading to the train station to send Alberto off to Bergamo to serve in a small parish. As he mounted his train carriage, Alberto tried to hug his mother, but she shrunk back. He told her that God would provide for the family even without him. Trust in God. Not to worry. Standing on the station platform Luigia wondered if all the Borgo men abandoning the family was somehow the doing of the evil spirit.

Luigia's sister Lucia could have escaped like Alberto. She was the prettiest of the three sisters and the sweetest; she loved children. *If Lucia married*, thought Luigia, *she would have many children and Luigia could go and help her and get away from the farm the way Alberto had.* A year ago, the butcher's son Renato asked Lucia to marry, but she turned him down. Luigia was devastated. She couldn't understand why Lucia didn't want to marry and live in the big house Renato's family owned above the butcher shop. Last month, Renato married Carmela Spolato. Luigia spied them walking out of St. Ambrose's with their families trailing behind. Luigia thought about how her life might have changed if it had been Lucia walking out of church with Renato instead of Carmela.

When Luigia finally arrived at the front of the Silvestri house she noticed something was different; the shutters were all closed, even those on the main floor. Usually, the house was only closed like this during the month of August when the family left for their vacation at the sea. Luigia walked around to the back of the house and saw the shutters on the upstairs windows closed as well. The door to the kitchen was open with the net-curtain gently billowing in the wind. Luigia knocked and called in to Teresina; the kitchen was dark, but the stove had been lit. Luigia waited and after a few minutes entered the room, calling again for Teresina. She heard footsteps above her and down along a staircase until finally Teresina appeared standing in front of her, red faced and puffy eyed.

"What is it, Teresina?" Luigia asked.

"A tragedy, an unbelievable tragedy," sobbed Teresina, "Signor Silvestri is dead."

"What?" Luigia asked.

"Il Signore is dead. He died in his sleep. Just like that, without warning," Teresina continued. "Dottor Giovannetti was called in during the early hours this morning when the Signora realized her husband wasn't breathing. He was still here when I arrived. There was nothing to be done," she added.

Luigia had never met Signor Silvestri. He worked in his studio in the house, but was never really seen except by his clients, much less would he ever be found in the kitchen. She had only seen him during the *passeggiata*, walking arm in arm under the porticos with his wife or seated at a terrace when they stopped for a drink. He was much respected in town because he was a judge and his family came from quasi-nobility, having lived in the town for centuries. He was much older than his wife and everyone spoke of the tragedy of them having been left childless. Teresina was sure that their infertility was not the Signora's fault; no one could be that young, healthy and pink and not be able to produce children.

For three days family members came to pay respects to the deceased Judge and his wife and then the funeral was held at St. Ambrose church. Luigia, her mother and sisters attended the service watching from the last pew. Eloquent eulogies were given for "il magistrato" while his wife and family sobbed quietly, the women's faces covered under dark veils. After the final blessing, a parade of black attired men and women, followed by Father Matteo, descended the altar behind the coffin. When Father Matteo reached their pew, he bent over and whispered to Beatrice, "I hear Alberto is coming to visit." A week later, Beatrice received a letter from Alberto telling her that he was being transferred to a parish in Ravenna and would be spending a month with them before taking up his new post.

After the funeral, life at the Silvestri house changed considerably. The shutters were permanently closed and black wreaths were placed on the windows and doors. Luigia made her deliveries only once a week, instead of twice, and Teresina would update her with ever more disturbing news. Signora Silvestri wasn't eating and rarely slept. She seemed to live in a comatose state, often wandering the house in her nightdress all day.

"She wants all the shutters closed and sits in the dark all day long," said Teresina. "Sometimes, when I arrive in the morning, I find her just sitting in the darkened reception room or in her husband's studio. I'm sure she's been there all night."

Luigia thought back to the day Signora Silvestri offered her the lemon water. How sweet and fresh she had seemed then. She couldn't imagine that beautiful face ruined by grief.

It was during those weeks that Alberto arrived. When his carriage drove up to the courtyard of the farm, Lucia and Luigia rushed out to greet him. Erica hung off his neck as he attempted to stand upright.

"Ah, the returning cleric. What news from God?" said a sarcastic voice behind them.

All three girls turned to find their mother standing in the doorway, arms crossed defiantly and eyes squinting from the rays of the sun.

"Mamma," said Alberto, "Don't talk like that." He kissed his mother and she smiled slightly as she led him into the kitchen.

"Lucia, make some coffee," ordered Beatrice.

Beatrice stood over the table sprinkling flour over the dough she was preparing for pasta while Luigia and her sisters interrogated Alberto.

"Why are you leaving your parish in Bergamo?" asked Luigia. "What will your parish be like in Ravenna?" asked Lucia.

"Why can't you just stay here at St. Ambrose?" asked Erica.

Alberto did his best to answer; priests are reassigned, Ravenna will have its share of saints and sinners, until his mother interjected, unable to keep her peace as usual.

"Why does God feel that he needs blackbirds to minister to his flock?" Beatrice retorted, "Everything we need to live by is written in the Bible—we don't need interpreters."

"Mamma, people are human, they have failings and faults, they need guidance," Alberto began to answer back.

Beatrice sighed heavily and opened her mouth to speak, but then stopped short turning her head to look outside at the fields.

They talked for several hours until Alberto announced that he wanted to visit Father Matteo before it became too late. Luigia told him about Signora Silvestri and Alberto said he would send her a note expressing his condolences. He remembered the day Signora and Signor Silvestri had married; he had been the altar boy at their wedding. He remembered how young Signora Silvestri looked standing next to Signor Silvestri with his gray hair, his handlebar mustache and his droopy jowls. He remembered that they had given him an envelope with some *lire*, a gift for serving at the wedding. Sometimes, to earn some pocket money, Alberto had run errands for Signor Silvestri; buying him a newspaper, having his shoes polished. Yes, Alberto thought, he would definitely send Signora Silvestri a note.

On Sunday morning, Beatrice sat coiling her long braid up into a bun and pinning it to her scalp. She pulled the last hairpin from her pursed lips and stuck it forcefully into the bun, sighing heavily and thinking how she detested having to go to Mass and listen to Father Matteo preach nonsense. Normally she never went, but this Sunday was different and Beatrice knew she would need to accompany her son to Mass. She took one last glance at herself in the mirror and then threw her shawl over her shoulders and headed downstairs to meet the others.

The whole family walked together under the early morning sun towards St. Ambrose. When they reached the main *piazza*, people were pouring out their doors and heading towards the church, except for the men who were delaying the inevitable by stopping off at the bar before Mass. People stopped to greet Alberto. It seemed odd to Beatrice to see people who had once treated Alberto with insignificance now defer to him with respect. *How hypocritical*, she thought; *had Alberto changed so much? What had transformed Alberto from a mere mortal to a near God? A white collar?* Beatrice smiled in acknowledgement at the people who greeted her as they all entered church. Father Matteo passed by their pew right before Mass and whispered something to Alberto, which he gently acknowledged with a slight nod of his head. From the back of the church Beatrice heard the swell of the organ music and the smell of incense permeated the church. Mass had begun.

After Mass, Alberto announced that he and Father Matteo were going to look in on Signora Silvestri. Father Matteo had been visiting Signora Silvestri ever since her husband's death, but he found that she was not accepting her loss and was becoming more and more distraught each time he visited. Father Matteo thought that maybe Alberto might be able to help. "After all," he said, "I am but an old priest. Maybe someone younger, with more spirit, would help."

Luigia, her mother and sisters agreed to meet Alberto afterwards at home for lunch and they began their walk back past the *piazza* and towards the outskirts of town. Beatrice turned to watch Alberto and Father Matteo as they walked away. Two heads bowed together in conversation, two black cassocks blowing gently in the wind.

While Alberto was home, he helped a bit on the farm, but after his Sunday visit with Father Matteo, Alberto went to see Signora Silvestri regularly during his stay. Sometimes he would stop in after lunch or sometimes he would visit her during the *passeggiata*, when everyone was out in town. Signora Silvestri still refused to leave her home and no one had seen her since the day of the funeral. Teresina told Luigia that the Signora wasn't eating and had lost even more weight. When Luigia asked Alberto about this, he became defensive and snapped back at her saying that she shouldn't listen to gossip. One morning, Alberto announced that Signora Silvestri had asked him around for dinner.

"Whatever for?" Beatrice inquired.

"She is feeling better. We have been reading scripture together and I have helped her to find words of comfort. She is just thankful, I would guess," replied Alberto.

"Is she really better?" Beatrice asked. "Teresina says that she still doesn't look well and that she is always locked away in a dark room except for when you visit."

"You shouldn't listen to gossip," Alberto snapped, "She is better spiritually, the physical healing will come with time."

Later that evening, Luigia accompanied Alberto into town; Alberto on his way to the Silvestri house for dinner and Luigia to the *merceria* to buy some ribbons for a dress she was making. Alberto seemed more silent than usual and he kept his gaze fixed on his feet and on the gravel path as they walked.

"What is the house like, inside?" asked Luigia.

"What? What do you mean? What house?" replied Alberto.

"The Silvestri house. I always wondered...I mean, when I make my deliveries I like to imagine what the inside beyond the kitchen is like.

It seems so grand from the outside," Luigia said.

Alberto laughed, "Yes, it is grand but also a bit somber. It reminds me of Signor Silvestri: old, established and staid."

"Really?" Luigia said.

"Yes, the house is not at all like the Signora. She is lighter in spirit than her husband was and quite sensitive. But her house is yes… heavy and a bit oppressive, I guess you would say," Alberto replied.

Alberto's description made Luigia even more curious. She had no idea what a heavy, oppressive house would look like. Arriving at the *piazza*, Luigia and Alberto parted paths. Luigia turned back once to watch Alberto and it seemed as if he had picked up his pace as he neared the pathway that led towards the Silvestri house.

It was a Friday morning and Luigia was due to make her deliveries to the Silvestri house. She went to collect the eggs and vegetables and placed everything carefully in her basket. When she went into the kitchen, Beatrice was standing over the stove cutting carrots and dropping them into a pot of stew.

"I'm off to the Silvestri house," Luigia announced. "Where is Alberto?"

"He had to leave early. He went to see Father Matteo. He said he wouldn't be home for lunch and would see us in town at the *passeggiata*," Beatrice replied.

The weather had turned cooler and the bright days of summer were beginning to fad. *Autumn would soon be here*, thought Luigia, *and Alberto would be leaving.* She pulled her shawl around her shoulders for warmth and kept walking. When she arrived at the Silvestri house it looked to her as it had for the past months. All the shutters were closed and the house itself seemed dead. Luigia went around the back into the kitchen and called for Teresina. No one answered. She stepped inside and saw that the stove had been lit and that someone had been deboning a chicken. "Teresina?" she called out louder this time but there was still no answer. She walked over and placed her basket on the table. Off to the right was a small workroom where Teresina did the sewing and mending. Luigia poked her head in and called out, "Teresina?" She noticed that some fabric and scissors had been left on a table, but she saw that the peg where Teresina's coat usually hung was empty. *She must have rushed out for something,* Luigia thought.

Luigia walked back out into the kitchen and fixed her eyes on the door at the far end that led into the main house. She thought of Alberto's words describing the house and how desperately she'd like to see what it looked like. Was it like Alberto described or how she had imagined? With Teresina gone and Signora Silvestri surely locked away upstairs in her bedroom, Luigia thought she had a chance to peek. Luigia checked the kitchen and the workroom again and then quietly began to open the connecting door. As the door opened a pattern of green, red and black marble began to emerge from the other side. Luigia slipped through the door and found herself in the entry hall. The pattern of the marble floor repeated itself over and over and over, seemingly endlessly. In the middle of the room a confection of crystal balls and triangles hung down from the ceiling. Luigia stood under the chandelier and twirled around slowly. As she gazed upward, thin shimmering rays of sunlight streamed through the tightly closed slates of the shutters, playing off the crystals.

In front of her were the massive entry doors of the house—two dark panels with intricate carvings of a coat of arms and two sets of initials intertwined above them. Across from the doors was a staircase made from the same dark wood. Luigia tiptoed over and ran her fingers over the carved figures of birds and foliage that lined the railing. Luigia thought it was the grandest room she had ever seen, grander than St. Ambrose. She wasn't sure what Alberto meant about it being somber or oppressive. On either side of the entry hall were two sets of doors, both carved in the same fashion as the staircase, with flowers so lifelike you could almost smell their perfume. Luigia looked back at the door to the kitchen and bit her lip. She was so curious and wanted so much to see what was behind those doors. Surely no one was here on the ground floor. Teresina was out and Signora Silvestri was certainly upstairs and, given recent events, wasn't likely to budge. Luigia quietly walked over to one set of the doors and ran her hands over the beautifully carved contours of the sashes. Just as her fingers were out-lining the door, she heard a slight sobbing sound coming from behind it. Luigia thought it sounded like a whimpering cat. She stopped for a moment and listened again, pressing her ear closer to the door. Luigia heard a rustle, like paper bunching together and then a methodical whimper and a slight groan. *Whatever was in there was in pain*, Luigia thought, and she really wanted to look. She glanced back into the entry hall to ensure that it was still vacant and thought to herself, *I'll only peek just for a moment*. She wrapped her hand around the smooth brass handle and, finding it unlocked, gently began to push the door open. She laid her head against the door so she could quickly look inside when suddenly the pressure of her shoulder against it caused the door to open widely.

Luigia stood wide mouthed as her eyes fixed on Signora Silvestri lying against the damask daybed, her bustier unhooked and her brown crinoline skirt crushed up around her waist. Alberto was knelling in front of Signora Silvestri, his naked back towards Luigia; head plunged into Signora Silvestri's bustier. Luigia felt herself grow lightheaded as she tried to steady herself against the door frame. Then three sets of eyes suddenly all converged and after an interminably long silence it seemed as if Luigia, Signora Silvestri and Alberto all screamed at once.

Alberto grabbed his cassock to try and cover himself. Luigia felt as if she would vomit. She ran out of the room and through the entry hall searching for the door that led to the kitchen. Half-dressed, Alberto followed her though the entry.

"Luigia, I will explain," Luigia heard her brother repeat over and over like a mantra. Luigia flung open the connecting door to the kitchen and spied Teresina hanging up her coat in the small workroom.

"Whatever are you doing here?" a shocked Teresina asked. Luigia just ran past her and when Teresina turned, she gasped at the sight of Alberto.

Luigia ran all the way home, her crippled leg aching as she pulled it with her hand from behind her knee—willing it to move faster. Once home, she bolted up the stairs and flung herself onto her bed. Beatrice heard her pass through the house, her eye catching the hem of Luigia's dress as it skirted up the stairs. Erica, aware that Luigia's footsteps had been too hurried and brusque to be normal, dropped what she was mending and followed her up to their room.

"Whatever is the matter?" Erica asked. Luigia hugged her and sobbed. "Leave me. Just leave me," she said. Erica wrapped her arms about Luigia.

"Tell Mamma nothing, just that I'm tired." Luigia begged as she rubbed her leg.

Erica nodded silently as Luigia buried her face into her pillow. Images of Alberto, the marble floor of the Silvestri house, Signora Silvestri, the chandelier all melded into one endless distorted dream running through Luigia's head as she slept. Every now and again she would wake and be sure that what she saw she had only dreamt, but then she felt the ache of her leg and remembered running home from the nightmare.

That night at dinner, Luigia stayed in her room while Alberto sat glassy eyed and unresponsive at the table, facing his mother and sisters. Lucia and Erica glanced back and forth at one another, not speaking a word throughout the entire meal. Beatrice knew that something bad had happened; Luigia refused to come down from her room and Alberto had returned before the *passeggiata*, disheveled looking and with eyes like a madman, refusing to join them for the evening walk in town. Now sitting silently at the table fingering her napkin, she tried to read her son's mind through his face. Whatever had happened, it was sure to bring an evil spirit.

It wasn't long before Beatrice learned the truth about Alberto and Signora Silvestri. And when she did, Beatrice threw five dishes, two large platters and one of her best bowls—aiming them directly at her son and not at the wall.

"Is this what God's work is about?" she asked him

"Is this how you helped Signora Silvestri with her grief?"

"Is this how you helped her heal physically?" she yelled, "You are as bad as your father... worse .... a priest, no less. Our reputation will be ruined."

Alberto did not even try to protest as he sat in silence, his mother's recriminations becoming his penance.

With gossip being the town's national pastime, it didn't take long for the news to spread. When Luigia walked into town now people looked away or lowered their eyes. The evil spirit that had descended on baby Carlo and Luigia had now spread to the whole family. Beatrice and the girls began losing more and more of their clients and fewer and fewer of the townspeople were willing to trade with them. Even Father Matteo had turned cool towards them. No one was ever going to marry any of Beatrice's daughters now; they'd all been tainted by Alberto's transgression. Luigia would fall asleep all nights counting and recounting sums in her head, trying to figure out just how they would make it through another month, while Erica would sob quietly in the bed next to her. Even Lucia had taken to lamenting that she should have married Renato.

Shortly after that day, Signora Silvestri left town and stayed away for three months. Alberto went back to Bergamo, presented his excuses to the church and officially had his life as a priest put to an end. Signora Silvestri came back to town only once to pack up her house and belongings; then she and Alberto met in Genoa where they boarded a boat and immigrated to Argentina. For a while after they left, it had seemed to Luigia that people were beginning to forget what had happened. *Out of mind, out of sight,* she thought. But that was wishful thinking; as more and more news began to arrive, Luigia noticed that the few faces that had just begun to acknowledge her again, soon turned away again. There seemed no way to stop the news from infiltrating into their small town, even from as far away as South America. The child that Signora Silvestri and Alberto had so desperately wanted born in secrecy soon came to light.

Alberto wrote his mother and sisters, begging them to join him to Argentina. He sent them letters with money every month, urging them to immigrate and make a new beginning with him in a new place. "No one here cares about who you are or what you have done. It's a new beginning, I swear," he would write. And, every month Beatrice would pocket the money, crumple the letters and toss them into the kitchen fire. *The evil spirit will visit your baby*, thought Beatrice.

"You wait and see, Alberto," she said quietly to no one as she watched the fire singe the edges of Alberto's script, "you wait and see."

Hillbilly Bikini Bottom

by Stephen Siciliano

*"Hillbilly Bikini Bottom" is a product of the author's two years as
an Italian-American New Yorker studying agriculture at
Arkansas State University back in the late 1970s.*

*His time in the American South was a culture shock, but much
was learned, some of which has been distilled into this short work
melding the topics of race, sex, and high school football
into something both serious and humorous.*

Jefferson Davis was in a fix.

It was towards the end of the fourth quarter already and the
natives were getting restless. Bugs swarmed in the high and bright
lights and the players' pads were soaked in Indian summer sweat.
Jeff saw Brenda Lee Underwood over by the south end bleachers, just
above where they liked to drink beers and nip at each other most nights
when football wasn't on.

The Little Honey was there with that prick who owned the
Camaro from up north of county line and didn't she just love anything
with pants on?

"Should've listened to Danny Joe Dean, the Highsteppers' bass player," he told himself, "when we was up at the Collection House and he said she wasn't worth the cheap dress she was burstin' out of."

Darnell Hampton was loping back to the huddle. He saw his mother standing in the north end, hands clenched in prayer, old before her time. There were others from the family and neighborhood standing frozen around her. Aunts and uncles come to see Darnell the Wonder Boy. He didn't need to look to know they'd all be praying, too. Or passed out already from delirium at the Jaguars' pending defeat.

The football religion was strong on both sides of the tracks and both sides of the tracks were simmering in disappointment.

This was no homecoming crosstown rivalry. It was a little 'ol Catholic school you couldn't even find in the Arkansas State high school football rankings. And here were the Jaguars sputtering toward the final gun, ready to blow a shot at the perfect season for 1979 in the first warm-up game.

Whitman High took a last time out. Coach called Jeff Davis to the sideline so he could draw up a play. As Jeff jogged in, he scanned the bleachers and saw Danny Joe Dean giving him the finger. Damn, he loved that 'ol boy!

Coach whipped up Xs and Os that had a shotgun, a pulling guard, and a wildcat something or other. He sent his quarterback out to hunt with those words, but Jefferson Davis hadn't heard any of it. He just nodded and jogged to the huddle.

His left guard, Ralph Mazzanti, looked like something come out of the meat grinder and Henderson, the right side tackle, was useless out of habit.

Jeff Davis looked at Darnell. "You hear that farm boy call you a nigger?"

Darnell looked out at the north bleachers and his praying people again. They kept all the stories, the terrible dark stories he had heard. Held them close and whispered to themselves.

Uncle LeRoy was gone, because somebody had to get the chicken and ribs for after the game. That's when they would all rush back to the other side of the railroad tracks to eat and sing and be apart from everything else happening in town.

Darnell was always invited across the track on football Friday nights, but before the clock clanged twelve he was back in the low shacks, a speedy Brougham turned brown pumpkin again.

"Ain't nobody called me a nigger all night 'cause they know I will kick a lot of serious ass if that was the case."

"Like Hayl," Jeff spit. "Number 77 called you a fast country nigger."

Darnell looked into the Maria Regina huddle for a Number 77. "He's black, you fool."

"So he's cool?" Jeff asked. "He can say it?"

"Mostly," Darnell practically whispered.

"It's true anyway," Mazzanti said. "The bit about bein' a fast country nigger."

"D'jou just call me a country nigger, Ralph?"

"Um, not direct-like. Not like, 'You, Darnell Hampton, are one very fast country nigger as per my words, Ralph Mazzanti.' No. I was paraphrasing."

Jeff knew Ralph picked up "paraphrasing" in Miss Keating's English class, because she wore patch pocket bellbottoms and they kept him focused.

Henderson knew none of those boys cared if one was green and the other blue so long as they could get a miracle touchdown, and avoid facing up to family and friends with so great a debacle. There were girlfriends on the line, scholarships...girlfriends!

So he put it out there: "Hayl, Darnell, Jeff's just a little hot-and-bothered about Brenda Lee Underwood and her being with that ol' boy from Paragould."

"Henderson, you are a useless piece of crap," Jeff Davis shot back.

"Maybe, but it don't change the veracity of what I said none."

Jeff knew Henderson picked up that word from Doc Hotstetler's dairy cattle judging class, where he talked about the "veracity of a heifer's udder."

He looked over at the south bleachers again and saw Brenda Lee kiss her new beaux.

Jeff would like to get a gun and kill her straightaway after the game. He thought he'd do it. Get a pistol, shoot all her friends, too. End her world, the little bitch.

And he was drifted back to that night in July down by the river when Tiffany James come up and told Jeff all about how sweet Brenda Lee was on him, and how she was over by the swimming hole swinging around on the rope hanging down from a tree. "You know the place," she tilted her head at him and pulled on a Busch beer. He almost didn't want to leave.

Jeff Davis went up river and he saw Brenda Lee hanging down from the rope, swinging, her cut-off blue jeans getting pulled up her butt like a hillbilly bikini and this about drove him wild. He watched her swoop out over the water and let loose, landing in the black oily splash. He licked his lips as she hit the surface.

Then, like a kinda swamp rat, this guy's head popped up laughing. Brenda Lee squealed and made like she was trying to get out of his arms and that's when she saw him, Jeff, standing there.

"Why, Jefferson Davis!" and Brenda Lee looked at him with a kind of challenge in her face, before she turned and kissed that 'ol boy that was in the river with her.

The ref came over. "Break it up," and blew the whistle, waving his right arm around like a whirlybird.

This was the moment. Jeff Davis had never given his troops the play, because he'd never heard it, and because of Tiffany James and Brenda Lee and that night down by the river. Same kinda night. Summer night. Bugs and gnats in the air, in your lungs.

He looked over at the bleachers. Again. Brenda Lee pulled herself out of a kiss with the Camaro Kid and stared straight at him. Her face had the same challenge in it as that July night by the river. Her little piglet-button nose pointing skyward.

And he was sparked. Hard. Not by the challenge of a Camaro, or a perfect season, but by the memory of that hillbilly bikini bottom.

Jefferson Davis turned to Darnell Hampton and looked at him across generations of blackness and whiteness and railroad track and said..." Go deep. I'll hit ya."

Peckerwoods
and Altar Boys

by Mark Spano

Peckerwoods and Altar Boys by Mark Spano
is part of a larger work entitled Kidding the Moon.
It is a memory story of a boy's Catholic upbringing in the inner city.

...the mouth, as "upper womb," is the birthplace of the breath
and the word, the Logos.
—Erich Neumann from The Great Mother

Italian Catholicism, I am happy to say, retains the most florid
pictorialism, the bequest of a pagan past that was never lost.
—Camille Paglia from Sexual Personae

I did not understand until I was grown that my childhood was
spent in a world in decline. I say "world" because the world outside me,
the world of my youth, was no larger than our downtown Kansas City,
Missouri neighborhood of the late 1950s and early 1960s. Though this
place was not so distant in history from Lewis and Clark, Daniel Boone,
and cowboys and Indians, it was all too distant in the mind's geography
from the southern European village life of our grandparents. We lived

in an Italian neighborhood that oddly had few Italians remaining. Most had moved from inner-city apartments like the one in which my family lived to brand new houses in suburbs north of the Missouri River. These shiny suburban developments were erected on what had been farmland for a hundred years prior and virgin prairie before that.

Our neighborhood was located about ten blocks south of the Missouri River. To the east, in what was called "The East Bottoms," were grain elevators, agricultural chemical plants, and railroad yards. To the west, just beyond "downtown" were the stockyards and packing houses in what were, imaginatively enough, called "The West Bottoms." On a summer night, given the direction of the prevailing wind, there were always smells. From the west, one night, we could be ingesting the dusty sick stench of cattle and pig manure coming from the stockyards. A night later, the packing houses might be emitting the sweet rank simmering of meat by-products in the process of becoming bologna or canned chili. From the east, there were insecticides, fertilizers, and a pollen-like fog that came off the grain pouring from elevator to train car.

These local industries required trucks and trains to do business. At every hour of the day and night, eighteen-wheelers rolled up and down Chestnut. (We called our street "Chestnut," not "Chestnut Street." This is how Kansas Citians talk.) The charcoal-colored dust of diesel exhaust covered everything, indoors and out. My mother could never stay ahead of the dusting in our apartment. Outside, you could almost always write your name on the cars. There was constant noise. No place was quiet. In the deep of the night, railroad cars were assembled into long freight trains. Only blocks from my bed, freight cars crashed into one another in a nightly thunder that I nearly grew to require in order to fall asleep.

The five of us, my parents, my sister, my brother, and I lived in a four-room apartment in about the same living space as double garage. We were on the first floor of a four-unit, turn of the century building. When the wind blew or when the trucks rumbled past, the windows shook in their dry rotted frames. We were located directly over the boiler for both hot water and radiator heat. We had no air conditioning. Winter and summer, our apartment was hot.

Orientation within Kansas City was based on the parish. It is how Catholics divided the city. The parish existed as a geographical unit just higher on the scale than the neighborhood. I learned later that Kansas City's old-time political boss, Tom Pendergast brought in the vote in our town parish by parish rather than by ward. My family lived in St. Ignatius Parish. We were part of a ragtag mix of city dwellers who gathered on Sundays and holidays in a seventy year old Catholic church. The interior of St. Ignatius church suffered under the most sentimentally ornate decor, while the building itself barely survived in a state of post blitzkrieg dilapidation. Each group that had passed through our neighborhood on that great journey to prosperity left some lasting and tasteless mark of new-gotten gains on the sad old church.

Nostalgic departing parishioners seemed always to endow St. Ignatius with gifts of dying Jesuses bloodied beyond the observability of the faint-hearted or infant Jesuses or Blessed Mothers draped, beaded and brocaded like Las Vegas showgirls. Never did these warmhearted departing St. Ignatiusians offer a cash gift to repair boarded-over stained glass, giant doors dropping off hinges, falling plaste, or decades of accumulated pigeon droppings mounting into new spires on the church's exterior. The St. Ignatius church building was a mess that might best be described as Western Missouri 1880's Irish Italian Gothic Baroque Rococo.

When I was in first grade, my sister was chosen to crown the blessed mother. To be chosen for this yearly May time ritual was considered, parish-wide, a very great honor. Because of my sister's unblemished virtue, a conclave of priests and nuns handpicked her for this privilege. Later, the conclave allowed a ballot of seventh graders to validate their decision. (This more creative approach to democracy functioned much like the political process within our county.) At age six, I took my sister's honor to be a great triumph for our entire family due to some overflow process of familial holiness. Father Corliss our pastor preached frequently on such issues. My theory on holiness overflow was less likely than the conclave's mistaken perception that my sister's incredible shyness sprang from some deep-seated and de-murring sense of virtue. But, holiness overflow seemed to have some merit because a few days later, I was also chosen to carry the holy virgin's flowered crown on a silk pillow.

After numerous rehearsals for both procession and choir perfor-mance, the big event was held on a glorious May Sunday. St. Ignatius was inundated with flowers, incense, desperately sentimental music and a hundred or so sniffling parents and grandparents. Later that after-noon, as I basked in the afterglow of my celebrity, I advised my brother that this event symbolized a recognition throughout the neighborhood that our family had achieved some manner of community leadership. My brother, the middle child and not chosen to participate in the May Crowning, differed heartily with my observation on the natural superi-ority of our family and ended his rebuttal to my proclamation by naming my sister and me, "a couple of suck-ups."

Many of the old people at St. Ignatius were Irish. The Irish were the original holders of the neighborhood. But, unlike the Italians who moved north of the River out of the old neighborhood, the Irish who had "made it" moved south in the city. They followed the Jesuits who had founded St. Ignatius but had left St. Iggy's for the greener pastures of a prospering south Kansas City upper-middle class. Having been edu-cated by some of those very Jesuits, I later grew to realize that the Jesuits knew a deal when they saw one, and St. Iggy's was no deal.

A few Italian families, like my own, remained in the neighbor-hood, somehow stalled in the anxiously awaited ascent into the middle class. The remainder of the neighborhood was grudgingly shared by Mexicans, blacks, and "peckerwoods." Peckerwoods were people from the country. They mostly drove trucks even when their jobs did not require the ownership of a truck. They also listened to "hillbilly" mu-sic. This fact alone served as irrefutable evidence that peckerwoods lacked aspirations to a better kind of life. Few peckerwoods had ever lived in the city before their arrival at the tired old brick and stone apartments lining the west side of Chestnut. Fewer still had ever re-sided in structures that touched adjoining residences at the top, bot-tom, or opposing sides.

On a Friday summer evening, as most of our neighbors watched from their porches, two tattooed country boys whaled the tar out of each other over not much more than having drunk too much of their paychecks. As their wives drug them inside, ending the evening's en-tertainment, I overheard old Mr. Fero say, "You know, you just can't stack peckerwoods."

But, their unstackability or truck-driving or "hillbilly" music or their ignorance in the ways of tenement living paled to the true offense of merely being a peckerwood. Peckerwoods were not Catholic, there-fore, cultureless in the eyes of the arbiters of such things in my neigh-borhood. Clearly, there was a hierarchy at work here. Italians were the best because we were Italian. There was little or no argument on this point. The Irish could be tolerated, for after all, they were Catholic as we were, and they aspired to some semblance of respectability. In fact, the Irish aspired to a good deal more respectability than the Italians in my neighborhood, but this was observed by my mother and her gaggle of canasta playing neighbor ladies as social pretense.

The Mexicans were Catholics, but their respectability quotient was quite low by neighborhood standards. Their looks and possessions never glistened with the glamour that was requisite to Italians. This branded Mexican Americans with comments like, "They're God-fear-ing people," meaning, "They may believe like us, but they sure aren't blessed like us."

Blacks were respected. The boys respected black boys because of their toughness. Every one of us knew that T.C. could throw further and fight harder. T.C. was clever with building things like go-carts and skateboards. He had physical prowess and strength. This was serious capital with neighborhood boys.

The girls and women had little contact with blacks because blacks did not live in our apartments. T.C. and his family lived two blocks away in what we considered slums. (Our own homes were very likely considered slums by those one rung up the economic ladder from us.) My mother had few dealings with blacks; yet, she was always heartened by their avid church attendance. My mother's occasional bursts of warmth were based on little firsthand knowledge. Understand that blacks were hated in my neighborhood simply because they were not white; yet, they managed to eke out a certain degree of respect under the existing rules of engagement. This was in sharp contrast to peckerwoods that were hated and garnered no formidable respect in our humble little community.

Contrary to the heroic efforts of Sister Mary St. Jude, the four foot ten-inch mother superior and school principal of the St. Ignatius parish school, esteem was measured only in tangibles, an occasional lapse into the sentimental on the parts of my mother, notwithstanding. Boys were measured by their toughness and brawn, girls on their looks, and marriageability. Wealth was measured by cars and clothes, not by good jobs or the size of one's savings account.

Parents may have paid some lip service to the tenets of right living, but as children, we understood that in their hearts, grown-ups really knew what counted. In our dull world of school, church, and hanging out, and in our parents' even duller world of mindless physical labor, lousy living conditions, and the unending joys of child-rearing, what counted was glamour. Glamour was the cause, the cure, the ultimate escape from the heavy boredom of our lives in a place that offered little else but cheap rent.

None of us knew enough of the world beyond our neighborhood to want to be lawyers or doctors or President of the United States. Few of us had met any lawyers or doctors. The ones we might have known didn't live where we lived, and the president existed only on television, no more real than Ward Cleaver. The grown-ups we knew worked in factories, tended bar, or drove trucks. Work was boring. Everyone knew that. We wanted to be doo-wop singers or prizefighters. We wanted cars with leather seat covers and gold watches. We wanted what the men called one another on the street as if it were a name. We wanted "Easy Money."

There were, of course, those who didn't work. Most of them gambled. Gambling as a career choice was not considered by my neighbors as a "true" involvement in crime and was, therefore, tolerated. Other rackets, such as prostitution and drugs, might not have been.

Buying stolen merchandise was a crime. My father would have killed us if we had done such a thing. But, other of our neighbors possessed little of my father's iron on matters of honesty, and a bargain, after all, was a bargain. Few of us probed deeply as from where such bargains came.

When I was in the fourth grade, Sister Mary Theresa was replaced as principal and mother superior of the St. Ignatius by the imposing though Napoleonically short Sister Mary St. Jude. Unlike Sister Mary Theresa who was a gentle and forgiving sort, Sister Mary St. Jude was a fierce enforcer of rules and a serious challenger to the values of both students and parents of the tiny parish school. This change was less a shock to the students of St. Ignatius than it was to our parents who, from Sister Mary St. Jude's point of view, exhibited a laxness in attitude that was certain to be the ruin of the oncoming generation.

Sister Mary St. Jude was, in fact, a very practical woman. I am certain that she'd have preferred easier duty. She must have wished to be mother superior in a wealthier, less hard-luck sort of parish. This, of course, was in the years before inner-city work had become fashionable with the liberal upper-middle class. Sister Mary St. Jude was no fool. St. Iggy's was a tough assignment. So, the new principal and mother superior could not hope for the joys of preparing her grammar school classes for private high school that might lead to Catholic college and professions or possibly even vocations.

Sister Mary St. Jude would not content herself with the luxuries of May Crownings and interscholastic sports. These two indulgences of time, effort, and money were the goodwill projects of Sister Mary Theresa, her predecessor. Sister Mary Theresa was taken into the hearts of the parishioners for her goodwill projects. Sister Mary St. Jude was not.

Sister Mary St. Jude did not believe there was time for the frivolity of such goodwill. Her job was to keep her students in school, and, God willing, impart to them a level of skills that might enable them to survive high school any amount of time beyond age sixteen, (the age one was allowed to quit school legally in Missouri). Her job was to keep the boys out of trouble with the police and the girls out of maternity clothes. Sister Mary St. Jude, I'm sure, wanted students with charm and intellectual curiosity, but she had few. So, she responded with a vigor that comes only from a strong sense of duty and an ability to view our world as none of us could.

Like all Catholic boys, we lived double lives divided between the sacred and the profane. The sphere of street kid seldom, if ever, overlapped into the mystical sphere of church. Such boys prayed profound and deeply heartfelt prayers, then, within that very hour, broke windows for fun. Such boys cursed and ranked one another, then donned cassock and surplice for Benediction. Such boys begged, cajoled, and lied to neighbor girls to engage in any amount of kissing and private touching, then marched from the choir loft to the communion rail singing, "Oh, Lord, I am not worthy."

Fortunately, few of us experienced any uneasiness with these behavioral inconsistencies. This was not simple good fortune; it was, in fact, a very great blessing. Boys who eventually grew to reflect upon this manner of moral ambiguity seldom found themselves comfortable or at home in a world that offered no reward for philosophical musings.

I never wanted to be an altar boy, but my resistance was broken by the extortion like persuasion of Sister Mary St. Jude. In fifth grade, my regular partner in vestments was a fellow named Philip Reppa. Philip was a good-natured big kid who looked at his altar boy's duties as less drudgery and more fun than I did. Philip considered the handling of candles and incense as a legally sanctioned opportunity to play with fire and explosives. He also pointed out that altar bread had the same edible consistency as fish food. We both agreed that altar wine was too sweet and that his grandfather made better.

I enjoyed Philip's good-humored approach to serving mass. Philip, though, was not always given to the self-discipline requisite for membership in the devout order of the Knights of the Altar. One winter Sunday, back when all the Sunday masses were high masses, Cecilia Cherubino was home sick with the flu and was unable to sing the six o'clock high mass that Philip and I were to serve. Rita O'Connor, the skinnier of the two ancient O'Connor sisters, was Cecilia's regular accompanist. In the young singer's absence, the frail, wrinkled Miss O'Connor volunteered her talents not only as organist but also as vocal soloist for that morning's holy sacrifice.

It was said that Miss O'Connor once aspired to the operatic stage and had even been awarded great honors for her virtuosity as a coloratura. That must have been many years prior to this early morning mass. Philip Reppa and I knelt at the foot of the altar dutifully reciting our Latin responses to the hoarse mumblings of Father Lagnusu, our assistant pastor who was visibly every bit as sleepy as we were so early on a Sunday.

When Miss O'Connor began her rendition of the Kyrie, the prayer that begs the Lord's mercy, it was more than abundantly clear to Philip and myself that only the Lord's mercy would get us through this octogenarian's screeching, cackling, and wholly unmusical version of this ancient Christian chant.

Try as I might, I could not ignore Miss O'Connor's animal-like liturgical squeals. Even harder to ignore was Philip kneeling with his head lowered toward mine, sputtering with laughter, through his "Mea culpas." Actually, at the first moments of laughter we were somewhat in luck. Our grinning faces were bowed toward the floor, but there was the Gloria and Credo to go, and for those, we had to be seated on either side of Father Lagnusu. We were dead men.

After the prayers at the foot of the altar, Father Lagnusu ascended into the sanctuary. Miss O'Connor was finishing off the Kyrie. As Father turned to the congregation to sing the opening bars of the Gloria, he had a look on his face that suggested great distress. He pulled his handkerchief from his sleeve, wiped his brow profusely. Father Lagnusu was a wan dreamy-eyed, fidgety man who could get rapturously caught up in his preaching on the goodness of the blessed mother and how the daily recitation of the rosary was the key to the gates of heaven. But, this morning, he was distraught.

It was clear that the goodly and nervous little priest did not find Miss O'Connor's performance nearly so amusing as Philip and I had. Now, facing the congregation, Father Lagnusu pointedly recited the first words of the Gloria. He did not sing. "Gloria in excelsis Deo." He spoke the prayer staring directly at Philip and me. Philip and I responded, "Et in terra pax dominibus..." and that was that. There would be no more singing the rest of the morning. That time, Philip and I were spared the wrath of the clergy, but this was not the case at the funeral of old Mr. LaFiamma.

Mid-week funerals were the best because we were taken from class to go to church and serve the funeral mass. We also got to ride in the black limo to the cemetery. From time to time, we were given breakfast, and most times, we were even paid for our services by the family or the funeral director. This was a serious bonus program.

Mr. and Mrs. LaFiamma had a house around the corner from us. They had a bigger yard than anyone else in the neighborhood. Their yard was full of gardens, grape arbors, and fruit trees, which, when ripe with fruit, were also ripe for raids by neighbor boys filching figs, peaches, cherries, apples, tomatoes, whatever we could eat.

After nearly ninety years of life, Mr. LaFiamma died from simply having lived too long or from having chased too many neighborhood children from his abundant backyard.

Philip Reppa and I were pulled from class to serve the funeral mass. Father Corliss gave his same "Angel of Death has winged his way into our community" sermon, and Philip and I rode in the limousine with Father out to the cemetery. After the graveside service, Mrs. La-Fiamma, an otherwise quiet little gray-haired neighbor lady, began to scream and wail like a wild woman. "Beddu, Beddu miu," she howled. Throwing herself onto her husband's casket, she lost balance and fell into the metal bars of the device that lowers the casket into the grave. In a breath, the tiny old woman slipped out of sight between those bars of the framework holding up her husband's casket and into the hole meant for the departed Mr. LaFiamma's remains.

As family and funeral directors scrambled to fetch the grieving widow from the ditch, Philip started to laugh, thereby causing me to laugh. Father Corliss noticed immediately, and before either Philip or I knew what hit us, Father had us both by the shoulders, offering us the sternest expression either of us had ever seen in our heretofore short lives.

The priest said very little to us the rest of the morning and through the excruciatingly long ride back from the cemetery. Father, of course, reported our breach of decorum to Sister Mary St. Jude, who kept us after school that afternoon. Sister gave us both a long speech about our insensitivity and disrespect. "I understand," Sister said in what we hoped was the conclusion of her long moral diatribe, "that the LaFiamma family gave you boys a thank you gift for serving the funeral mass. If I were either of you, I would feel too much shame to spend that money on any sort of personal treat. Actually, it might be a very good idea for you both to contribute your money to the mission collection as penance for your poor behavior today."

Though my face and Philip's too showed great remorse, these were emotions related less to our offense than to having been caught. I knew deep in my heart and guessed that deep in Philip's, that unless Sister Mary St. Jude actually forced us to fork over our cash, the African missions would not get so much as a nickel of it.

No Fix, No Pay.

by John Suriano

Want to have a difficult problem fixed, and only pay when it's completed?
Sounds reasonable enough. Except, sometimes the solution provided can
exceed the solution needed, with a dire and supernatural outcome.

By the time I thought about it a hundred times, I still couldn't figure out what made me buy the paper. More specifically that paper. The
New York Times, May 3, 1948. For you see, I bought the Daily News my
entire life until that day.

It was only after I bought the paper that I saw that front page
photo of the young boy greeting General Dwight David Eisenhower to
his new home in Morningside Heights, on the day he retired from the
US Army. The humor of the photo took some time to emerge. It was
when I saw just what the neighborhood boy was greeting him with in
his arms. He was holding a plastic machine gun toy. Ironic that our
great general was welcomed to the neighborhood into his home by a
piece of plastic weaponry. But I digress. I have no idea why I bought
the Times that day.

When I sat down to have a coffee at Pete's Diner I saw that tiny
ad. The kind they always had back then, on the very bottom of the

front page of the Times. It was below the bigger ad for the sale of Churchill's War Memoirs. (I guess he got to writing them as soon as it was over). It's still fixed clearly in my mind, all in capitals: WILL FIX PROBLEMS. NO FIX, NO PAY. DONT BE SHY, HAVE A TRY. CALL PEnn 5-3061.

At that point, I had been looking for a lost package for the past week. I went everywhere—the freight forwarder, the post office, my landlord, my neighbors, on and on—that package was gone; vanished. As it contained the only remaining objects of my dear departed Uncle Ray, shipped from Ohio, I was not about to give up easy. So I came home, waited for the elevated train to rumble by, and called.

On the lull between the second and third ring, she picked up. As I came to know later, she was called Janice. She said hello in a gentle but confident voice. I inquired whether this was the service and could she transfer my call. I could hear her teeth clack as she made it clear, a touch firmly, that there was no one to transfer the call to. She was the service. Embarrassed, I explained what I was looking for. She agreed to meet with me and pick up my shipping papers the next day, and would then quote a price.

Early the next morning I was waiting for her at Pete's, sipping the usual murky strong coffee, when she walked over, asked my name, and sat down. She was no more than forty, but certainly not less than thirty. Well dressed, wearing a modern cut dress, hat, and a red flower in her lapel. And a thin briefcase. After some perfunctory chat about the lost parcel, and giving her the papers, she promised that she would call me as soon as she found the parcel. Not whether she would find it, which I found odd. And we agreed on an almost comically low finder's fee. She insisted happy first time customers always return.

Two days later, I sat across from her again at Pete's as she slid the parcel across the table. In my surprise, I almost forgot to ask where it was. She explained it wasn't lost, just needed to be unplugged from where it was stuck. She waved away any more questions, took my payment, and with a mock bow made her way out of the cafe.

It was a month later that I came across my old baseball glove, at the back of my closet. Actually it had belonged to my older cousin Bob, until he gave it to me. It got me thinking about him. I hadn't seen him for years. He moved somewhere out west when I was fifteen. And then poof—he disappeared. He sent a letter years letter to say he wasn't dead, but wouldn't be seeing anyone in the family again. Some argument he had with his father, which like many escalated beyond whatever reason it originally had. Except he lumped the extended family into it. And he told us he had another name now, and the letter didn't have an address, so we couldn't get in touch. I think I was the only one in the family he liked, so I took it hard. I often thought of looking him up, but for the impossibility. Then like most people who leave one's life, he faded from my memory.

On a whim, I picked up the phone, then put it down. Any price she would charge would be prohibitive. And for what? To say hello to Bob? Then like some unseen hand moving me, I found myself holding the phone again, and the line ringing. Before I could hang up, Janice's velvet voice came on. And I found myself saying more than I expected to. The quote she gave me was as if she knew exactly just how much I would pay, then she came a smidgen below that. I gave her nothing more than his name, age and "last seen somewhere on the west coast many years ago". She said she'd let me know on Monday. It was now Friday. I hung up and laughed.

At this point I was becoming busy with my new business, importing cheap TV accessories from Hong Kong in bulk—rabbit ear antennas, felt covers for the channel switch, that sort of stuff—then selling it to five and dime shops. I didn't have time to think about Janice and my cousin.

Until Monday. When she rang me up, and asked to meet at Pete's.

There she was in her usual sharp cut dress, hat and red flowered lapel. She explained how unsuccessful dropout Cousin Bob Richards became Jack Egbart, the still unsuccessful dropout. He washed dishes in a restaurant in a small town in Northern Montana, did odd jobs around town, and generally survived through the support of his girlfriend.

Then she handed me a small black and white photo of Bob, now Jack. I laughed at Jack, as that was the name he called all male strangers when we were kids. He had a thick beard, and I could just make out his distinctively arched eyebrows. And Janice handed me a slip with his phone number. She encouraged me to call him from the phone booth, but I declined. Shocked that she found him so quickly, I ignored that, and passed over her payment. She bid me adieu.

I went home, picked up the phone, and dialed the number. The moment his gruff voice came on, I hung up. I wanted to see that he was still alive, and he was. That's all.

This was astonishing. Three days and she plucked him out of the middle of nowhere! With a photo!

This was worth telling my friends, but no. Best not to let the secret of this magical fixer out into the world. Even though she was advertising on the front page of the New York Times.

After a few days of being astonished, I forgot about Janice. Weeks and months went by. My business was picking up. More and more stores were ordering my various goods. I had to get a warehouse, and hired five staff. This was no longer a one man operation. I moved into a bigger apartment, got a nice car.

And then one day business started to flatten out, and then drop. My salesmen would be told by customers our products were too expensive. Or they could find better for the same price. Then my own orders from Hong Kong were delayed. Taking longer to arrive. Or items were not available.

I found out it was a new competitor in the Bronx, Universal Components. Sam Morris. I needed to know how this competitor was getting his product quicker and how he was selling it cheaper. Then I realized Janice would do this.

I called Janice. I knew she'd find out exactly what I need to know. But this time she did something she didn't ask before. She asked me how important this was. I said it was very important. This was my livelihood, and that of five employees. She quoted a price as before, just below the maximum I'd pay, as if she was reading my cards in a poker game.

Two days later she asked that we meet at Pete's. She told me that Universal was closing down next month. I should call back all those clients we had lost. I was shocked as they were going strong and had just hired one of my star salesmen last week. And she said that Universal was getting all their products through a middleman, Simon Cheung, who was paying off factory owners in Hong Kong to sell through him first. I passed across her payment. She did her usual bow, and walked off.

Sure enough, when we started to call back those customers we had lost, they were more open to hearing from us. I drove by the Universal Warehouse one day, and it was shuttered. I made some inquires. It seems Morris had gone missing. Around the time I asked Janice to look into his business. No one knew where he could be. The police were put on the case. It made the papers.

Was this something I put into motion? It seemed mad, so I left that idea alone.

Morris was never found. The police case was closed, his business liquidated, his employees out of work. And my business doubled.

Then one day I was having issues with my girlfriend Diane. More specifically she was no longer wanting to be my girlfriend. I was out at McCann's having a few beers. And maybe a shot or two of whiskey. Drunk, to say it bluntly. I sat at the bar, looking at the payphone. Staring. Fiddling with the coin in my pocket.

I walked over, and dropped in the coin. Dialed the number. I got scared, and began to hang up the receiver. As always, she picked up after the second ring and I heard her voice. I hesitated, then spoke. I explained that Diane had left me. I needed to know why. Was it another man?

Janice then asked, as she did last time. How important was it that Diane come back to me? In my drunk, maudlin state, I said more important than anything. She said she couldn't charge me. She had a policy of only three sales to a customer. I protested that was a crazy policy. What business person would do that? I insisted I'd pay her, she refused and said that was her policy. But she'd do this one for free, me being a loyal customer and all. Then she was moving on.

The next morning I woke up, totally hungover. The phone rang. My friend Chuck, whose wife was Diane's best friend, said Diane was in the hospital. I dragged myself out of the house, and drove over to the hospital. I walked in; family and friends were already there.

Diane was in the bed, comatose, but breathing. They said she was found on the street, in a state of shock, unable to speak or move. Otherwise uninjured, but she soon became unconscious. I hung around for a while, made some small talk, then left. I had a bad feeling. Something I couldn't shake off.

I walked home, went upstairs and looked at myself in the mirror. What had I set in motion?

I called Janice. It was disconnected. She was gone. Upped sticks.

A week later I got a call from Chuck. Diane was out of her coma, and asking for me. I had stayed away, out of a fear I would make her situation worse by just being near her. I went to her bedside. Her hair was going gray on the sides, and she looked older than she did a week before. She grabbed me by the arm and said she'd never leave me. I asked her what happened. She said all she remembered was a woman with a flower in her lapel came to her on the street, whispering in her ear. Telling her only I could save her. Then blackness. Diane looked at me oddly, and I could swear I saw a red rose shining in her eye. We were inseparable from then on.

Years later I was down south. I had expanded into manufacturing, and I was buying a factory in Alabama. When I woke up in the hotel, breakfast was brought in and a copy of the Montgomery Advertiser with it, a local newspaper.

I sat down to have a coffee and opened the paper. I glanced at it briefly, then noticed I was running late. I was about to throw the paper in the garbage pail, then I saw it. Tiny ads on the bottom. I laughed, thinking they stole that idea from the New York Times.

I looked closely, and turned white.

WILL FIX PROBLEMS. NO FIX, NO PAY. DONT BE SHY, HAVE A TRY. CALL PEar 7-4285.

Excuse Me

by Tim Tomlinson

"Excuse Me" involves young Anglo-Italian-American
Clifford Foote in an experience of two kitchens:
his Italian-American mother's where everything comes out of a can or a box,
and the local pizzeria, where preparing food is magic and music and mystery.

Mom didn't like to cook and rarely did. One night, Dad had it.

"I'm hiring a cook," he said. "Three nights a week."

"No," Mom said, "you will not." She removed that night's dinner from the freezer, four boxes of Swanson's Turkey and a bag of Ann Page Krinkle-cut French Fries.

Dad said, "Look, I come home, I want dinner on the table. And not that crap. I want real nutritious food."

Mom said, "This is not a restaurant."

"It will be when I hire a cook."

"You will not bring a cook into this kitchen."

Dad said, "Why not?"

She spread tin foil over a narrow tray and folded the edges neatly around the tray's corners.

"Because I don't want anyone in my kitchen," she explained.

"OK," Dad said, "but excuse me. Why not?"

"Because I don't, that's why."

Dad said, "What do you care? You never use it."

Mom peeled the foil back on part of the TV dinners and slid them onto the oven's wire rack.

"I do not want anyone in my kitchen," she said, "and that's it."

Dad's stomach growled.

"You hear that?" he said.

She said, "I didn't hear anything."

Dad said, "Boys?"

I said, "I heard it."

Wally said, "In Rocky Point they could hear it."

"Look," Mom said, "I'm not having this conversation. There is nobody coming into my kitchen, period."

Dad said, "You're not making any sense."

She said, "It makes perfect sense to me."

"Boys," Dad said, "is your mother making sense?"

Wally said, "Nada." Wally was in fourth grade. He was taking Spanish.

"Stay out of this," Mom said, "the two of you."

I said, "But we don't understand."

"Really?" Mom said, untying the apron at her back. "Do you understand this?"

She threw the apron on the floor, clomped past the dining table and turned toward her room. In another moment the door slammed.

Wally said, "Don't pick that up, Cliff. Let her clean up her own mess like she always tells us."

"All right," Dad said. "Remember, she's your mother."

Wally said, "How could I forget?"

Dad said, "Enough."

He turned off the oven and put the TV dinners back in their boxes. A few minutes later he one-knuckle knocked at the bedroom door.

"I'm taking the boys out for pizza," he said.

She said, "I don't care what you do."

"Do you want to join us?"

Wally frantically waved his arms. "Dad, no," he whispered.

Dad ignored him.

He said, "Well?"

We heard her get up, heard a closet door slide. Wally muttered, "Fuck." He was lucky Dad didn't hear him or he would have been sucking a fresh bar of Lifebuoy past his tonsils.

· · · · · · · · · · · · · · ·

We loved going for pizza. And we loved where it was made. At the Big 'N on Route 25A near Radio Road. The N stood for Nick, and that made sense. Nick made the pizza. The "Big" made sense, too. Nick was almost as big as Dad. He wore a sailor's cap and white t-shirts underneath a sauce-stained apron. He wore a mustache, which Dad didn't like, but he didn't make too much fuss about Nick's. Maybe because Nick served in the World War. If you served in a war, Dad could overlook things like your mustache. He overlooked Nick not shaving, too, and the way he smoked even when he was pounding out the pizza. From Nick's lower lip, a Lucky Strike always hung. The smoke made him squint while he knuckled out dough. But something didn't make sense—the apostrophe before the "N." I asked Dad about it.

Dad said, "You have to ask Nick."

So one time I did. I said, "Hey Nick, how come there's an apostrophe before the N?"

Nick said, "Hay is for horses."

I said, "Yeah. But what about the apostrophe?"

Nick said, "I didn't go to no college, boys. I served in the US Navy and you can put that in your flat hat and smoke it."

Wally said, "You ever hear of an apostrophe."

Nick said, "You ever hear of the USS Boise?"

Wally shook his head.

"See?" Nick said, "You're not as smart as you think."

. . . .

Dad turned into the Big 'N's gravel parking lot. We parked right at the entrance. On weeknights, most families took their pizza home in boxes.

"Go say hello to Nick, we'll be right behind you," he said, and we ran inside.

And there he was, behind the counter.

"Hey," Nick said, squinting over a Lucky, "it's the Marine Corps kids."

"Flip the pizza, Nick," we cried, and the few other diners at tables looked up and smiled.

Nick said, "What do I look like, some clown on Ed Sullivan? I toss, not flip."

Wally said, "Whatever."

Nick picked the dough off the stone countertop. He fingered white flour onto the stone and slapped down the dough, which he pressed out with his fingers, then smacked with flat palms. And then it was aloft, up above his head like a flying carpet, spinning until it landed, softly, onto his fists. And the fists spun it some more until it seemed to take off and rise again off his knuckles and float against gravity on top of smoke from the Lucky Strikes.

Dad said, "Why don't you quit fooling around and throw some sausage on that thing."

"Aye aye, sir," Nick said, winking. "Extra cheese?"

Dad said, "Why not?"

"Anchovies?"

From a table in the corner Mom shouted, "No anchovies!"

Nick looked at us.

"What she got against anchovies?"

Wally said, "What she got against cooking?"

Dad said, "All right, the two of you, sit down, go join your mother. I'll bring you your Cokes."

Mom sat against the wall smoking a Chesterfield, her gaze turned toward 25A. It was still light out. You could see the faces of the people in the cars that drove by. Mostly men going home from work. One sang along with the radio, his arm out the window. Another smoked with both hands on the wheel. They stopped at the traffic light. When they looked into the Big 'N, they seemed embarrassed when I waved. They looked back to the road even though they weren't going anywhere.

Each booth had a tableside jukebox on the wall above the napkin dispenser. Dad dropped coins into ours and pressed some buttons.

"I hope you're not playing those songs again," Mom said.

Then, from the PA system, we heard the booming voice of Jerry Vale: *My love forgive me, I didn't mean to have it end like this...*

When it got to the part Jerry Vale sings in Italian, Nick started singing along. Everyone was laughing. *Amore scusami, se sto piangendo...*

Wally said, "Look, is Nick crying?"

Nick stopped pressing dough and opened his arms wide. *E se mi penserai ricordati...che amo te.* Little teardrops pressed through his closed eyelids.

"I forgot," Dad said, getting misty-eyed himself. "He spent a year after the war on shore patrol in Naples."

"What's that supposed to mean?" Mom said.

Dad said, "You wouldn't understand."

"Well, excuse me for asking," Mom said. "I think I'll go wait in the car."

Dad said, "Sit down, the pizza's coming."

She said, "You know I can't stand these stupid songs."

"They're not stupid," Dad said, "they're Italian."

"Italian my foot," she said.

"But you're Italian," I said, "Mom, right?"

Dad said, "Cliffy."

"But isn't she?"

"Don't call your mother she. She's your mother," Dad said, "And yes, she's Italian."

"I'm American," Mom said. "We're all American."

Nick came with the pizza on a big silver metal tray. He set it in the middle of the table and from his apron he pulled a circular blade for rolling the pizza into slices.

Wally said, "Can I?"

Nick looked at Dad and Dad nodded.

"But careful, you hear me?"

Wally pressed the roller into the pizza but it didn't go smooth.

"Look," I said, "he's ruining the cheese."

Wally said, "I'm gonna ruin you."

"Gimme that goddamn thing," Dad said.

He wrenched the blade from Wally's hand and handed it back to Nick.

"You gotta do it fast," Nick said. "Watch."

First, he pressed the roller into the fat crust. Then he rolled forward in one swipe. "You see what I'm saying," he said. Then he pressed out a second and third. He was about to finish off with the fourth when the ash from his Lucky Strike fell right into the middle of the pizza.

"Jesus H. Christ," Dad said. "Are you kidding me?"

Nick said, "Take it easy, marine, I'll make youse a new one."

• • • • • • • • • • • • • • •

We kneeled on stools and watched Nick make us the next pizza, the white flour on stone, the slab of soft fat dough, slapped once, flipped over, slapped again, his fingers pressing into the middle, pressing out, and the fat dough getting wider and skinnier. He dipped a ladle into a silver cylinder of red sauce and dumped the sauce into the center of the dough. He made circular motions with the ladle and spread the sauce out like ripples from a stone until it reached all the surfaces of the pizza. Then he stuck his hand inside a plastic bag filled with pieces of white cheese. He removed a fistful and sprinkled the white cheese over the red sauce. He fisted sausages on top of the cheese, then more cheese on top of the sausage. He reached for a long handled pizza peel, slid the tray across the stone underneath the pizza, turned and opened the wide oven door, and slid the pie all the way to the back of the oven. He moved a couple of other pizzas already cooking closer to the front.

"Won't those get burnt?" I asked him.

"Not if I'm careful," Nick said.

Wally said, "Why were you crying?"

Nick said, "When was I crying?"

"When Dad played that stupid song."

"*Amore scusami?*" Nick said. "That's not stupid."

Wally said, "OK, but how come?"

Nick shrugged. "You're young," he said. "You don't know how sad love is."

I said, "Does Dad know?"

Nick said, "All too well, my young friend. All too well."

I said, "Are you American?"

Nick smiled wide. One of his teeth was the American flag.

"Cool," I said.

"You're not Italian?" Wally asked.

"I'm Italian-American, and proud of it. So are you."

I said, "We're just American."

Nick said, "Says who?"

Wally pointed to our table. "She said so."

Nick said, "Don't call your mother she. She's your mother."

Wally said, "Yeah, everyone keeps reminding us."

Nick said, "So don't forget it."

He reached the peel into the oven and slid out our new pizza. The cheese bubbled and blistered around the sausage.

"I'll slice this one over here," Nick said.

This time, Nick's cigarette curled smoke from an ashtray near the cash register. "Sherry Baby" played on the jukebox.

Wally said, "Can I try again?"

Nick looked over at our table.

"You gonna do it right?"

Wally said "of course," and he did, all four rolls for eight slices.

Nick set the tray on our table. Then he pulled four Cokes out of the refrigerator.

"On the house," he said.

Dad said, "No."

"Yeah," Nick said, "on account of the you know."

He reached across the table and dropped two quarters in the jukebox.

"H-8," he told Wally. "Press it for your old man. Then you pick one."

Wally pressed the buttons. Inside the jukebox window, records flickered back and forth, then clicked to a stop. A 45 slid out, then spun onto the platter. Mandolins and violins filled the speakers, and Dad was out of his seat, his arm over Nick's shoulders, and together they sang, *Al di là del bene più prezioso, ci sei tu.*

"All right," Mom said, pushing back from the table, "I'm waiting in the car."

"Jackie," Dad said. We all of us watched her push through a screen, then the outer door.

The song kept playing—*Where you walk, flowers bloom, when you smile all the gloom turns to sunshine*—but the room felt strangely silent.

"Jeez," Nick said. "Who does she like?"

Still looking at the door and shaking his head, Dad said, "Eddie Fisher."

Nick said, "The Jew? You're sh—, you're kidding me."

Dad felt behind the jukebox. "This thing unplug?" he asked.

Nick hit the jukebox with the heel of his hand. The record scratched off.

He said, "I'll get you a box for the pie."

. . . .

Later that night, I thought I heard noises in the kitchen. Mom sat at the window blowing smoke through the screen. Her face looked strange in the night light.

"I wake you up?" she asked. "I was trying to be quiet."

The toaster oven pinged. She reached in and pulled out a metal tray. A slice of pizza sizzled on top.

"Watch your ashes," I told her.

She set the plate down hard and shook her fingers. "Damn thing's too hot."

She took out a knife and two forks.

"You want a bite?" she asked.

I asked if there was any Coke.

"Coke's not good this late. It will just keep you awake." Then she said, "All right, but just a small glass, OK?"

I said OK.

We chewed our pizza. Now the crust was crispier. The extra cheese made it chewy and hard to separate with my teeth.

She watched me eat and continued to smoke.

She said, "You understand, don't you?"

I said, "Understand what?"

"What do you mean what?" she said. "Why I don't want anyone else in this kitchen."

That reminded me of where this night had started. I finished my Coke and pushed the glass forward. I waited until she refilled it.

I said, "Yeah, I guess. Kind of."

"I thought so," she said. "You're the smart one."

I belched. I didn't say 'excuse me.'

Brothers In Arms

by Robert Trotta

Two Italian American soldiers form a brotherly bond
in the waning days of the Vietnam War.
As military police officers assigned to the US Embassy in Saigon,
Bobby Collozzo and Tony Frongillo talk of traveling to Italy after their tours
to see the country and visit Tony's grandparents who live in Taormina.

For Bobby it would be a dream come true
to visit the country of his ancestors.
For Tony it would be a return to his Nonna
and the place he spent summers during his youth.

Would the North Vietnamese Army and the Viet Cong
have other plans for these two brave young men?

— For Ann Blanshaft —

CHAPTER ONE

It was another hot and muggy day as Staff Sergeant Robert Collozzo left his quarters at the US Embassy in Saigon. Before going to roll call, he would stop, as usual, in the Military Police office and peruse the latest telexes to learn of any special instructions for this evening's patrol. Collozzo was the senior NCO at the 504th Military Police Detachment at the Embassy. It was the middle of April 1975 and everyone knew that it was only a matter of time before the North Vietnamese Army (NVA) and the Viet Cong would reach the city. The war would soon be over and Bobby's main concern was to ensure the soldiers in his platoon were safe, complete their tours of duty and return home to the States in the same physical condition as they were when they arrived in Vietnam.

The 504th Military Police Detachment was assigned to the US Embassy in support of the US Marines but was tasked with the additional responsibility of patrolling the city of Saigon and assisting the local police in maintaining law and order among the thousands of US military personnel assigned to MAC-V (Military Assistance Campaign-Vietnam), and the soldiers who came to Saigon on R & R. (Rest & Recuperation). Originally, the 504th was structured like most US Army Companies; a Commanding Officer with the rank of Captain, an Executive Officer and Admin. Officer, both of whom were lieutenants, and three platoons of 30-40 enlisted personnel led by a senior non-commissioned officer. Since February, no replacements had been assigned, as soldiers rotated back to the States upon completion of their one year tours of duty.

The marines were responsible for the interior of the several buildings in the compound and also served as protection for visiting dignitaries and sometimes as drivers. There were also several civilian security personnel that Collozzo assumed were either state department or CIA (Central Intelligence Agency).

Everyone at the embassy knew the war was lost, and since the Tet Offensive in 1968, the tide had turned in favor of the Vietcong (VC) and the North Vietnamese Army (NVA).

The Command Officer, Captain Steve Auditore, and his Executive Officer, Lt. George Olsen, were the two remaining MP officers. They both relied on Collozzo to oversee, assign, and deploy the remaining military police officers in the 504th. In addition, he was responsible for maintaining a working relationship with the Saigon police and the ARVN (Army of the Republic of Vietnam) officers in the capital.

After retrieving the latest Telex, Sergeant Collozzo made his way to the muster room. The MPs working the 0700 - 1900 shift were milling about waiting for the platoon leader to call them to attention and read their assignments. Among them was Specialist 4th Class, (Spec 4) Louis A Frongillo, who everyone called Tony. Tony, like Collozzo, had been in the country almost as long as he and was always assigned to drive the platoon leader. As the only two Italians in the platoon, they bonded well from the first day they met. The rest of the platoon called them the Wop brothers but not to their faces. Bobby especially took exception to any ethnic slurs and was quick to use his fist if he heard any derogatory remarks from anyone. He earned his reputation as a bad ass during his first week in Saigon. While breaking up a bar fight between several marines and soldiers, one marine noticed his name tag and called him a grease ball. Bobby, who stood at 6'2", weighed about 190 pounds of muscle, asked the marine to step outside and then beat him like a rented mule. The marine, who was about 2 inches taller and outweighed Bobby by twenty pounds, had a reputation as being the toughest jarhead in Saigon. Bobby made short work of him, thereby setting his rep as someone you do not mess with.

Collozzo had only been in Saigon about a month before Tony arrived. After roll call, the three other two-man teams left the muster room, went to their assigned military police vehicles, and started their patrols. Collozzo felt it best to keep the same teams assigned to the same areas of Saigon. Spec. 4, Greg Adams, and his partner PFC, Bob Shaefer, were assigned to the area around Ton Son Nhat Airport. Sergeant Lou Schneider and Spec 4, Walker Verne, patrolled the red light district around Bui Vien street and Collozzo and Frongillo patrolled Cholon, Saigon's Chinatown. They liked working the area and became friendly with several local merchants. Tony had met and fallen for a young Chinese girl named Yim Ling, but he called her Alice. Fraternizing with the locals was not permitted by the MPs but Bobby covered for his driver and friend.

Over the months, the two became close friends. Tony was from Framingham, Mass. and his parents and older siblings were all born in Taormina, Sicily. Taormina, on the east coast of Sicily, was located in the province of Messina. Growing up, Tony spent his summers visiting his Nona and Papa there. His father was a plumber, as were he and his brothers. When he received his draft notice, he decided to enlist rather than be drafted so he could choose his MOS (Military Occupation Specialty). By enlisting he added another year to his service commitment but he believed that the extra year would not matter if he could choose his MOS. He chose the MPs, knowing that if the Army knew he was a licensed plumber, he would spend his entire enlistment fixing toilets, which is something he did not want to do. Back home in Framingham, with the help of his older brothers, the family plumbing business grew. Frongillo & Sons Plumbing was now a large commercial plumbing contractor with about two dozen employees. Tony knew that his father would want him to return to the business once his enlistment was up but Tony had other ideas. He would talk to Bobby about returning to Taormina, maybe living there. He would talk on end about how much he loved it there and wanted Bobby to visit with him. Bobby, for his part, was second generation Italian American and although raised in a typical Italian household in Brooklyn, he never traveled to Italy. All of his grandparents emigrated from Naples around the turn of the century. Tony was fluent in Italian, or, at least, the Sicilian dialect of his grandparents. Bobby only knew a few curse words but their friendship grew, and Bobby enjoyed Tony's stories and dreams of Taormina. They spoke often of traveling through Italy from north to south and then to Sicily. During their patrols through Saigon and Cholon they would talk about the places they would see, the people they would meet and especially the great food they would eat.

"Do you know there are parts of Northern Italy where you would think you were in Germany", he would tell Bobby. "It's called the Alto Adige. The towns have both Italian and Germany names. The people wear those goofy Lederhosen. I went there with my cousins a few years ago to hike the Dolomites." Tony would go on and on about all the places they could visit and see once they got out of Nam and the Army. He was such an upbeat guy. Bobby really enjoyed his new best friend.

CHAPTER TWO

During the last week of April, the entire military staff at the Embassy was placed on twenty four hour alert. Nonessential personnel were evacuated, and a sense of doom permeated throughout the company. Most Vietnamese civilians who worked for the Americans were trying desperately to seek asylum inside the Embassy or make their way out of the country. On the morning of April 28th, Collozzo could hear the thunderous sounds of cannons and howitzers firing on the villages surrounding Saigon.

Collozzo ordered his men to dig in. The teams worked hard placing sandbags around the interior perimeter of the compound and digging foxholes to prepare for an attack. To Collozzo it seemed surreal, as locals were seen leaving town carrying as much of their belongings as they could fit in their vehicles or horse drawn carts. Smoke was billowing from Tan Son Nhat International Airport just miles from the Embassy. Boeing CH-47 Chinook helicopters were flying in and out taking personnel to the super carrier USS Kitty Hawk (CV-63) in the South China Sea.

Prior to these current events, most of Collozzo's duties involved setting schedules for his platoon and patrolling the streets of downtown Saigon, breaking up fights between drunk servicemen on R & R or fights between servicemen and locals. Orders were not to interfere with the local authorities. If a service member got into a scrape with a local or refused to pay a hooker, it was his problem. But Collozzo had a good working relationship with the local police commander, Colonel Tron. The monthly bottle of Johnnie Walker Black that he gave the commander went a long way. Most disputes with locals were settled with a payoff by the offending GI.

Prostitution was also rampant but the military had a hands-off policy as long as violence was not an issue. STDs were common among the soldiers stationed in Saigon, mostly cases of the clap or crabs, which could be treated by the medics assigned to the detachment. "Yep," Collozzo thought to himself, "I had a pretty good run here compared to what other guys went through." This would be the first time he would face danger from the enemy as opposed to some drunk GI, who wanted to fight the cops. Collozzo was good at using his baton to get a drunk's attention. In most cases a whack on the knees was enough. The military had a separate drunk tank in the local police station where they would let GIs sleep it off. Only in the most severe cases would charges be filed. The policy was especially lenient toward soldiers who had spent time in the field and needed to let off some steam.

CHAPTER THREE

On April 29th, the NVA had reached the outskirts of Saigon. At the Embassy everyone who needed to go was gone. Ambassador Graham Martin was the last civilian to leave. In the embassy, pandemonium reigned as soldiers and marines kept busy shredding documents and destroying telecommunications equipment. Hundreds of Vietnamese civilians were crushing at the gates, hoping to get in and be airlifted out. Collozzo had several marines and MPs on the gate trying to hold back the throngs of screaming civilians. He knew, as did they, that once the city fell, they would be executed for working for the American government. While he sympathized with their plight, there was not much he could do.

He now had to ensure the safety of his own men. The first shell that landed inside the compound killed Captain Auditore and severely wounded Lt. Olsen. Collozzo knew that he was now in a position to make decisions that his life and the lives of his men depended on. To say the scene was chaotic was an understatement. People were running in every direction. One Chinook was hit with an RPG (rocket propelled grenade) but managed to stay aloft and make it out of the range of fire.

Collozzo did not know if he and the remaining MPs would get out. From his position inside the compound, he could see that a company of ARVN troops had arrived in a deuce and a half truck. They were mostly pushing the people around the gate trying to gain access to the compound. Collozzo, like most GIs, had very little respect for the ARVN. Their officers were incompetent to a man and were corrupt, as well. The soldiers, themselves, were poorly trained and most were becoming sympathetic to the VC and NVA. Using his PRC-25 radio, Collozzo contacted the Kitty Hawk and gave a situation report (Sit-Rep). He was ordered to make sure no American civilian remained in the compound. They were to hold off the enemy until another Huey (Bell UH-1 Iroquois) could be deployed to extract the remaining soldiers. Armed with only a 45 caliber pistol, Collozzo made his way around the compound. He reported casualties and wounded to the carrier and requested med-evac ASAP. Most of the civilians who were trying to gain entry had left as the ARVN pushed them away and took positions both inside and outside the gate. Smoke filled the compound and Collozzo noticed a civilian who worked in the commissary, a local they all called "Dinky Dow" coming from behind the main building carrying a backpack. Collozzo knew in an instant that he was about to toss the satchel full of explosives at one of the foxholes his men were in. Without hesitation, he fired several rounds at Dinky. The backpack exploded and Dinky was blown to bits. The soldiers in the foxhole turned to see just as Collozzo yelled, "Get down, incoming."

Collozzo wondered how many more "friendlies" would turn against his men. His ears were ringing from the explosion, but he made his way to the foxhole and ordered the men to follow him. They would make their way to the back of the compound and await evacuation. He tried to survey the area to ensure any wounded and dead were not left behind. Four medics with stretchers carried the bodies of Captain Auditore and Lt. Olsen.

Once again, Collozzo radioed the carrier for air support. "Get some fire power outside the Embassy. Get us the hell out of here. We will be in the rear of the compound by the auxiliary chopper pad. Don't know how much longer we can hold them off."

Collozzo was surprised how calm he was. Here he was just a twenty three year old, had just killed for the first time and was attempting to save the lives of the remaining soldiers under his command. He could see several black pajama clad VC scaling the main gate. It was then that he first saw Tony, who had not been in his thoughts for a long time. Tony opened fire killing several of the VC. Looking in Collozzo's direction, they made eye contact as he waved Tony over to his direction. Tony smiled, nodded, and ordered the others to head towards the rear of the compound while Collozzo laid down covering fire. Tony started to follow his squad as Collozzo continued to wave him over. Just then the explosion from an RPG tore into the compound. It played in slow motion as Collozzo saw his friend fly into the air and land about ten feet from where he last stood. Without hesitation, Collozzo ran toward his stricken comrade, dodging left and right to avoid enemy fire. When he got to Tony, he could see his friend lying in his own blood with his left leg gone and his intestines oozing out of his torn fatigue shirt. For a brief second, Tony looked up at him with a wry smile on his face. "We are still going to Taormina, right Bobby?"

"Yeah, Tony, we are gonna go, just like we planned."

" Just hang in there. I'll get you out of here." Hang on, Tony. Hang on."

Collozzo picked up Tony's AR 15, just as two VC ran towards him. He fired a burst of the 7.62mm rounds and both insurgents fell but not before he felt the hot sting of a round pierce his left shoulder and upper arm. "Shit," is all he said. Overhead he could hear the thump, thump, thump of the helicopter. Two Hueys, choppers, were laying down suppressing fire as the med-evacs and one Huey flew into the compound. The other marines and MPs provided cover and the VC were now coming over the gate and walls at will. One of the Hueys flew over, riddling the VC with a .50 Caliber round from the door gunner.

Again, that surreal feeling came over Collozzo as the chopper was blasting music, The Doors' "Riders on the Storm." Collozzo could see the door gunner's face, grinning as he mowed down VC, his Grateful Dead baseball cap turned backwards. This gave him time to carry Tony back to the rear of the compound just as the med-evac was landing. Bleeding badly in two places, a medic who he knew as Doc Brown, bandaged both his wounds. Collozzo did not know he had been hit with shrapnel from an RPG.

"You're lucky , Sarge. No vital organs damaged but your shoulder may need some surgery. Can't say the same for your buddy here," he said looking at Tony. "He's a goner." Tony still had that wry smile on his face. That smile would stay with Bobby Collozzo the rest of his life. As the chopper lifted off, Bobby cradled Tony's head in his arms and tears streamed down his face.

Chapter Four

Collozzo spent the next several weeks in an army hospital in Osaka, Japan. Once his wound started to heal, he was given some physical therapy to restore the power to his damaged arm. A day did not go by when he didn't think about his friend, Tony, and their plans to travel to Italy and visit Taormina, the city Tony's parents came from and the place he visited so often as a boy. He promised himself he would visit Tony's family in Framingham, Mass. and tell them how their son died a hero. He promised himself he would visit Taormina and see for himself all the places Tony had told him about.

Bobby Collozzo was healing from his wounds, but he wondered if his injury would keep him from his lifelong dream of becoming a NYC Police Officer. He had taken and passed the written exam but wondered if he would be able to pass the rigorous physical exam. Each day he worked out to strengthen his arm and shoulder back into shape. One day while returning from therapy he was told to report to the main muster room on the first floor of the hospital. When he walked into the large day room, he was surprised to see several other soldiers in pajamas sitting in wheelchairs or on crutches.

Vice Admiral, Robert Cullen, CO of the Naval Hospital in Osaka addressed the assembled group. There were several other ranking officers from all of the other services. "Men, I am here today to award medals to those of you who have displayed courage and gallantry in the face of a hostile enemy." As he called out each soldier's name, he would walk over and pin a Purple Heart on their pajama top and shake the hand of the receiving soldier. "You men have served your country and shed your blood for all free people of the world." Collozzo thought it was a bit melodramatic. He was a bit shocked when the admiral continued and said, "To Staff Sergeant, Robert Collozzo, I am hereby awarding a Bronze Star with "V" device for actions taken on the 29th -30th of April 1975 at the US Embassy in the city of Saigon, Republic of South Vietnam. Sergeant Collozzo, please come forward and be recognized." The admiral then read the Special Order that detailed the actions Collozzo had taken on that fateful day. He shook his hand as he pinned the Bronze Star on his fatigue shirt. He also handed him his Purple Heart. Bobby knew he would be getting the Purple Heart, but the Bronze Star came as a surprise. Not knowing what to do, he just shook the Admiral's hand and went back to his seat. Several soldiers started to clap and Bobby felt his face flush. The Admiral continued with posthumous awards and Bobby was pleased that in addition to a Purple Heart, Tony was awarded a Bronze Star with "V" device. Bobby was unaware of the actions Tony had taken at the front gate as the VC started to overtake the compound but when the Admiral read the narrative, Bobby knew his friend died a hero.

After the admiral and his entourage left, coffee and donuts were served by USO volunteers. These "donut dollies", as they were referred to by GIs were young, attractive, friendly, and eager to chat up soldiers with the usual questions, "Where's your home, handsome?" Or questions like that. Bobby appreciated their effort. It took courage on their part to volunteer and support the troops in the very unpopular war. An Army major, whose name tag read, "H. Finn," came over to Bobby and congratulated him on his bravery. Bobby could see from his insignia that this major was a medical doctor. Bobby asked him if he thought his injuries would result in any permanent damage to his arm. He told Major Finn of his plans to become a police officer.

"Any police department in the country should be proud to have you as a member, Sergeant. For a man your age you demonstrated great courage and leadership under the most difficult of circumstances."

Bobby just shook his head and pointing to the medals on his jacket said, "Major, how or who, I should say, reported my actions at the Embassy?"

"Like most awards today, other than the Purple Hearts, your fellow GIs made the recommendations." Bobby said nothing and looked down at the bronze medal with the red and blue banner. The major handed him two cases, one for each medal. Inside each case was a copy of the special order awarding the medal and a bar for his dress uniform. "I'm sure you want to wear them on your way home," he said.

Bobby looked at him with surprise. "What? I'm going home?"

"Yes, you are well enough to travel, and your enlistment is up next month. Here are your travel orders to Wrightstown Air Base in New Jersey. As you can see, you are out of here in forty eight hours. So, if I were you, I would go back to your ward and start packing."

CHAPTER FIVE

Bobby did not call his parents until he arrived at Wrightstown Airbase in New Jersey. During his time in Vietnam he was pretty good about writing home. His letters were very broad in scope. Words like "I'm doing fine, it's very safe here at the Embassy, I saw this movie or that movie last night." He never went into details about his MP duties much less his combat experience during the last days in Saigon. His dad read the papers and knew in his heart that Bobby had played down his experiences but did not share his views with his wife who worried constantly and prayed for Bobby every day

Bobby got his discharge orders after two days at Ft Dix. The Army had a bus traveling to Ft. Hamilton in Brooklyn, not far from his home. The only issue was that he was apprehensive about traveling in uniform. He had heard stories from other GIs about the poor treatment they got from the civilian population. Taunts like "Hey, soldier, kill any babies today?" Or "You're a freaking war criminal." Bobby knew these comments mostly came from young people but many adults, even veterans opposed the war in Vietnam, a war in which he fought and was awarded a medal for bravery under fire. It was going to be hard to be home, as he saw it. He knew his younger sister, Rosie, would not greet him with open arms, as if he could have controlled his situation. No, it wasn't going to be easy.

CHAPTER SIX

Bobby arrived home a few days later. On the bus ride to Ft. Hamilton he sat next to a lifer (army slang for career soldier) Master Sergeant who had just completed his third tour of duty in Vietnam and was now going to be stationed in Germany. His name was Caswell Bridges. Bobby liked him right away and never harbored any racial prejudices. He was not raised that way and he had a few black friends in high school. Bridges was a heavy equipment operator and could operate any vehicle the army had, Jeeps, Deuce and a half's, bulldozers, backhoes, and even cranes. He could not only operate these vehicles but could do repairs. He told Bobby that he had just gotten promoted and was going to be the new First Sergeant of an engineering company stationed outside of Frankfurt. He had been in the Army for twelve years and would stay and do twenty, at least. When they arrived at Ft. Hamilton, Bobby said goodbye as they exchanged addresses. Bobby told him he planned on traveling to Europe before he joined the police department and would look him up in Germany.

CHAPTER SEVEN

From Ft. Hamilton, Bobby got a cab to take him to his parent's house, which was about two miles from the fort. The cabbie, a Korean War vet, did not charge him for the ride. "Wow," Bobby thought, "that was nice." As he pulled into the street where he grew up, it seemed the houses were smaller than they were when he left just thirteen months ago. There was a huge hand- made sign reading, "WELCOME HOME BOBBY" in bold print suspended from two telephone poles on either side of the street. As the cab pulled into the driveway of the single family brick home, the cabbie honked his horn. Out came Bobby's mom and dad, followed by his older sister, Ann and several aunts and uncles, all smiling and carrying small American flags. Hugs and kisses, pats on the back and "Welcome Home" wishes abounded. It made Bobby feel good as he saw his mom, sister, and aunts all teary eyed. He was practically carried into the house and right away he noticed his younger sister, Rosie, was not among the well-wishers.

"Where's Ro?" he asked.

His mom looked at his dad and before he could answer, Ann said, "Don't worry about her, Bobby. She is one of those hippy anti-war idiots. It's just as well she's not here. She's changed since you saw her last. She moved into an apartment on 4th Avenue with one of her girlfriends about a month ago. We don't see much of her these days but she does call mom, when she wants something or needs some money," said Ann in an annoyed tone.

"She's going through a phase," said his mom. "You know how these kids are today, with the war, the drugs. This whole society is breaking down. But let's not talk about that now, Bobby. You're home and you're safe and your dad and I are so proud of you. That's all that matters. I made lasagna and your Aunt Mary made some of her famous meatballs and sausage. So, let's all have a good time. You must be starving; you look so thin."

So, for the next several hours Bobby ate, talked to his aunts and uncles, cousins and neighbors and tried to keep the conversation light.

He did not want to talk about the thirteen months he spent in Vietnam and his family members were savvy enough not to bring it up, all except his Uncle Phil, his father's younger brother. Phil was a paratrooper during WWII and parachuted into Normandy hours before the invasion. He never spoke of his experiences during the war but the family knew he suffered what was then called "battle fatigue." Today it would be called PTSD. He took Bobby aside and asked him how he really felt.

"I'm okay, Uncle Phil. I'm happy to be home and back in civilian life."

"I'm glad you're home, too, Bobby. I was just wondering if you had any thoughts or issues you wanted to share. After all, I think I'm the only one here who was in combat and I noticed the Bronze Star ribbon on your uniform. I don't suspect they give those away to MPs for good police work," he said with a smile.

"Well, it did get a bit hairy the last couple of days at the Embassy, but if it's all the same to you, I'd rather not talk about it just now. I hope you understand, Uncle Phil."

"Sure I do, Bob. Come on, let's grab another beer."

After the family left, Bobby sat outside with a couple of his buddies who had stopped by. Most of the guys he hung out with had been drafted earlier or were able to join the National Guard; however, the conversation was mostly about the future. Most of the guys, like Bobby, were waiting to be called by the PD or fire department. They too knew the benefits of a civil service career. After everyone left, Bobby took another shower and went to bed. It felt a bit strange to sleep in his old bed again and just as he was falling asleep, there was a knock on his door.

"Bob, are you awake?" It was his sister, Ro.

"Yeah, sure. Come in."

She had changed in the year and a half since he last saw her. Her hair was long, almost down to her butt and the once curly, brown hair was straight and had blond highlights. Her eyes were a bit glassy. Bobby figured she was high. He had seen that look on plenty of GIs on R & R.

"I'm sorry I didn't write you more often. I am glad you're home and out of the army."

Bobby could sense that she was about to go on about how horrible the war was and how the country and the politicians are all corrupt, so he just said, "Come here, Ro. Let me give you a hug." As she approached, he got out of bed and hugged his kid sister. "I'm really beat. Let's catch up in the morning, okay?."

"Sure. Have a good night, Bobby and again, I'm so glad you're home and safe."

CHAPTER EIGHT

Over the next few days, Bobby tried to adjust to being home. He tried to find out when the city planned to appoint a new class to its police academy. The city, however, was in the midst of a fiscal crisis and a hiring freeze was ordered by the mayor. Bobby decided that as long as he had the time, he would do some traveling. He had saved enough money while in the service to buy a car. His dad helped him out and he bought a 1971 Buick Skylark convertible. He decided he would drive to Framingham to visit Tony's grave and maybe his family. He then wanted to travel to Sicily and visit all the places in Taormina that his friend had spoken about. He did not have the Frongillo's phone number, but he figured he could look in a phone book and find either a home number or certainly a business number. When he arrived in Framingham, he found both in the local directory. He called the home number first. His hands were sweaty as he dialed the number. He had rehearsed what he would say over and over on the drive from Brooklyn to Framingham.

A female voice answered after a couple of rings. The voice had an Italian accent.

"Hello".

"Mrs. Frongillo?" He paused.

"Yes, who is this?"

"Mrs. Frongillo, my name is Robert Collozzo. I was a friend of Tony in the Army." He did not want to say, "Vietnam." He didn't know why. Again, he paused. "I live in New York and I wanted to pay my respects at Tony's grave site." It seemed like an eternity as Bobby waited for a response.

"You're Bobby Collozzo," she said, with a bit of excitement in her voice. "Tony mentioned you in all his letters. Are you calling from New York?"

"No, ma'am, I'm here in Framingham."

She mumbled something in Italian and holding the phone away, he could hear her speak to someone else in the house.

"You can comma here for dinner, no? My husband and sons and family will all be here and want to meet you. You come, say around six tonight. That's okay?"

"Well, yeah, I guess, sure." Bobby was a bit dumbstruck. He really didn't expect this, but he thought to himself had the situation been reversed, his mom would do the same thing.

CHAPTER NINE

On his drive to the Frongillo house Bobby spotted an Italian bakery and bought a dozen assorted pastries. The uneasiness Bobby felt soon disappeared as the family greeted him as one of their own. After introductions, Mr. and Mrs. Frongillo took Bobby into a small den off the main dining room. Pictures of Tony were on the end tables and fireplace mantle. "Bobby, we feel like we know you," said Mr. Frongillo. "Tony mentioned you in his letters." Looking at his wife he continued. "We have so many questions but we both agreed that maybe it's best not to trouble you with them."

"No, it's OK, you have made me feel very welcome, and I must say I was very apprehensive about meeting you all. I think about Tony all the time and wish there were more I could have done, you know, to save him."

"We saw the medal they gave him. We know he died saving his buddies. But it doesn't make it easier for his mom and I." They both started to cry, and it made feel uneasy. He just sat there trying to think of something to say.

"Tony and I planned to travel to Italy, to Taormina, where you all come from. He told me so much about his summers there that I feel like I have been there myself."

"We still have family there," said Mr. Frongillo. We will give you their names and address if you want. They loved Tony so much, they would love to see you too."

It seemed dinner never ended. Pasta followed by a fish dish with assorted Italian veggies. On the table was a gallon jug of Mr. Frongillo's home made wine. The food was familiar to Bobby but prepared much differently. The sauce for the pasta was much thicker than his mom's sauce. The Frongillo 's called it "gravy". They went back to the dining room table for dessert and coffee. Mr. Frongillo place several bottles of after dinner drinks on the table: Sambuca, Anisette and his home made Grappa. He explained to Bobby that he made the Grappa from the dregs of grapes used for making his wine. Most of the conversation during dinner was in Italian and Mrs. Frongillo had to remind her husband and sons that their guest did not speak Italian. They would apologize to Bobby who just shook them off, but their conversations, mostly about the business would revert back to Italian.

CHAPTER TEN

The Frongillos insisted Bobby spend the night. Although he mildly protested, he was relieved that he would not have to drive back to Brooklyn or look for a hotel. Strangely enough they did not offer Tony's room but rather a sofa bed in the basement. "There was a bathroom and a TV, so it was better than Tony's room," they explained. For Bobby it was fine, although he felt they wanted to maintain Tony's room as it was. By 9 PM the brothers and their families had left and both Mr. and Mrs. Frongillo said their goodnights. Bobby turned on the TV but all he could think about was the wonderful people he had met this day. They treated him like one of their own. He knew it was because of his relationship with Tony. He only hoped that after he left, the pain he saw in their faces would not be exacerbated by his visit. He awoke the next morning to the aroma of fresh bread baking in the oven. He showered and dressed and upon entering the kitchen Mrs. Frongillo greeted him with a hug and a kiss.

"My husband left for work, so I made you a nice Italian breakfast." She took a piece of the fresh made Italian bread, cut out the inside, placed it in a skillet and cracked and egg and laid it inside the hollowed out piece of bread.

"That was delicious, Mrs. Frongillo and I can't thank you enough for your hospitality."

She just looked at him and giving him a hug, she started to cry. "My poor baby, I miss him so much, why did he have to die? Why did God do this to me?"

Bobby felt awkward and patted her on the back. "I miss him too Mrs. Frongillo. I think about him every day. I promise to visit your family in Taormina and tell them about Tony. He said his goodbyes and started the drive back to Brooklyn. He would travel to Italy and he would never forget his Paesano.

Dies Irae
(The Day I Got Mad)

by Leo A. Vadalà

*"Dies Irae - The Day I Got Mad" could easily be
a follow-up to "The Viewing," Leo Vadala's short story
that appeared in Volume Two of "A Feast of Narrative."
In fact, it could just as easily be titled
"The Viewing – Part Deux."*

*In "Dies Irae" the author again displays his grotesque
and somewhat cynical sense of humor as the hero
of his short story attends yet another Italian viewing.*

*Just fasten your seat belts and prepare yourself to enjoy
"A Feast of Laughter."*

The phone rang. It was Tony, Tony Ruello, a friend from way back; we talk two, three times a week, just shooting the bull.

"Hey, Tony, what's up?"

He was quiet for a couple of seconds then he mumbled: "You heard anything?"

I said: "What do you mean?"

He went on, subdued like: "No, no, I mean, nobody called you yet?"

I said: "No, why? What's going on?"

"You haven't heard about Santino?"

"No, what's he been up to?"

"He's dead!"

"**WHAT!?!...**" —I screamed.

Tony kept talking: "Yeah, there was an accident on the job... He's dead!"

My jaw must have dropped about a foot. I mean, Santino was the last guy I'd expect to die. Not that I keep a list of guys I expect to die, but you know what I mean.

I mean, a guy is around all the time, strong and healthy as a bull, you see him two, three times a week, only yesterday you were talking to him—**last night,** for Christ sake!—and all of a sudden you pick up the phone and—**BOOM!**—somebody tells you he is dead. I mean, what gives? Which is why I almost flipped out.

"Are you kidding? Are you kidding me?..." I kept saying, as if somebody would joke about something like that.

Then Tony went into the gory details. Seems like Santino had been working at the shore on some construction job, one of those goddamned condos they're putting up all over the beach, I swear they are ruining the damn place. Anyway, some rope had snapped and he had fallen off the scaffolding from the twelfth floor, him and two other guys who had been killed too, of course.

We went back and forth talking about life, death, here today, gone tomorrow, what's life all about, no use making any plans, blah, blah, blah, all silly stuff, even though we meant it. Finally I asked Tony to let me know about any funeral arrangements. He said he would as soon as he'd find out.

Santino Catalano had come over from Italy some eight or nine years ago. He was a friend who had joined our card-playing group, although most of the times he was a no-show.

Come to think of it, I'm pretty sure he had played only once, lost maybe a couple of bucks, and that's the last we saw of him. We always invited him, but he always found some excuse for not coming.

Did I say he was a friend? Scratch that. I really didn't care for him all that much. I saw him occasionally, usually when he asked me for some favor but I hardly ever socialized with him, we never exchanged confidences, never talked about sport, never swapped jokes or bantered around.

He knew squat about sports. As for jokes, forget it—**zero** sense of humor, absolutely zilch. I never once heard him tell a joke, good, bad, clean or dirty, never heard him make a funny comment, a wisecrack, a double entendre, never even saw him laugh at someone else's jokes. He just didn't get them.

True story: once we were watching a TV show at my brother's house, and some comedian made a mother-in-law joke that went something like this "When my mother-in-law came to live with us I told her 'Mom, you're not just a guest here. You are in your own house'... (Pause)... So she sold it!" It was a mildly amusing joke that got a laugh from all of us. Santino was there. His English was still nonexistent, but since he had heard us all laugh, I politely translated the joke for him.

His comment? "Real estate laws must be different here than in Italy!" which in a way was funnier than the joke on TV, except that Santo was dead serious, I swear.

Like I said, we were not buddies, still I felt sorry for the poor bastard. Much as I didn't like him, I had to admit he didn't deserve to end up like that; hell, nobody does. I mean, I knew the guy had worked his ass off all his life, and I mean Work, Work with a capital W, real Work, "sweat" Work. Personally, I work in a bank, I've been working there for the past twenty five years. It can be aggravating as hell at times, but at least the hours are pretty regular and you work in air-conditioned comfort. Santino, on the other hand, he did mostly construction work plus any other type of work he could get, yard work, hauling, cleaning, whatever.

Man, could that guy work! Seventy, eighty, ninety hours a week, that was average for him; Saturdays, Sundays, Christmas, New Year, any time, anywhere, any job, he was sure to show up as long as there was a buck to be made, and I do mean one buck, literally, that is one hundred pennies.

Like I said, I didn't care for him all that much. At the same time, I am not too proud to admit it, but I envied him a bit. That's because I knew that after eight years or so in this country he had already managed to stash away over forty-five grands in the bank. I knew that because he had his savings account at my bank.

He made deposits just about every day, sometimes as little at two dollars at a time, driving my tellers crazy. Little by little he had managed to accumulate over forty-five thousand bucks, which is about forty-four thousand five hundred more than I have managed to salt away for my old age after forty-six years in the good old US of A, land of plenty and opportunity. And that's why I envied him.

True, there are good reasons for my anemic bank account. For one thing I am married, have two kids, a big mortgage, car payments, insurance, and so on. Santino was single, lived in a ramshackle room in a cheap boarding house, had no car, and he simply didn't like spending money.

He was such a miserable goddamned miser you would never believe it. Me, on the other hand, I've lived a little, I've been around some. Not so much now because I have a family and can't afford it, but when I was single I was always on the road, I went places, saw things, took vacations, went to museums, the theatre, stage shows, and the movies. On the other hand, Santino spent his few leisure hours mostly in his room—understandably, of course, because one needs some rest after working so many hours.

As for female companionship, I am pretty sure he was celibate. He had mentioned once he had a girlfriend in Italy, they were engaged and he would marry her and raise a family when he went back in a few years.

Very touching, I thought, but still, eight years without a woman, you know what I mean. I'm sure even his fiancée would have understood if he'd plunged his dipstick in another engine a few times while away from her. Actually, this is pure speculation on my part—for all I know, maybe he did, but I doubt it. To start with, looks-wise, he didn't get his fair share—honest to God, he looked like a turtle. Furthermore he had little or no conversational skills in Italian, and practically zero in English, even after eight years in this country. Let's just say his chances of hooking up with some girl were slim or none.

He could have hooked up with a hooker, of course, but I doubt he ever did because they cost beaucoup money, or so I'm told, and Santino just wasn't the big spender type.

The word entertainment just wasn't in his vocabulary. Just saying, but would you believe that he had never been to the movies? Not even once, here or in Italy? Can you believe it? I mean, OK, his English was still very poor, so why waste money if you can't understand what's going on; plus one could argue that with the kind of junk they show at the movies nowadays the guy showed remarkable intelligence by not going, but Christ!, come **ON,** once, just once for Christ sake, if only for the novelty of it, just to see what it was about, I'm sure he could have done that. But no, he never did.

I happen to know this because he told me so himself once, when I took him to the movies. Whoa, hold it right there! I know exactly what you're thinking—why did I take him to the flicks when I could hardly stand the sight of him?

Rest assured I had no intention of introducing him to the wonders of the silver screen. What happened was that I had gone to the mall to buy some stuff, I forget what, some swimming trunks I believe. While looking at something at Macy's, reflected in the store window I saw Santino wandering about in the mall.

I tried to make myself as inconspicuous as possible and silently I pleaded: "Please God, please don't let him see me..." But God didn't hear me; he never does when I really need him. Santino had eyes like a snail and, with about a million people in the mall and my back turned to him, he still spotted me. That's the kind of luck I have!

He tapped me on the shoulder and said hi. I acted very surprised-like and asked him what he was doing there.

Actually I wasn't acting all that much. I mean, I was really surprised because being at the mall means shopping, and shopping means spending money, and let's just say that Santino's spending never made a significant contribution to the American economy. Furthermore, I knew his favorite boutiques were the Goodwill Store and the Salvation Army, not at the mall.

He said somebody had told him some store in the mall was going out of business, he needed some underwear, and that's why he was there. About two minutes of this and that, and I was mulling how to get rid of him. He came to the rescue when he asked if I could give him a ride back home. I told him I couldn't because I was on my way to see a movie that started in about five minutes. It was the best lie I could come up with, because I knew he would rather have parted with a healthy tooth than with five bucks, that's how much tickets used to cost back then. Anyhow, that's when he told me he had never been to the movies.

I thought he was kidding but he said no, he had never been to the movies, and he asked me what they were all about. I explained it was the same stuff you see on TV except the screen is much larger, the show lasts about two hours, 'and it costs five bucks to get in', you sit with a bunch of other people, 'and it costs five bucks to get in', it's all very dark and smoky in there, 'and it costs five bucks to get in'.

You get my drift, of course, trying to be as negative as possible, nonchalant like, movies ain't that big of a deal, that kind of stuff, because I had this uneasy feeling I knew what was coming next. Which it did, of course. Like clockwork. Swiss clockwork.

He asked me: "Do you mind if I come too?"

Let me tell you, you could have knocked me out with a feather! And no, not because he had never been to the flicks, I mean, after all, who gives a shit? But because now I was forced to act out my lie, and in **HIS** company. O sweet Jesus, Joseph, and Mary!!!! Talk about a royal screwing!

Well, I swallowed hard and said sure, come along, why not? I mean, what else could I say? I had no choice, really.

When we got to the box office I reached for my wallet to pay for my ticket. I never really expected him to reach for his wallet, I don't even think the guy had a wallet, but I kind of looked at him from the corner of my eyes just to see what he would do, hoping against hope. Miracles do happen now and then, or so they say.

Not that time they didn't, pal—he didn't fail me that time either. The bastard never even **attempted** to go for his wallet, assuming he had one. And so, poor, little, unmitigated, **TOTAL** asshole **ME** wound up paying for both tickets.

But the afternoon wasn't over, not by a long shot, no way José! God, in his infinite wisdom, had decreed that I should pay in more than just money for my little white lie. He wanted blood. And by God, He got it!

The theater happened to hold a revival of Ingmar Bergman movies, in Swedish of course, which is one of about two thousand languages I don't know at all.

Let me tell you, it was inhuman. Savage. Brutal. What the Nazis did to the Jews in their concentration camps was a Sunday picnic compared to what I went through that afternoon. To this day I don't know how I got through that experience, not only alive but with my sanity.

Picture this: me, struggling to read the subtitles, and him next to me, tugging at my sleeve every fifteen seconds asking 'Chi dissi?. Chi dissi?.... Sicilian for 'what's he say, what's he say?'...And since Bergman—the bastard!—never comes out and says black is black and white is white, I was also forced to come up with an impromptu lesson on the significance of allegorical imagery in Scandinavian cinema. And, of course, in terms comprehensible to a guy who'd quit school after repeating the second grade three times!!! Honest to God, to this day I still get the urge to go **YAAAAAAAHHHHHHH!!!!** whenever I think about it.

By the time the movie was over—about nineteen hours at least—I was ripe for the guys in white. I was seeing things, talking to myself, crying inside, sobbing, even laughing a short, eerie laugh, cackling softly like a chicken that knows she has been selected for tomorrow's dinner.

You read all the times about guys, regular guys, meek guys, gentle guys, who all of a sudden grab a gun or a pair of scissors and start punching holes in people passing by. You've read about them, I'm sure, it happens once or twice a year. The newspaper guys always interview the neighbors, and to a man they will say 'Who, Tommy?...No way! He's the kindest man I know, a regular guy, always volunteers for this and that, he is a good, pious, reliable, helpful, gentle, generous man, my kids play with his kids, blah blah blah....'' You know the kind of guys I'm talking about. Well, I know exactly who they are and why they do it, I learned it that afternoon. They are the little people, the ones who spend their worthless and pathetic lives giving, giving, giving, and taking nothing but shit, and shit, and more shit in return, and they take it, and take it, and take it, always in silence and with a vapid smile on their faces, until something inside their brain goes **BOOOOOOING!**, and then it's big, humongous front-page headlines all over, '**BANK MANAGER KILLS 8, WOUNDS 14.**''

Yes, I now know who they are and why they do it, and they all have my full sympathy, support and understanding. And I'm telling you right now that if I'm ever called on jury duty and one of those poor shmucks comes up for trial, he'll walk. Guaranteed.

I know I didn't sink my fangs in Santino's windpipe that day because God, that same God who had so fiendishly punished me for my little white lie, had decreed that he should crash to the ground, but believe me, I was ready. And willing. I'm not sure about the 'able' because Santino was a big mother and I'm not much of a fighter, but that afternoon I could have taken on King Kong.

Instead, when we came out of the movie I didn't say a thing, typically. I thought about coming up with some other pathetic lie but thought better of it. In a hurry. I figured—Christ!—if God did that to me for one measly white lie, I didn't even want to think what the big guy had in store for me for a second one. So I said what the hell, and took him home.

That night, I went home, popped about 4 or 5 Zantacs, washed them down with half a bottle of scotch and cried myself to sleep.

And that's the kind of guy Santino was—a good worker, yes, a great worker, I won't take that away from him. But he was also very cheap, thoughtless, and ignorant.

Tony called me the next day to inform me that Santino's viewing was going to be on Monday night at the Arcaro Funeral Home from 6 to 9, and the funeral on Tuesday morning at 10 AM at St. Anthony's Church.

I wasn't too crazy about going to the viewing or the funeral. Let's face it, both viewings and funerals are not exactly fun occasions. In both cases, there's always a large display of grief and tears—even genuine, occasionally—and anyhow, they just ain't my bag. But I had to go, it was expected of me and it would have looked bad if I hadn't, him being a 'paisan' and all.

When I walked inside the funeral home I was nervous as hell. I mean, a viewing is not a social event, even though you get to meet a bunch of friends and relatives.

There's nothing like a death, especially a tragic one, to bring out the crowds. I'm telling you, it's better than a circus—in fact, **IT IS** a goddamned circus.

Most people—and Italian people particularly so—view death with an unbelievably disgusting air of solemnity, all the more disgusting because in the vast majority of cases it's faked. Look, I'm not being cynical, but my guess is that, except for the immediate relatives of the deceased—and frequently not even them—very few others are really all that shook up about somebody's death.

Actually, if you have a decent sense of humor, you can have a good time at a viewing.

You can't believe the incredibly trite remarks you hear. Invariably, the most inane is: "Look at him, he seems to be sleeping."

And, inevitably, perfect strangers will come to buttonhole you to give you their private pearls of wisdom. One perennial is "Heh! What can you do?!."—murmured dejectedly, and with just the right shrug of the shoulders. If I don't hear that one at least ten times, I feel like I've wasted my time.

Another winner you will unfailingly hear, especially at the viewing of someone who has died suddenly, is *"Si sa quando si nasce, ma non si sa quando si muore.* (One knows when he is born, but one never knows when he is going to die)", this pearl stated somberly, with a long, deep, meaningful look straight in the eyes.

And, of course, the recipient of this little nugget of wisdom has to go along with the charade. He will open his arms in a gesture of total agreement and infinite understanding, and will solemnly nod and sigh to indicate we are mere pawns in the hands of a superior power. He doesn't recognize that statement for the piece of shit it really is, so he doesn't waste any time repeating it to somebody else.

At Santino's viewing I heard that particular gem at least four times and, I'm telling you, I wished I had more guts, because the last time I heard it I was so, so, so tempted to sneer: "Well, I am **pretty** sure our recently departed *'paisan'* knew **exactly** when he was going to die—**WHILE HE WAS PLUMMETING BETWEEN THE SECOND AND THE FIRST FLOOR OF THAT FUCKING CONDO, FOR FUCK SAKE!!**"

I walked in and signed my name on that album they always have parked on some lectern, which is something else that drives me fucking bananas.

Can somebody please, please, please with sugar on top, please explain to me just why the hell people do that? You mean to tell me there are people who, after the funeral, actually pore over that list to find out whose ass was present and whose wasn't? You mean somebody actually gives a shit? Somebody please tell me it's not so. Somebody please tell me it's just another gimmick for the funeral director to pad the bill, somebody please tell me nobody from the family actually requested it, and I'll die happy. And then you can come and sign **MY** album.

It's a bit of financial legerdemain by the undertaker, that's all it is. All things considered, business is business, I can relate to that, and who's going to notice another little item lost in the confusion:

Embalming—$2,000.00; Casket—$1,500.00; Flowers—$750.00; Remembrance Album—$100.00 – **ZAP!**.... Nobody will notice.

Anyway, I signed my name and just walked in. Oh! By the way, once—I swear to God—I signed in as Benito Mussolini, as a joke of course, not to be disrespectful to the guy who'd died, absolutely not. Hell! He was a damn good friend of mine and I would never have slighted him. I did it because the guy had a great sense of humor and, politically, he stood left of Lenin. I was sure he would have appreciated it and I bet he chuckled in appreciation when I signed in as Il Duce.

When I walked in Arcaro's funeral parlor, first thing I did I looked around to see who was there. The closest relative Santino had was his brother Johnny, and he was there of course, right next to the casket. I walked over to him, shook his hand and mumbled something about how sorry I was, the usual stuff. He mumbled back something I didn't quite understand and I then moved over to see the remains.

The casket had been set up at one end of the room, in an alcove-like depression in the wall. It was a bit elevated and, from a distance, you could hardly see what was inside. As I got closer, however, I saw the whole corpse. First thing I did I thanked God he looked all right. I mean, he was dead and all, but he didn't look too bad. Not that I'm squeamish, or anything like that, but I had half expected to see a pizza laid out there, and I wasn't too pleased at the prospect. Instead, by some miracle, his face hadn't been messed up by the accident. Either that or the Arcaro people had done a marvelous job in face reconstruction. I'm sure the rest of his body was hamburger—I mean, we are talking twelve stories here. The only visible sign of trauma was a slight bruise on his right cheek, and that's about it. The messy parts, if there were any, were covered by a fancy-looking blanket that went from one end of the casket up to his shoulders. All around the casket there were flowers galore from everybody. His brother, of course, his fellow workers, the Order Sons of Italy, friends, all had sent some kind of flower arrangement. I did not, I just don't send flowers on principle, it's just a big rip-off. I remember when my brother-in-law died the whole family was gathered at his house, his brothers, his sisters, they were all there to grieve together and to console his widow and the two kids.

They had called a florist who got there in no time at all. Like a trained vulture, the son of a bitch brought out his catalogues and started showing them around. You had to see it to believe it—gorgeous flower arrangements in the shape of a cross, of a broken heart, of a rosary, they even had arrangements in the shape of whatever the deceased might have been fond of, like a guitar, a book, a car, whatever! And if you didn't see what you wanted in the catalogue they would custom make it for you. At a price of course, a hefty price! I fully understood and shared everybody's grief. Hell, I was crying myself, and meant it. My brother-in-law and I were good buddies, we'd played tennis together a thousand times, and we got along famously. I was grief-stricken like all the others, but not to the point that I wasn't aware of what was going on. And I knew damn well what was going on—the florist was just trying to make as much money as possible.

So I tried to warn them, look, this guy is just pushing for the high-priced stuff, let's not go overboard here. I didn't flat out say the guy was taking advantage of their semi-impaired mental state, even though he was, but I just told them to be careful. Man, they all looked at me with some disgust, like I was a leper, even my wife, so I backed off and mum was the word, no pun intended.

They all made their selections and we arranged to have all the bills sent to me. Afterwards we would all split the cost, of course.

Three days after the burial the bill arrived—it was nearly $4,000.00! That's for flower arrangements from 8 families, mind you! Even my wife was just about wasted! I told her, honey, I hate to say I told you so, but I told you so!

She is under strict orders now—if I croak before she does, I don't want one single solitary flower, not even a dandelion. It's a rip-off!

I couldn't get next to the casket right away because people were waiting in line ahead of me to express their condolences just before viewing the remains. And—Italians being Italians—they couldn't just murmur a quick "I'm so sorry" and move on. No sir! Italians may start with a more or less sincere "I'm so sorry", but that's just as an appetizer. What follows is a first course of going on and on and on and on about what a marvelous human being the deceased was, then a second course of how cruel destiny is to have taken him so young and finally, without fail, as a dessert they will compare that tragedy with something that happened to them or to a third cousin of theirs about half a century ago. And the entire charade is seasoned, of course, with the appropriate gestures, yet another trait totally mastered by Italians.

Two hundred people behind them, some of them glancing repeatedly and impatiently at their watches and silently cursing because they know they will miss the opening kick on the TV? Fuck them!

I swear when I see something like that I want to grab the inconsiderate bastard, stuff him/her in the casket and close the lid. But in our so-called civilized society that would be considered uncouth. And so I quietly waited my turn.

Now, don't get the idea I'm some kind of ghoul or a weirdo, but I got to say this—I have always wondered what people say or think when they kneel down in front of a corpse. I mean, it's not like I lose sleep over it, but it does cross my mind now and then, especially when I'm waiting in line. I wonder, do they pray? Do they think, who knows? *"Will I be next?"* There but for the grace of God go I? I mean, there they are, as close to eternity as they will ever get without actually being there, and I want to believe their mind doesn't wander on some mundane thing, like, how did the Yankees make out last night, did I turn the gas off before leaving home, who's that blonde chick with the boobs at the head of the line? Who knows?

At this point, I suppose you'll want to know what memorable thoughts come into my mind, right? Well, I'll tell you. Nothing much comes into my mind, honest! The whole idea, the entire scenario of a viewing is so unreal to me that I try to minimize my thought process; my mind enters a neutral stage, sort of.

I have in fact perfected a ritual that helps me get through that scene almost mechanically, like a car on the assembly line. This robot-like routine goes into overdrive as soon as I'm in the presence of the corpse. Once I'm out of viewing room and with some friends and relatives, everything returns to normal. First off I adjust my face to the basic, quintessential grief-stricken look. Remember a while back I was telling you about the faked solemnity of the Italians? Might as well tell you the brutal truth—in that department I can out-wop anybody. **ANYBODY!!!**

So, try to imagine the real, living, walking, Oscar-winning picture of solemn grief, and that's me approaching the casket.

When I get to that padded thing in front of the casket—what's it called, a kneeler?—I kneel down, and first thing I do I curse under my breath because I got a bum knee from my soccer playing days and it hurts like a son of a bitch every time I bend it.

Then I automatically start reciting the prayer for the dead, the old "*Requiem Aeternam*" I learned as a kid which, incidentally, I know just in Latin and which, by the way, I don't even know what the hell it means which, I suppose, is piss-poor grammar, but who cares at this stage of the game.

When I finish the *Requiem*, I recite it one more time for good measure because, as prayers go, it's rather short, and you can knock it off in about five seconds, an indecently short time to spend in front of a casket. Not that there's any conventional etiquette about it, and I'm sure Emily Post never gave the matter much thought, but I've always believed there should be a decent interval between the time you kneel down in front of a corpse, and the time you get up, cross yourself, and then make your way toward a group of friends who are already on their third cigarette.

How decent is decent? To each his own, of course, but I got my own rules, I've set my own time limits—to me a decent interval is between thirty seconds and one minute. Many variables, of course, can affect that time frame one way or the other, to wit, how closely related you are to the stiff, how grief stricken you really are, how many people are waiting in line, and so on.

After I finish with the two *Requiems*, then it's simply a question of me counting one, two, three, four, five and so on until I've filled out the thirty second to one minute time allotment. When I've finished, I get up, cross myself, give one last mournful look to the deceased, shake my head disconsolately and solemnly walk away.

With Santino I used that same time-tested technique. He was strictly a thirty-second job, of course, and with overtime at that. I mechanically recited the two *Requiems,* and I figured they had used up, what?, only about 10 seconds, so when I finished the second *Requiem* I started on the tail end of my programmed routine, counting pretty fast to twenty.

And here's where things started getting weird. I think it was when I got to about 9 or 10 that I got this strange urge to raise my head and look closely at his face. I don't know why I did it—maybe it was that same morbid fascination that makes us look when we drive by a bad car accident, you know, you see a car smashed up real bad, cops all over, ambulances wailing away, and you want to see if somebody got hurt real bad. And, crazily, I looked.

In death he was pretty much the same as when he was alive, ugly as sin. I swear, compared to him Quasimodo was Cary Grant! He could have nosed out a gargoyle in an ugliness contest. Talk about noses, he had a schnozz you could hang a suit from. He had these big, fat lips like two pounds of liver, huge bushy eyebrows still flaked with dandruff, Mickey Mouse ears, practically no forehead. A real loser, honestly, no wonder he never got laid. I mean, even hookers got some standards, I suppose.

What struck me the most about the corpse was its total stillness. It's to be expected, of course—I mean the guy was dead and all—but it looked so unnatural. It was as still as only a corpse can be, stiller even than a rock that, somehow, has some vitality.

A blanket covered him, and I tried to visualize the horrible mess underneath. I pictured pieces of bones sticking out all over, and some gooey stuff oozing out. The gooey stuff damn near did it. I tuned it out immediately, and just in time too, or I would have puked all over him, and wouldn't that have been some scene!

What happened next cannot be explained on a dimension of human logic. The only explanation I can give is that I believe all of us—God, I hope it's not just me!—all of us have at some time or other felt, or believed, that we just may possess some latent superhuman power, and we just need the right occasion and the right time to bring it out. Either that, or I'm just fucking goofy.

You hear all the time that, barring a miracle, everything that happens has a rational explanation. I used to believe that, but not anymore, not after what I did. What I did was beyond irrationality, it reached the outer limits of spaced out lunacy, it went into uncharted ding-dong territory, it can only be described as the essence of distilled, good to the last drop cuckoo madness, so don't ask why I did it—I told you, maybe I was just fucking goofy. In fact, no maybe about it. All I know is that, all of a sudden, out of the blue, I began thinking, **SERIOUSLY** thinking: "Wouldn't it be nice if I would wake him up?"

Would—get that?—not **could**! Now, temporary insanity comes and goes and, in and by itself, a stupid thought does not really constitute insanity. I'm sure we all at some time or other have fantasized about the most bizarre happenings, we all have indulged in the most fanciful, unattainable daydreams. Of course we have! Hell, if it weren't for that all state lotteries and the PowerBall people would be out of business!

Like I said, thinking crazy thoughts is tolerable, acceptable, even human. But I didn't just think it! Since I have been a crazy mother from day one, I actually gave it a try. As true as I am standing here talking to you, I actually had the nerve to do it, I actually told him to wake up. I actually went ahead and...No, no, wait! Let me run it through for you from the very beginning so you can appreciate and follow the smooth flow of events better.

OK, fasten your seat belts. I go inside Arcaro's, I sign myself in, I see his brother Johnny, I go over to him and say very sorry, blah blah blah, he says something mumble mumble, I say yeah, yeah, that's tough and go to the casket, I wait in line, I kneel down on the watchamacallit, I mumble goddamn (the knee, remember?), I start *Requiem Aeternam* blah blah blah, then again *Requiem Aeternam* blah blah blah, Amen. Then, One... Two... Three... Four....

Five... Six.... Seven.... I raise my head, I see his ugly puss and finally —**BLAST OFF!!!** I actually tell him: "Come on, Santino, wake up, what's the matter with you, you got no business being dead, ain't your time yet, come on now, get the hell up, you hear?"

Friends, Romans, countrymen, and fellow inmates, that's exactly the way it went. Now, I did not declaim that, of course, I just whispered it, but I actually said it, and if you want to call the guys in white, be my guests.

Oh, but wait, that's not all. I told you about madness coming and going, right? That one time it didn't even leave the room. I had my hands clasped in front of me because I was praying, loosely speaking. So, what I did, I unhooked my hands and, shielding them from view with my body, I actually snapped my fingers to sort of jolt him out of his sleep. I swear to God I did it, softly of course, but I did it.

And you know something? For one terrifying millisecond, make that a nanosecond, for one microscopic piece of eternity, I actually believed he was going to wake up. I really thought he would start stirring just like Frankenstein when they turn on the juice, all the more so because he did look a bit like Frankenstein.

Man, I almost shit in my pants! In that one nanosecond I prayed to God the juice of one thousand prayers, the root essence of everything I'd learned in Catholic school, all condensed into a few, short, powerful, pleading words: "**DEAR. GOD. CHRIST. BABY. GOD. JESUS. SON OF THE VIRGIN IMMACULATE MARY AND THE HOLY GHOST!!**" —I begged silently—"**Please, no! Don't let it happen, I was just kidding. I swear to God, I was just blowing smoke! I'll never do it again! I promise.**"

Nanoseconds do pass, even when they last a lifetime, and eventually I regained my composure. Quite a few seconds had actually passed, well over a minute probably—way, way, **WAY** over my self-imposed limits.

People waiting in line probably thought I was grief stricken, I'm sure they figured me and Santino must have been asshole buddies. Under ordinary circumstances I would by now be talking to my friends and be halfway through a cigarette. And let me tell you, I really needed one even though I'd quit smoking many years before. Madness, however, wouldn't let go of me, the bitch! And so, for some perverse reason, I decided 'what the hell, let's give it one more shot,' and I did. The promise I had made ten seconds before? What promise?

I whispered all my exhortations all over again and, again, I snapped my fingers, this time just a bit louder. I thought perhaps the first time he hadn't heard it. Again, nothing happened, the bastard just wouldn't respond. And then it hit me, I knew **exactly** what I was doing wrong— I remembered where I'd seen it done, probably one of those goddamned Cecil B. De Mille movie I'd seen ages ago. I remembered that the proper technique for those happenings was for me to stand up, extend my arms over the body, intone some kind of chant, and then **COMMAND** him to rise up from the dead.

Relax, guys! Sanity, or whatever tiny fragment had remained, prevailed. I had a **pretty** good idea that, had I done that, there would have been a **HELL** of a commotion in there. Not to mention what would have happened had the trick worked, so I chickened out and didn't do it.

Afterwards, on my way home, I alibied to myself a lot. I told myself 'what the hell, let sleeping dogs lie, it was his turn to die, rest in peace,' and a bunch of other stuff, but they were all face-saving, self-serving words, I know that.

Still, I swear I was a bit annoyed that nothing had happened. More than a bit annoyed actually—I was pissed off.

OK, maybe I hadn't used the right technique, but I had at least tried, hadn't I? My heart had been in the right place. I mean—come **ON!**— when I snapped my fingers, **twice** for good measure, I felt it warranted something, some kind of response, some kind of acknowledgement on his part—just a twitch of a finger perhaps, a fluttering of the eyelids, a little grunt maybe, something, **ANYTHING!**

Maybe not a full scale resurrection, with trumpets blaring, saints and angels galore, those pretty rays of light piercing through the clouds in glorious Technicolor, the Mormon Tabernacle Choir singing Halleluiah, maybe not that, but something. Anything.

But no, nothing, zilch. And that really pissed me off.
I was so pissed I even skipped the funeral.

Nanu

by Elizabeth Vallone

*Have you ever thought of what you would do, or how you would
feel if suddenly you were thrust into the role of breadwinner?
Nanu describes the life of a young southern Italian boy
who must do just that. Overnight he must become a man.
Why, you may ask? How does it become necessary for him to do this?
Where will he go to find work?
Only 14 years old and this burden he must bear.*

On March 5, 1938, my parents and I took the train to the Naples Central Station from Molfetta. From there we walked the mile to
the dockyards.

The buildings in Naples were taller than those in Molfetta, a town
on the south-east coast of Puglia just below the spur of the booth. The
Neapolitans were as noisy as we were. There were people everywhere—
mothers calling to their children, fishmongers calling to patrons, an occasional sputtering car, braying donkeys, men in doorways laughing and
talking and children all over.

From where we stood outside the rail station, we could see the
harbor below with a fort in the distance. I had never seen such an omi-
nous fortress,

"Look at the beautiful Bay of Naples and that structure in the distance," said pappa. "It is called Castel Dell'Ovo."

"The Egg Castle?"

My father heard the astonishment in my voice.

"I know it's a wimpy name but it was built by Emperor Frederick. You know, the same one that built Castel del Monte near us," he said.

I nodded recalling that our school took us to the octagonal-shaped castle, which was about a half-hour by bus from Molfetta. It's situated at the top of a mountain that was surrounded by vineyards. I remember the beauty of the design—eight towers forming a perfect circle. The rectangular garrison in the Bay of Naples was massive and did not have the flair of Castel del Monte, which was designed by Frederick himself.

In spite of the excitement of the sights of Naples, my legs felt numb with fear. I forced myself to move forward to keep up with my parents who walked 'a braccetto', arm in arm. My pappa's knee was paining him and he leaned heavily on mamma, who basically pulled him along.

She whimpered softly as she walked, "Please God, protect my only son. Protect my only son."

Mamma had been crying since the day pappa came home saying I was going to be a deck boy and that the ship would be leaving port shortly. At the waterline in Naples, my pappa shouted out to anyone within earshot. "Apollo? Where's the Apollo?"

A man pointed to a dilapidated ship that was obviously very old. The name Apollo was barely decipherable on the hull.

Seeing this, my mamma broke down. "Enzo, no! This ship is too old. Look at the tanks on top of the deck! What must they be carrying? Petroleum? Chemicals? No! It will be certain death if this ship should hit rough seas. Please, please don't send him away. We've already lost two children, pleeeease!

"Elize, we need him to work! You know we can't survive much longer if he doesn't bring money in to the family. He doesn't make enough as the druggist's errand boy. We can't subsist on fish soup and a piece of bread with a squashed tomato on it. Think of Maria, she is so tiny probably from malnourishment. She should be much bigger for a three-year-old. Nanu should be bigger too for a boy almost 15 years of age."

"No! No! Enzo pleeeease!" She erupted. "God damn the day you crossed paths with Magarelli and learned of the opening on the Apollo!"

Unhooking his arm, he almost lost his balance as he stepped away from his wife.

· · · · · · · · · · · · · · · ·

Grandfather was my hero. Everyone called him 'Brigadier' instead of his name Michele (Michael). He was known for his toughness, and after the war of unification rose through the ranks of the police force quickly. He was the Chief of Police all of my 14 years. We would sit side by side in the evening. He with his newspaper, which he read with a magnifying glass, and me with my Braccio di Ferro (Popeye) comic books. I'm sure I developed my love of reading from being with my nonno.

My father was a merchant marine his entire life. Most of the Molfettese men were. You were either a farmer, merchant marine, or a fisherman. If your family was in the trades, you would do exactly as your kinfolk did; carpenter, plumber. Salaries were very low.

If you came from money, you went to school and became a professional—doctor, lawyer, pharmacist, accountant. There were very few of these 'professional' men in a town of 30,000. Only the oldest families with inherited money had the means and could give their sons advanced schooling. Although, there was always the Church that was looking for brilliant young men.

Pappa was at sea most of my growing up years. When he did come home, after a six month stint on the ship, he only stayed until it was time for him to leave again, which always came up fast. He was like a stranger to me, an ugly stranger. His face was totally pot-marked from a bout of small pox he had as a child. Even though he was kind to me, it was my nonno who I would run to with my joys and tears.

Everyone would laugh. "This is your father!" my mother would say, but I just didn't know him. That is, until his illness started.

I was maybe about 12. It was just after my elder brother and sister died. They stay things come in threes. Well, for us tragedy certainly came in threes. My brother died of meningitis and the following years my sister died of diphtheria.

My father was between assignments and went fishing with his brother Alfredo. Upon their return, my father fell and banged his knee on the mooring and collapsed. The knee swelled up like a balloon and the pain was searing. He couldn't move. Alfredo had to carry him home to mamma.

She and my grandmother tried every cure they knew to help reduce the swelling and pain. After a week of his being immobile and in constant pain, they sent for a doctor.

Doctor had no idea what was wrong, but gave us salve to put on the knee and said, "Keep the knee warm. I will send someone to teach you, Signora, how to give him some physical therapy."

When he left, we did as the doctor ordered, but day after day, night after night, my father got no relief. He was running a fever and mother was very worried.

I sat with my father when I was not in school and held his hand. I could see how much he appreciated it in his eyes. It was the only time his eyes shone brightly—when I sat close to him. It was if all the love he had for me was shining out to me. I would squeeze his hand harder.

He would watch me doing my homework and the tears would begin to flow. At the time, I didn't comprehend he was crying for me. I just thought it was the pain. Then one day, when Alfredo came to help him walk around the house and do the exercises the doctor prescribed, he thought I was out of earshot and said:

"Alfredo, you must find Onofrio a job, any job. We are running out of money and must find a smaller, cheaper, apartment. I don't want Elize to do it. She's upset enough knowing the boy will have to be pulled out of school."

My grandparents were beside themselves at my father's ailment. Father was always a strong man and now he just hobbled along, could put barely carry any weight on his leg though the swelling had gone down.

Uncle Alfredo found that the local druggist needed an errand boy. He came for me and introduced me around and I stopped going to school. Each morning I would dress, have a little coffee and a small bun for breakfast. Mother would give me a piece of cheese and fruit in a sack for lunch and I went to the drugstore across town.

She whimpered softly on the dock repeating the same litany as before.

"Please God, protect my only son. Protect my only son."

"I should have never brought you here! I should have never spent money that we could ill afford on the train fare.

You're making the boy afraid!" His booming voice and mamma's cries attracted the attention of some of the men hanging over the ship's railing and the purser, standing, clipboard in hand, at the water's edge.'

"Porca Miseria, he has to go!" Pappa bellowed, seeing me tremble next to mamma.

I could tell he was disappointed that I was not braver, that I didn't want to get away from the poverty, and from his reoccurring illness that left him useless. All I knew was that I would miss my mother and my grandfather, whom I adored.

"Elize, if I thought anyone would hire me with this leg, I'd take the job myself, "he repeated. "You know no one will hire me!"

Mamma started crying again. "Enzo... my boy... I don't want to lose my boy!" She choked back bitter tears.

Pappa grabbed my shoulder and pushed me forward. He wobbled toward the man dressed in blue and black at the gangplank which led to the deck of the Apollo.

"Onofrio Palombella!" Pappa stated over my head.

"Good, good," the man said. We shove off soon and I was afraid we would be one deck boy short."

Looking down at me I saw tears in his eyes. He patted me on the head and said, 'Vai, vai, Nanu!"

I had not heard him call me Nanu since I was a little boy. It had always been Onofrio. I obeyed and moved up the walkway. Turning, I watched my parents embrace. Mamma's howls were even louder now and I tried not to show any emotion. There were men along the rail watching me.

On deck the ship looked larger. There were big trawlers anchored in Molfetta's harbor all the time, but nothing, absolutely nothing, was as big as this. It had a three-story helm and on the opposite side of the deck two enormous tanks stood side by side—each the size of 20 barrels.

What was in these containers and how on earth does this ship stay afloat? I wondered.

Running along the deck were pipes attached to the tanks that ran along the deck and disappeared below deck.

Did they go all the way down to the bottom of the ship? A fellow near me saw my puzzled look. "Metal tubes for siphoning in chemicals and for draining them out."

A quiver shimmied down my spine and my mouth went dry. *Madonna! I thought. I'm on a ship full of chemicals! This is a death trap. How could they put me on this kind of ship?*

The boatswain, Giovanni Guerrini, was a tall man with a massive chest. He introduced me to others on the top deck who were obviously sailors judging by their threadbare uniforms—tattered dark pants, collarless shirt that was probably white at one time, and jacket to match their slacks. They grunted 'ciao' as did the other three deck boys, who were still in civilian clothes like me.

With the wave of the boatswain's hand, we deck boys followed him along. I kept my back to my parents still on the dock, lest I break down crying. I knew I was embarking on a new life and that my family was depending on me. I didn't cry, but I shook all over. I knew I was leaving the only life I'd ever know and it would be months before I'd see my family again.

TIZIANO THOMAS DOSSENA
— Editor of A Feast of Narrative —

Tiziano Thomas Dossena is the Editorial Director of *L'Idea Magazine* since 1990, and the founder and Editor-in-Chief of *OperaMyLove* and *OperaAmorMio* magazines.

He is the author of *"Caro Fantozzi"* (Scriptum Press, December 2008), *"Sunny Days and Sleepless Nights"* (Idea Press, 2016), *"The World As An Impression: The Landscapes of Emilio Giuseppe Dossena"* (Idea Press, 2020), and the co-author of *"Dona Flor, An Opera by Niccolò van Westerhout"* (Idea Publications, 2010).

His work as an editor and publisher at Idea Press, and his articles on Italian traditions, art, and music as well as his articles on Italian Americans, are aimed at divulging to the greater public the importance of Italians in the American society as much as to focus on the difficulties Italians had to face and overcome to be part of this great nation.

In 2012, he was awarded the "Globo Tricolore Award," considered the Italian Oscar of the publishing industry, for his outstanding journalistic work. In the same year, he was asked by the City of Yonkers to read poems at the 9/11 Memorial ceremony. Dossena is the recipient of the 2019 Sons of Italy Literary Award.

His works have appeared in more than 100 magazines and anthologies in Italy, France, Greece, Switzerland, India, Canada and the United States.

ABOUT OUR
AUTHORS

CYNTHIA HERBERT BRUSCHI ADAMS, Ph.D.

Cynthia Herbert Bruschi Adams, Ph.D. is the product of an American GI and an Italian mother whom he met and married in Roma in 1945. She lived briefly in Italy as a child and has frequently visited her cousins in Italy. She is a Professor Emerita from the University of Connecticut and a retired psychologist. She has authored a textbook with Peter Jones, MD, numerous journal articles, two trade-books and in 2019 published *Italian Spices: A Memoir*. Her first novel, *The Farmhouse on Cemetery Hill Rd* was published in October 2020. She and her husband, Roger, live in Connecticut where their extended family is also located.

BILL
AIELLO

Bill Aiello is a retired postal worker with two books, poems and numerous articles to his credit. He is a performer, amateur photographer, salesman, and the Executive Director of the Miss Queens Organization, a local pageant in the Miss America system.

Proud of his Italian heritage, he has made two trips to Italy. He also searches out Italian-American history in his travels around America. He has been a member of The Sons of Italy in America and Bella Italia Mia, a cultural organization in New York.

Bill marched in Columbus Day Parades in Manhattan in 2017, 2018 and 2019 and twice in parades in Howard Beach, NY.

Bill credits his mother Concettina and his maternal grandparents with instilling pride in his Italian heritage. His upbringing in an Italian family has been the inspiration for the books he has published and his devotion to the natural world around him.

LUCIA
ANTONUCCI

Lucia Antonucci always enjoyed writing and throughout her life she kept a journal containing her works of short stories and poetry. In 2013, when Lucia was age 83, her grandson decided to publish some of her works. This sparked Lucia to write more consistently. Fast forward to 2020, Lucia, now age 90, is an accomplished author of five books, and continues to earn five-star ratings on Amazon.com. Lucia gains inspiration from her life experiences, her strong faith and her Italian heritage. She has won the International Library of Poetry and Poetry.com's Editor's Choice Award for her poem entitled, "Park Angel," which was published in *The Best Poems and Poets.* Her vignettes and poetry have also appeared in various newspapers and church publications throughout New York City. In addition to writing, Lucia enjoys cooking; speaks Italian fluently and lives in Brooklyn, New York.

Lucia Antonucci was also a contributor to "A Feast of Narrative: An Anthology of Short Stories By Italian American Writers, Volume Two."

ANGELO
BUMMER

Angelo Bummer lives with his wife and daughter in the San Francisco Bay Area and is a dual citizen of Italy and the United States. He works as a professor for the English department and Umoja Community at Las Positas College, where he also teaches Italian Conversation. He grew up in East San Jose, California where he worked as an agricultural laborer as a teen and young adult. In 2010, he earned an M.A. in World and Comparative Literature for his study of Italian and Argentine literature. In 2018, he completed a fellowship with Stanford Global Studies and the Educational Partnership for Internationalizing Curriculum. His fellowship project focused on designing community college curriculum that showcases contemporary Italian literature from authors of African descent.

MARIA TERESA DE DONATO, Ph.D.

Born and raised in Rome, Italy, Maria Teresa De Donato, Ph.D. moved to the States some 25 years ago. After having started writing and getting published at a very young age, Maria Teresa studied Tourism and Foreign Languages at T.T.I. "J. F. Kennedy" and later Journalism at Scuola Superiore di Giornalismo "Accademia". Once in the States, she graduated (BS, MS, Ph.D.). from the American College of Journalism and the Global College of Natural Medicine (Holistic Health). She is a Naturopath, Classical Homeopath and Life Coach.

Her extremely versatile and eclectic nature, and her holistic and multicultural approach to health and to life itself, enabled her over the years to publish works on various topics.

All of her publications–including two novels–can be found on Amazon.

Maria Teresa De Donato was also a contributor to "A Feast of Narrative: An Anthology of Short Stories By Italian American Writers, Volume One."

DEBBIE
DiGIACOBBE

Raised in an Italian American community in South Philadelphia, by parents of Italian descent, Debbie learned that family is at the heart of everything. Inspired by her parents, she learned the importance of hard work, persistence, and of her responsibility to help make the world a better place.

As a teacher, she has been committed to educating and inspiring her students. She has drawn on great books and literature to create programs that motivate students to read, write, think, and be curious. Currently, an adjunct professor at Temple University, she continues her goal to help young people reach their greatest potential.

She is an advocate for the homeless, leading a ministry at her church and working with nonprofit organizations to help fight homelessness. She is a voracious reader and enjoys writing about issues that are important to her. Debbie is inspired by authors like Adriana Trigiani and Lisa Scottoline.

Debbie DiGiacobbe was also a contributor to "A Feast of Narrative: An Anthology of Short Stories By Italian American Writers, Volume Two."

DAVE
DILILLO

Dave DiLillo lives just outside Boston. He is a second generation Italian American and all four of his grandparents immigrated to America in the early twentieth century. He is a retired sales engineer in the semiconductors and power electronics industry in New England. His second career started full time in 2018 focusing on work as a SAG union actor on Hollywood films and television series shot around Boston. He is also very active in live theatre and has appeared in several live theatre productions in and around Boston, independent and student films and television pilots and even did a little stand up comedy. In retirement, he has focused on acting, reading great fiction, taking writing classes in Boston, and working to hone his writing skills.

MIKE
FIORITO

Mike Fiorito is currently an Associate Editor for Mad Swirl Magazine and a regular contributor to the Red Hook Star Revue. In 2019, he was nominated for the Pushcart Prize by Ovunque Siamo Press.

Mike's fourth book, *Falling from Trees* (Loyola Press), is due to come out at the end of 2020. He has another book slated for publication in 2021 (Bordighera Press).

Mike's other books are: *Call Me Guido* (Ovunque Siamo Press, 2019), *Freud's Haberdashery Habits* (Alien Buddha Press, 2018) and *Hallucinating Huxley* (Alien Buddha Press, 2018).

He was also a contributor to "*A Feast of Narrative: An Anthology of Short Stories By Italian American Writers, Volume One.*"

Mike is currently working on a novel.

https://www.pw.org/directory/writers/mike_fiorito

CECILIA M. GIGLIOTTI

Cecilia M. Gigliotti is a writer, musician, and travel photographer, as well as the only Italian-speaking member of her family. Much of her work deals with pop culture, medical trauma, and things famous people have said when they thought no one was listening. Her essays, poems, short fiction, and photography have appeared in *The Atticus Review, The Route 7 Review, RiverCraft, Outrageous Fortune, Blue Muse, DoveTales, Uncomfortable Revolution,* and *Boudin,* among others. She also runs a culture blog called *Così faccio io* (cosifaccioio.com). A native New Englander, she is currently based in Berlin, Germany.

Find her on Twitter (@CeciliaGelato), Instagram (@c_m_giglio), and YouTube (Lia Lio).

Cecilia Gigliotti was also a contributor to "A Feast of Narrative: An Anthology of Short Stories By Italian American Writers, Volume Two."

JOE GIORDANO

Joe Giordano was born in Brooklyn. His father and his grand-parents were immigrants from Naples. He and his wife, Jane, now live in Texas.

Joe's stories have appeared in more than one hundred magazines including *The Saturday Evening Post, and Shenandoah*. His novels, *Birds of Passage, An Italian Immigrant Coming of Age Story* (2015), and *Appointment with ISIL, an Anthony Provati Thriller* (2017) were published by Harvard Square Editions. Rogue Phoenix Press published *Drone Strike* in 2019 and will publish his short story collection, *Stories and Places I Remember*, in 2020.

Joe was among one hundred Italian American authors honored by Barnes & Noble to march in Manhattan's 2017 Columbus Day Parade. Read the first chapter of Joe's novels and sign up for his blog at http://joe-giordano.com

Joe Giordano was also a contributor to "A Feast of Narrative: An Anthology of Short Stories By Italian American Writers, Volume Two."

THOMAS LOCICERO

Thomas Locicero's short stories have won international, national, and regional awards. His poems have appeared on all seven continents in such literary magazines as The Satirist, Taj Mahal Review, The Pangolin Review, Roanoke Review, Boston Literary Magazine, Bindweed Magazine, Antarctica Journal, Poetry Pacific, The Ghazal Page, Birmingham Arts Journal, Boomer Lit, Hobart, and vox poetica, among others. He resides in Broken Arrow, Oklahoma.

Thomas Locicero was also a contributor to "A Feast of Narrative: An Anthology of Short Stories By Italian American Writers, Volume Two."

LINDAANN
LOSCHIAVO

Native New Yorker LindaAnn LoSchiavo, recently Poetry Super-Highway's Poet of the Week, is a member of SFPA and The Dramatists Guild of America.

The stage version of *"A Worthie Woman All Hir Live"* [1 M, 1 F] has been published by Santa Ana River Review (Feb. 2020 issue) and is available for licensing.

https://sarreview.ucr.edu/a-worthie-woman-all-hir-live/

Her poetry collections *"Conflicted Excitement"* [Red Wolf Editions, 2018], *"Concupiscent Consumption"* [Red Ferret Press, 2020], and Elgin Award nominee *"A Route Obscure and Lonely"* [Wapshott Press, 2019] along with a contribution in *"Anti-Italianism: Essays on a Prejudice"* [Macmillan in the USA, Aracne Editions in Italy] are her latest titles.

Her YouTube channel, "LindaAnn Literary," features poetry from her latest books recited by an actor.

LindaAnn LoSchiavo was also a contributor to *"A Feast of Narrative: An Anthology of Short Stories By Italian American Writers, Volume One."*

ANTHONY MICHAEL MALARA

Anthony Michael Malara was born in Chicago and then moved to California, where he still resides. Currently he works in Learning & Development for a financial institution. His passions include cooking, gardening, writing and travelling. He publishes the blog *www.vinofindsbydonantonio.com*, where he tastes different wines and pairs them with a story.

MARIA
MASSIMI

Maria Massimi holds a B.A. in French Literature from Marymount College, Certificat d'Etudes from Lausanne, Switzerland, an M.A. in Curriculum from Columbia University, and an M.A. in Administration from College of New Rochelle. Department Head of a public high school, she taught French, Italian, Spanish, with a knowledge of Latin. She served as advisor to clubs, trips, and honor societies; had co-ordinated a Sardinian middle school exchange program and headed the first American group to travel throughout that island, hosted by dignitaries and school officials there. The group was invited to the NATO base, Secret Service School, numerous sites, and to Caprera.

Upon retirement, she served as supervisor and mentor to new teachers, taught on a college level and in the Bronxville Schools. Founder of a private high school for girls, she served as its first principal. A first-generation born Italian American, she resides in Larchmont, N.Y. with her husband.

Maria Massimi was also a contributor to "A Feast of Narrative: An Anthology of Short Stories By Italian American Writers, Volume Two."

STEVE
PIACENTE

Steve Piacente is an award-winning novelist and former Washington correspondent who serves as Training Director at *The Communication Center* in Washington, D.C. Steve has also worked as a speechwriter in the U.S. government, teaches writing at American University and is a certified life coach and owner of *Next Phase Life Coaching*. He holds a Masters in fiction from Johns Hopkins University and has published three novels and a self-help book. Steve grew up in Long Island, New York, and has roots in Southern Italy.

PAUL
SALSINI

The son of Italian immigrants, award-winning author Paul Salsini has written seven books—novels and collections of short stories—all set in Tuscany. Among them is the six-volume "A Tuscan Series," which follows a group of characters from World War II to the year 2000. He received the 2011 Sons of Italy's Leonardo da Vinci Award for Excellence in Literature.

Paul Salsini was also a contributor to "A Feast of Narrative: An Anthology of Short Stories By Italian American Writers, Volume Two."

MARYLOUISE
SERRATO

Marylouise Serrato (nee Musso) was born and raised in San Francisco in an Italian American family. Her father's family is from Piemonte and her mother's family from Friuli. She studied marketing at University and worked for 10 years in public relations and advertising in San Francisco prior to moving overseas in 1994, first to Brussels, Belgium and then Geneva, Switzerland where she and her husband raised their three children. While in Geneva, Marylouise taught English for Berlitz and ran a global non-profit, advocacy organization, American Citizens Abroad. Marylouise is currently the Executive Director of Americans Citizens Abroad. Returning to the United States in 2012, Marylouise splits her time between Europe (Switzerland/Italy) and the US. She currently resides in Washington, D.C. where she dapples in writing and continues to advocate on behalf of millions of Americans living and working overseas.

STEPHEN
SICILIANO

Stephen Siciliano is a writer living in Los Angeles. He worked 38 years a journalist for the Bureau of National Affairs, Inc., and Bloomberg Law. He has published two novels: "Vedette or Conversation with the Flamenco Shadows" and "The Sidewalk Smokers Club." He is currently shopping his manuscript, "The Goodfather," about the life and times of Congressman Vito Marcantonio.

MARK
SPANO

Mark Spano is working on a screenplay and developing two documentaries. He is traveling the U.S. and Canada with his feature documentary entitled *Sicily: Land of Love and Strife*. His recent novel *Midland Club* published by Thunderfoot Press has received two awards and significant critical acclaim. He recently adapted *Midland Club* for the screen at an artist's residency in Seaside, Florida. He is presently putting together a development team for the film of *Midland Club*. He is hoping to see his book *Kidding the Moon* published in the near future.

Mark Spano was also a contributor to "A Feast of Narrative: An Anthology of Short Stories By Italian American Writers, Volume Two."

JOHN
SURIANO

John is a filmmaker and screenwriter. His most recent film, Archie's Last Drive, is a family drama set within the classic car restoration world. He has written numerous screenplays, primarily in the historical drama genre.

TIM
TOMLINSON

Tim Tomlinson is the author of *Requiem for the Tree Fort I Set on Fire* (poetry) and *This Is Not Happening to You* (short fiction). His prize-winning story, "Another Lydia Davis Story," appears in Columbia Journal, August 2020. Other recent work appears in CHILLFiltr Review, Passengers Journal, Text (Australia), *Poet Sounds: An Anthology Inspired by the Beach Boys'* Pet Sounds, and *A Feast of Narrative:* Stories by Italian-American Writers. He's a co-founder of New York Writers Workshop, and a professor in NYU's Global Liberal Studies.

Visit Tim at timtomlinson.org

ROBERT
TROTTA

Robert Trotta is a retired NYPD Detective. After his career in law enforcement, Trotta co-founded T&M Protection Resources, an international security, consulting, and investigative firm. Trotta is the author of several security related articles and has published two novels: Murder in the Gardens (2018) and Murder at the Florida Classic (2020). All four of his grandparents emigrated from Italy in the late 19th century.

LEO
VADALÀ

Leo Vadalà has been active in the Italian community of Wilmington, Delaware, and a member of the Giuseppe Verdi Lodge, OSIA (Order Sons of Italy in America) since 1975 serving as Treasurer, Vice President and President. In 1995, he also founded the Lodge's monthly newsletter, "Va Pensiero," editing it and providing all articles for the first 7 years. He relished the editorial functions in 2002 but still provides monthly articles.

In 2015, the Lodge honored him as "Man of the Year" with the "Dr. Vincenzo Sellaro Distinguished Service Award" for his contributions to the Lodge.

His novel "Some Grief, Some Joy" was published in 2018 by Idea Press. He is a contributor to all three anthologies of Italian American writers, "A Feast of Narrative."

ELIZABETH
VALLONE

Possessing a B.A. and an M.S. degree, Elizabeth Palombella Vallone is a graduate of Montclair State University and Long Island University.

She is a columnist for L'Idea Magazine and has been a contributing author to four anthologies: *Imprints of Rockland County History* (1983), *Curragia: Writings of Italian-American Women* (1998), *A Feast of Narrative (Volume 1) – An Anthology of Short Stories by Italian American writers* (2020), and *No Distance Between Us - The Next Collection* (2020), *A Cultural Anthology of Italian American Poets of New York* (2020.)

Ms. Vallone published three novels: *Beyond Bagheria* in 2005, followed by *Barbarossa's Princess* (2011) and *Heaven, Hell and Hoboken* (2015.) She is also the author *Just Call Me Lucky*, a biography of Hezekiah Easter, the first African American Legislator of Rockland County.